THE CHILDREN OF CLEMORA HOUSE OF FRIENDS HAD DISAPPEARED FROM THE FACE OF THE EARTH.

As if mesmerized, they moved out into the dampened grass of the yard, where they herded together in a posture of confident waiting.

Perhaps it wasn't really more than a minute before *it* happened. The light...*materialized*. First it wasn't there; then it was.

It was roughly circular and of indeterminate size, seeming to shift, bubblelike—almost breathing. It swayed from side to side, and it moved persistently toward the waiting children...definitely directed by *something, somewhere*.

The children waited patiently, placidly, unafraid. They stood in unreal calmness as the shifting, shining light widened gradually to encompass their small bodies.

Then, descending, it *swallowed* the children —and vanished....

Also by J. N. Williamson

Horror House

THE BANISHED

J.N. WILLIAMSON

PLAYBOY PAPERBACKS

THE BANISHED

Copyright © 1981 by J. N. Williamson

Cover illustration copyright © 1981 by PEI Books, Inc.

All rights reserved. No part of this book may be reproduced, stored in a retrieval system or transmitted in any form by an electronic, mechanical, photocopying, recording means or otherwise without prior written permission of the author.

Published simultaneously in the United States and Canada by Playboy Paperbacks, New York, New York. Printed in the United States of America. Library of Congress Catalog Card Number: 81-80781. First edition.

Books are available at quantity discounts for promotional and industrial use. For further information, write to Premium Sales, Playboy Paperbacks, 1633 Broadway, New York, New York 10019.

ISBN: 0-872-16920-0

First printing November 1981.

For my immediate family, Mary, my wife, and my serene son John, and for my "adopted sister," Nancy R. Parsegian. To each, thanks for being you.

Prologue

Nine days until April 22, 1984
10:15 A.M., EST

Venus, they say, is the planet of love. Venus Hill, a suburban satellite of Indianapolis, was surely labeled with misplaced optimism or a curious sense of humor. In the half century of its forlorn existence, Venus Hill has thrived on murder, robbery, and rape. Most of the murders are kept in the family—Mom killing Pop, and vice versa—presumably following a tradition that says the family that slays together stays together.

Nor does Venus Hill ban the gentler crimes, such as car stripping. Hulking teen-agers apprentice themselves thusly on the way to bigger things. Locals remark with a measure of perverse pride that if the fuzz want to locate missing parts, even entire vehicles, they have only to prowl the grassless, graceless backyards of Venus Hill—Indianapolis's own Central Park. There, half of Detroit's products seem to be littered with a delicacy approaching *sang-froid*.

When forced to go there, one reaches Venus Hill by wending a route southward along chuckholed Gary Avenue. It is a perilous journey, since neighborhood motorists appear hell-bent on stocking their parts department through firsthand contact. You careen high above railroad tracks abandoned by the Penn Central and forgotten by a preoccupied mayor, dodging (prayerfully) grimy, wraithlike children whose playground the area must be. With a magic that Merlin would have envied, you cross the invisible boundary between proudly residential Indianapolis, a City on the Move, to enter a section that causes the chamber of commerce to blanch.

Here you are lost, both literally and in a metaphysical sense. Street signs have long since been removed to decorate hastily conceived dens. The streets themselves are labyrinthine, a welter of mazes that threaten to capture you and hold you prisoner forever, doomed to the barren fate of the very poor who inhabit the neglected realm.

Down one of the wider boulevards of Venus Hill —the direction is impossible to determine by now —you pass garishly painted ramshackle houses, then vacant lots. Some of the latter may well contain such points of interest as weed-shrouded corpses, sweetly decaying in the warmth of the new spring sunshine. The sole living children who play here are those from large families, families that can afford the loss of one or two offspring. The less said about the state of mind of their befuddled, poverty-eaten parents the better.

If you are even slightly bigoted, you will be surprised to know that most of the inhabitants of Venus Hill are white, Anglo-Saxon, Protestant— not black.

At the top of the potholed hill, on your right, you are startled to discover an entirely whole, functioning, even pleasant, brick two-story. A building, not a house. It wouldn't be particularly noticeable on North Meridian Street, say, or in the Glendale

Shopping Mall, but here in Venus Hill, well, you're surprised.

The legend in raised letters on the face of the building clears the mystery away, if you're able to identify the name: CLEMORA HOUSE OF FRIENDS, it states, emblemed with the image of a dove. If you're an Indianapolis resident, you know this is not a Quaker retreat but a combination home and school—for the mentally retarded.

Clemora is here in Venus Hill for some good reasons. The occupants are sixteen hopelessly retarded youngsters between the ages of nine and fifteen, several of whom were not professionally identified as retarded until after various antisocial acts. In all cases they are thought not to grace the middle-class-and-up neighborhoods from which they came. It seems that the influence carried by wealth has not reached down to them; were they adult and well-to-do, they might be considered merely—eccentric. Their presence here, miles from home in most cases, enables their parents to place them that much farther out of mind and necessitates, for a visit, a trip that acts as its own effective excuse.

Since Venus Hill's impoverished families can't possibly afford the Clemora House of Friends, they tend to resent the place if not, precisely, the children themselves. This is entirely all right with everyone else, since Venus Hill people carry no clout of even the lowliest lobbying kind with anybody.

When Lionel K. Hartberg built Clemora, he understood all these important factors and more. He knew that the place needed to be modern, well equipped and well staffed, and expensive enough to salve the consciences of the troubled, distant parents. It needed to appear *substantial,* both in the sense of durability—to suggest they would keep the children until the twenty-first century if necessary—and in the sense of being able to *restrain* the children so they wouldn't be popping in to civic-minded teas and pleasantly sloshed cocktail parties. Since Mr. Hartberg never for a minute intended Clemora as a nonprofit institution—he would have been horrified by the very suggestion—he was happy to oblige in all particulars.

The land itself he acquired for what passes for a song—call it a vamp and three quick bars. He hired Venus Hill labor, both to create goodwill in the community and because it cost him only another note or two of the melody. After the place was built—solid and safe on the surface, if no more—Mr. Hartberg assembled a staff of youthful teachers who were so eager to have a start that their minimal salaries kept him humming all the way to the bank. And, in the three years of its existence, Clemora provided Lionel K. Hartberg with a bank account worthy of grand opera and Pavarotti himself.

This day, however, some minor chords were to be struck. . . .

The sixteen children of Clemora House of Friends attended class simultaneously but in four separate classrooms. Unlike in the public schools, a given class wasn't convened on the basis of age but on intelligence quotient and educational attainment, however dim. This had been the suggestion of Dr. Stacy Bennett, staff psychologist, Mr. Hartberg's young chief assistant. She had made other proposals, which he accepted in an equally grudging manner, the mutual resistance based on the indecent fact that lovely Stacy made no bones about how much she cared for the youngsters. To

THE BANISHED 11

Hartberg's horror, she *liked* them. The clashes between him and Stacy were legend within the tight confines of the institution. Stacy remained at Clemora because it had been her first job after leaving the university, because her salary was more than she felt she could get elsewhere, and because she seriously feared what might happen to the sixteen children if she left.

For his part, Hartberg put up with Stacy both because he knew she was damned good and because he'd have to pay *more* to a male replacement. Mostly, with characteristic economic prudence, he kept her on for reason number two.

The quartet of students assembled in Room 1A had a group leader named Clyde Lucas. Clyde was only ten, but he had earned the respect of the others with a certain unfounded, sunny confidence that motivated them to try, too. Clyde, just now, was passing out pencils under the teacher's watchful eye, humming loudly to himself.

In Room IB, Elizabeth was the leader. Elizabeth answered to no other name and suffered from sporadic silences that superficially bordered on the catatonic. But at fifteen she was both an elder spokesman and the brightest in the building in terms of societal attainments. Dr. Stacy Bennett nurtured the unspoken hope that Elizabeth might go home someday. This moment, this fateful day, Elizabeth was showing little Timmy Browne for the thousandth time how to make the letter A. The teacher marveled, as always, at Elizabeth's angelic patience.

On the second floor, Lionel K. Hartberg was sitting safely ensconced in his luxurious office, pondering the acute problem of how to locate enough dormitory space for two more beds. He had uncovered parents who asserted that it would be worth "almost anything" to enroll their children at Clemora. Those were words that made Mr. Hartberg feel God was still in his heaven and all was well with the world, words of lyrical beauty indeed. They were motivation aplenty for his shrewdness to surface creatively and explore spatial possibilities with the eye of a manic engineering genius.

In Room 2A, DeWayne Johnson was making life quite rough for little leader Willa Corman. DeWayne, age thirteen, had raped two girls and caused them almost to bleed to death before his parents grudgingly agreed with his psychiatric results. Those tests, along with his IQ scores, indicated an intellect rather above the imbecilic, somewhere in the grayish region of the moronic. And they reckoned fully without a lone-animal cunning, which had helped DeWayne hide his other crimes. Barely into his teens, DeWayne was a large and powerful lad with hunched, rock-hard shoulders and hammerlike fists, the victor of countless skirmishes with younger and frailer children. One of them, to DeWayne's delight, had actually died; it remained his proudest secret to this day. And now, at this same moment that we are exploring, eleven-year-old Willa was striving mightily, even desperately, to get the attention of Miss Rinehart. DeWayne had finally made his resentment of her leadership known to Willa.

Room 2B was located between the girls' rest room and the girls' dormitory. Here, while the same instant began inexorably to enmesh them all, Dr. Stacy Bennett watched with pleasure as leader Susan Renick guided Phillip Hanzlik's round, lineless hand in a perfect circle. Only last September, Phillip had been fearful of bodily contact. The faintest hint that he might be touched provoked howls of terror that hung in the air like the awful whine of a dying dog. A timid, gentle youth, he was one of those Clemora unfortunates whose intelligence could scarcely be detected and evaluated. Still evacuating in his clothes at the age of fifteen, frequently diapered, Phillip offered a warm and ingenuous smile as his dull eyes trailed the every move of every adult. If only there were *something* behind that watchful, harmless stare, Stacy thought again, toying with a pencil trapped in her long brown hair. If only I had *some* idea what to do with Phillip at the end of the year, when he'll be too old for Clemora.

Stacy knew about the strictures, the solid advice against becoming attached—however briefly—to a retarded student. Such affection turned, like a mad dog, and rent one's spirit. One settled instead for the tiniest, most microscopic progress and rarely permitted the hope of normalization to intrude.

Stacy sighed, her gaze returning to the boy. There was something so marvelously endearing about Phillip Hanzlik, a certain strange radiance of personality that shimmered like a silver fish beneath the usually vacant surface. It seemed to insist that there was a functioning human *mind* there, irretrievably locked away in some unreachable chamber of his tortured brain.

Now Phillip put the yellow pencil down, half wrestling it away from little Susan playfully.

She didn't mind. Perhaps she didn't notice, because both children were staring, without any warning whatever, into space.

That was uncommon. *One* of these children, enraptured abruptly by some vagrant notion of the untrammeled imagination, might stare at nothing and no one would wonder about it. But they scarcely ever *shared* their wisps of unreality.

Stacy Bennett's gaze met that of the room's teacher, Whitlow Clark, in shared puzzlement. He had seen it, too; he saw them now, Phillip and Susan, avidly gaping at the mystery of nothingness. What *were* those two looking at?

No, Stacy thought then, shaking her head, that isn't it. They aren't *staring* at all.

They're *listening*. With all the rapt attentiveness every teacher at Clemora incessantly sought from them. Listening, Stacy thought with a measure of anxiety, as though their lives depended upon it.

She, too, listened intently, concentrating on noises beyond the boxy room. But she heard nothing unusual, only the distant rumble of broken-down cars lurching along the street and an occasional tired, raucous shout.

Yet the two children continued to stare, to *listen*.

And now the other two in the group began doing it as well, one smiling as if she liked what she heard. Another, though, appeared afraid.

Yet all four, a quartet of little persons mesmerized by apparent nothingness, arose smartly from their seats at the table and began walking steadily toward the door.

"Where are you going, young people?" called Mr. Clark, unmoving. Perhaps in his surprise he was incapable of movement.

The children shut the door behind them, quietly, gently, a polite gesture of good-bye.

In Room 2A, tiny Willa Corman moved swiftly away from the dangerous DeWayne Johnson and led the other two children from her class right out the door.

DeWayne Johnson, his viciousness oddly rebuffed, remained seated, left out. His lower jaw, already dark with five o'clock shadow, hung stupidly. DeWayne was thwarted, clearly confused.

The trio of youngsters from Room 2A met the four from Room 2B at the stairwell without saying a word. Then, silently, the seven of them walked at a rather brisk pace down the staircase, as purposeful as any parade of obedient businessmen to a Monday morning conference. At the foot of the stairs they met Elizabeth, Timmy Browne, Clyde Lucas, and the others from Rooms 1A and 1B, not saying a word.

Above them, converging at the top of the stairs, Whitlow Clark and Mrs. Rinehart looked down in speechless befuddlement. Mr. Clark cleared his throat as if to speak, but nothing occurred to him. Neither moved swiftly, because there was nothing remotely defiant about the children's departure, nothing at all unruly. Indeed, it was as if they were reacting *obediently*, the source of their direction unknown. Stacy Bennett, quick to sense when there was something wrong with the children, had gone immediately to the office of the director, Lionel K. Hartberg.

On the first level the fifteen students of Clemora House of Friends—all but DeWayne Johnson—opened the front doors and stepped softly along a lane fringed by red and white flowers. At last they moved out into the dampened grass of the yard, where they herded together in a posture of confident waiting. Thin little Elizabeth tapped her toe in the grass and watched the tennis shoe color. Phillip Hanzlik, impassive, closed his eyes and, still standing, seemed to go to sleep.

"Get back in here!" shouted Lionel Hartberg from his office. His head, seemingly deprived of a body, materialized in an open window, his face full of open contempt. Like a warden, he knew insurrection when he saw it. "You heard me!" he cried. "Get *in* here, *all of you!*"

Beside him, Stacy Bennett's pretty face appeared in the window, registering considerable concern. Really, it wasn't warm enough for them to be outside without their jackets. Just for a moment she started to duck inside, to hurry downstairs and go out to them, urge them to come inside for the sake of their health.

But something held her there, *gripped* her.

It was a lambent feeling that a climax to this bizarre march of the Clemora children would occur very soon now. An explanation, she sensed, was coming and, whether she liked it or not, it was best that she watch.

"God*damn* it, you miserable little bastards! You un*grate*ful brats!" yowled Lionel K. Hartberg, face purpling. He had never been defied by anyone, anywhere, before. "Get your little asses *in* here, *now!*"

Not a single child moved so much as a fraction of an inch. Stacy wasn't sure they were being disobedient. It was hard to tell, but it seemed that they hadn't heard the director at all. Half the people in Indianapolis, of course, must have heard what the old loudmouthed bully had said. The kids, though, might well have been so absorbed—in *something*—that they had succeeded in blocking him out totally.

Drawn by shouts that were clearly from sources other than their own crude number, some of the Venus Hill residents began forming a crowd on the sidewalk at the end of the lane. Their rubbernecking was open, rather genial, and appreciative; but they weren't sure whether they should root for the dumbo students or the furious upper-class director. It was a can't-lose situation for the onlookers, since they didn't like anybody in Clemora.

The day was cloudy. There was a nip in the air, but the children didn't shiver, nor did they budge. Stacy ached for them without quite knowing why. Poor little Phillip appeared to be sound asleep. Stacy noted that tiny Elizabeth was supporting the boy. Later she would wonder why Whitlow Clark and Miss Rinehart had stood frozen into immobility at the entrance to the building, from whence, theoretically, they could have dashed forward a few yards and drawn the children back inside.

Perhaps it wasn't really more than a minute before *it* happened. Perhaps *it* actually happened in unforgettable seconds after they were all at their doors and windows, watching the children.

Afterward, *it* was the only thing that seemed to matter.

The light . . . *materialized* where it had not been. First it *wasn't* there; then it was.

It was roughly circular, of an indeterminate size because it seemed to shift, bubblelike, almost breathing; it swayed from side to side, and it moved persistently toward the waiting children. Stacy wondered later why she hadn't been terrified, at least for the boys and girls, wondered why she simply had gone on thinking, observing, and appraising. It wasn't so much white, she noticed, as it was colorless on the verge of *being* white. And it wasn't so much threatening as purposeful, directed. Yes, definitely directed—by *something, somewhere*.

No sound rose from the circular light as it loomed nearer the children. Indeed, as everyone who was there later reported, there was no sound left in the world just then. All those remaining were to remember the way that traffic noises, the untutored bunch on the sidewalk, nature's chittering sounds, and even one's own familiar *breath* were muffled totally, until Clemora had become a world of the stone-deaf.

And yet the children waited patiently, placidly, unafraid; they stood in unreal calmness as the shifting, shining light widened gradually, *grew,* to encompass their small bodies.

Then, descending, it engulfed, hid, *swallowed* the children—and vanished.

Whitlow Clark, the teacher, barked a shout of terror and consternation that shattered the silence and made the heart begin to race in response. Miss Rinehart promptly fainted; it was overdue. Stacy Bennett screamed, once, a rather ladylike scream that no one even heard.

The children of Clemora House of Friends had, putting it plainly, disappeared from the face of the earth.

Except, that is, for one.

Burly, sadistic, secretive young DeWayne Johnson had seen everything happen from Room 2A, looking down, slack-jawed, with Neanderthal eyes.

Now those dull eyes were wet, soggy with unaccustomed tears. He had wept before, rarely, but never for anyone but himself. Today was no exception.

When they had gone, DeWayne sank heavily into a chair at the table, alone in his empty room, the last of a vanished and exceptional tribe. His immense knuckles kneaded his damp eyes, and his broad shoulders quivered with emotion.

"Didn't *want* me," he blurted into the silence, the aloneness, his ill-designed brain certain of only the one, significant fact. DeWayne sobbed from the depths of his impoverished heart, the salty tears flowing down his coarse cheeks as he struck the table with a hammer fist in despair and humiliation. "He just didn't want *me!*"

1

Eight days until April 22, 1984
8:24 A.M., EST

Jedediah Norman Westphal raised his anniversary cigarette to his lips, suppressing the usual morning cough, and peered distastefully down at his anniversary breakfast. The limpid, undercooked egg yolks looked unblinkingly back, like something from a Brian DePalma film. The two slices of toast contented themselves with being, respectively, charred like a stick and barely browned. His coffee would have been all right, except that the milk he'd dribbled into the cup had gone sour yesterday, along with Jed himself.

"I haven't lost a wife," he muttered aloud, pushing it all back, "I've gained a diet."

Beside Jed in the solitary breakfast nook lay the still unsigned, uncashed check from his literary agent and an unopened bottle of bargain champagne. The check had arrived the day before, on anniversary eve. Celebration of his first successful writing venture had seemed fitting at first; then all the artificial, pumped-up joy seeped from his thirty-three-year-old spirit like sawdust from a broken doll.

The framed picture of his ex-wife and his son, the glass greasily thumb-marked from being lugged all over the house for five weeks, was sitting up straight again. He gave it a wan frown, perplexed. Must have righted it himself sometime during the nightly insomniac special. The *anniversary* insomniac special. Jed squinted, again striving to look only at little Darren, but he failed. For the thousandth time he wondered if there wasn't some way to trim Rosalyn out of the picture without cutting away part of Darren. He'd always felt, superstitiously, that if you nipped at an ear or an arm in a photograph, the actual person would feel the pain. And he didn't want to give Darren any more pain just now.

Jed sighed, inhaling cigarette smoke and, simultaneously, a suggestion of unwashed clothes that lingered in the air. Soon he would simply have to take a load down to the washer—and just maybe he'd get in with the clothes and wind things up in style. Writers liked to die in different ways.

From somewhere on the block came the broken-glass shrieks of children at play; and, remembering the many mornings he'd prayed for a chance to sleep late, without disturbance from Darren's shouting, Jed snatched up the sour coffee and drank it down in a single, suicidal gulp.

Satisfactorily punished but still living, he turned the photograph facedown on the table and groped for the morning *Star*. The *anniversary* morning *Star,* he corrected his thinking sardonically, ignoring the rest of his inedible breakfast and starting to read.

Reading and writing—they were Jed Westphal's escapes, his dual means of avoiding the pushing proximity of reality. Prudent about his sanity, he'd developed each ability to an almost obsessive level of skill. He could read more and write faster than anybody he knew—facts of only passing interest until lately. But each skill had played a role in the events that had caused Jed's universe to implode.

It began with Rosalyn's discovering that he wasn't really driving to a job he claimed to have taken. She learned that, instead, he drove to the parking lot of a closed-down restaurant, where he'd sit in crabbed isolation, alternately reading for inspiration and outlining a short story with a twist that really turned him on. When Rosalyn found out, she lived up to her threat. She allowed the divorce to become final, instantly arranging to take Darren to visit her folks in Greenfield.

Rosalyn had actually begun divorce proceedings about three months before, but when he swore that he'd find work, when he promised to do his best to bring some money into the house, she'd moved back in with him. Platonically, which was better than nothing.

He still remembered how it had been five weeks ago today, when she discovered he had lied about going to work. Her indignation was so genuine and, worse, so understandable that he put up no defense at all. He was quite sure that she would never understand the special *prominence* his new story had in his mind, nor his private conviction that people who practically *forced* you to lie had no one to blame but themselves when you did.

Engaging in a rare silence meant to project dignity, Jed had merely draped his five-eleven against the bedroom door, avoiding sentimental thoughts so that his eyes would remain clear, untearful. There wasn't anything he could do about the heartache as he watched Rosalyn pack to leave.

God, she'd been in such a *rush!* It was as if she'd wasted enough of her precious time on Jed Westphal. She stuffed things in brown grocery sacks, one inside another for durability, because, he realized, they'd always been too poor—through nine years of marriage—to buy any luggage. It would have been foolhardy, anyway, since they never went anywhere. Rosalyn had packed with an alacrity and dexterity for which Jed would scarcely have given her credit, which was reasonable, since nobody in town had given them credit for years. She was a dizzying tornado of single-mindedness, reminding him of how quickly she always tried to get sex over, too.

Not that Rosalyn's actually leaving him had been a shock. Jed always believed she would go one day, because he had a writer's doomed sense of the inevitable and felt that this was their proper ending. They simply weren't the kind of people who wound up in a funeral home with one going, one staying, tears streaming down the old face and little ones hugged to the bosom.

They were modern people, he supposed; and modern folks finished their lives alone, drifting off on Viking boats or in cleansing crematoria with a hearty, hand-brushing "That's that!"

But he *had* mentally written a number of classy good-bye scenes to play, and Rosalyn, as usual, insisted on doing her own dialogue.

"You can stay here awhile. You don't have to leave until we get back." She had seemed to swell with the pride of her own munificence, then swirled downstairs with her arms full of packed sacks and rather more pomposity than their ongoing poverty seemed to warrant. He picked up her purse from the bed, helpfully, feeling effeminate and useless as he followed her to the stairs. She was saying, over her hurrying shoulder, "You have six weeks to get somewhere else to live, or whatever it is you call what you do."

That had been a surprise, a pleasant one. While

his mind had blanked out totally on where in the world he could go, he'd fully expected her to kick him out right then. Trailing down the steps after her, the purse looped and dangling from his wrist, he had muttered, "Thanks for letting me stay awhile. I have no money, as you know. Nowhere to go. Even six weeks——"

"*That* is *your* problem, Jedediah," Rosalyn had said, heading toward little Darren to change his shirt. Jed hated the way she did that, manipulating their son's arms like some inanimate manikin's, close to hurting the boy. She didn't even seem to notice the bewildered expression on Darren's round face.

Pausing from scanning the morning paper, Jed could still see Darren's face that day, and it pained him. Sometimes, when the nightmares came, he would see the child's anguish as Rosalyn dressed or undressed him; once, in a dream, an arm came off completely. Lord, Darren had taken the parting so *well!* Like such a *man!* The boy knew they never shouted at each other or called names, yet there was a finality about the scene that gave him a sudden, first comprehension that froze his mind and nerves like interior statuary. Jed remembered how Darren began hearing *all* the brutal things Rosalyn said that day.

"Where you live or *if* you live is your problem, and I'm *thrilled* not to be part of it any longer," she fired, thrusting the boy's bare arm into a clean, starchy shirt. "You can give up this literary fantasy life of yours, grow up, and get a decent job, or you can live with your father. Or, for that matter, Jedediah, you can simply go to hell." She hurled a fierce, wounded glance directly over Darren's flabbergasted head. "Just be out of our lives for good when we return."

Live with your father. Jed sniffed in surprise at the suggestion. That was the same thing as giving up writing; there was no difference. Dad Westphal kept constant company with a faded drop-in redhead with matching beach balls under her sweater and at the seat of her pants. She was fifteen years Dad's junior. Both Dad and she keenly opposed Jed's literary efforts, even more than Rosalyn. Dad was a retired bookkeeper: if it didn't add up, you didn't do it. Jed had left home to marry Rosalyn almost as much to have a place to write as because he thought he loved her.

He cleared his throat to get her attention. "What if I make it as a writer—really big—someday?" he asked her at last, gauging her level of security need, her remnant of affectionate interest, too. "Would you come back to me then, Ros?"

Her back was a silken shield as she combed Darren's hair, careless of the tangles. He could see the metallic clasp of her bra jabbing against the dress and remembered the first time he'd been permitted to unhook it, ten years ago. "By the time *that* happens," her words shivered like ghosts over her turned shoulder, "I'll be an old woman, probably widowed from my third husband. *You* will be a memory, like Santa Claus, Ed Sullivan, Sir Cedric Hardwicke, *Forever Amber,* and—and the Pet Rock."

"You never had any confidence in me," Jed said as she bustled to the front door and opened it, silk rippling on silk. It was an accusation. "That's part of the reason it didn't work."

"I stayed with you nearly *ten years,* buddy," she said simply, with eyes staring and angry. Then the door closed quietly behind her, instead of slamming violently as he had expected.

Nothing was right about it.

The next two hours flickered like images seen poorly through an ancient slide projector: Darren bursting back through the door for a final hug; their good-bye kiss (ex-wife, yes, he thought, but ex-*kid*?), tears intermingling like two rivers coming together; Darren beginning to see what was happening. Then Rosalyn and Darren seen in a furtive, dramatic glimpse through the yellowed curtains in front of the picture window. (Darren did not "press his Charlie Brown face against the rear window, a crazy-house mirroring of a distorted crazy-house break-up," the way Jed wrote the version in his writer's mind.) There were the two awful moments when his worst enemy, actuality, cruelly intervened in the guise of nearly psychotic emotional statements. Jed still trembled when he recalled those moments.

There was the astral-projection thing, or something maddeningly *like* that, when he seemed to be standing outside his body, witnessing his dreadful isolation at the second of their exodus. He'd been standing with locked knees in the living room, between the coffee table and Rosalyn's chair; and he saw that poor, dumb fool clearly, something Stan Laurelish about the blubbering, tearful face, even his maimed dreams and his ridiculous, childlike innocence of spirit. When Jed was *in* his body again, he'd nearly fainted.

Then there was the moment of undressing for bed alone for the first time in more than nine years. Part of it was the realization that sex had just been cut away as surely as though he'd been castrated, and he'd cupped his testicles with his hands to see that they were still there, still warm. But mostly it was the sheer, physical loss of a softly sleeping body curled comfortingly beside him in the manifold experiences of night.

Other, dread images had pursued him since. Awakening that first night with a nagging toothache and groping for Rosalyn's comfort only to find his fingers sinking into his own sweat-soaked sheets. And getting a phone call from an acquaintance who didn't know and asked them both for four-handed pinochle. Trying to choose between his rudimentary cooking knowledge and dining solitarily in a restaurant crammed with chatting couples.

But there were other events from that day, five weeks ago, which Jed recalled as well. An hour after Rosalyn took that large segment of life called Darren away from him, the mail had arrived.

There, he found the letter from Roy, his agent. He'd been unable to open it until he first went to the bathroom to relieve himself, his hands shaking so violently that a rude splash sounded on the linoleum tile.

Confused, he'd gone back downstairs, sat down, opened the letter slowly, and learned that he'd sold his first novel, *Robert + One*.

The impressions flooding in at the time were bizarre, a mixture of *déjà vu*—for he had envisioned that moment a million times, until it felt real—and a terrifying ambivalence that would not clearly intrude itself, announce itself as gaiety or as ironic despair, leaving the writer winded and drained, as if he had run hard miles in hot sun. He'd peered through the window at the street and looked for signs of change.

Finding none, he almost ran to the phone to call Rosalyn at her parents', not to brag, but because notifying Rosalyn of everything that happened to him—large or small—was the way things had been done for nine years.

Immediately he regretted his impulse. It was

necessary to chip his way through Mom Nugent's towering iceberg of immense dignity and maternal vengeance. Finally Rosalyn herself was at the other end—unfamiliar location; she should be near him, or he should be somewhere calling her *here;* gross sense of dizzying distortion—monosyllabic and noncommittal. She murmured a frigid "Congratulations" that gave Jed the further unbalancing impression that he'd somehow merely imagined the sale again.

Fingers dug into the phone; lips almost touched the mouthpiece. "Rosalyn," he began, "does it make any difference?" He could hear Darren's aimless chatter in the tinny background; the boy seemed to be pounding intermittently on a pan. "Does this make a difference?"

She didn't pause. "Only to you, Jed," she replied. "Only to you."

Which meant, of course, that the success meant nothing to anyone.

When he realized she had hung up, he rested the phone on the table without replacing it in its cradle and again squinted at the letter from Roy, reading it with enormous attention to detail. He *had* to be certain. "Check on its way within two weeks after you sign contract," read Roy's terse message. "Jed, you're on your way *up!*"

He nodded and picked up the phone again. People going in that direction always told other people; that was the Right Thing. And Jed had always tried to do the Right Thing, so long as it did not diminish his creative flow.

He telephoned three friends that day. One was in conference. Another said he was nervously on the precipice of unemployment. The third was so preoccupied with his own business transactions that he accidentally referred to Jed as "Jack." It was midday in a commercial week, and everyone was already sealed in his own tomb of unreality, his own pretense at importance.

Only to you.

He decided then to hold off on the real celebration—and on reporting the great news to the local book review editors, for a bit of free publicity—until the check came, until everything was truly definite. By then, surely, pleasure would be permitted.

Now, having glanced at the headlines and trying hard to concentrate, Jed knew that half the advance money from his publisher was already earmarked, already gone forever. Barring his taking a job, there'd be no more cash from the novel until publication, when the book would, of course, reach the best-seller list. How could anyone in this position conceivably think of seeking employment? "Hello, there, I'm Jed Westphal and I'll be a famed author in six months. Is it OK for me to sell ad space at one-fifty a week until then?" Unthinkable.

But soon he would need to find both a place to live and a topic for his next book. Neither was easy to come by, mostly because Jed made no effort toward achieving either goal. A man was entitled, he told himself several times, to a few lousy weeks of mourning when his whole damned family broke into little pieces.

There was a week to go before Rosalyn would want the place for herself and Darren. "Would you accept a roomer?" he found his imagination plotting the scene. "I'm quiet, sober, and capable of providing excellent references. Or I could have, that is, until my wife booted me out. How about it, honey?" And she would laugh merrily, throw her arms around his neck, and——

You're a child, Westphal, he told himself, looking back at the newspaper. *You need more help to get along than Darren does!*

The story was on the front page of the *Star* beneath a report on the president's latest attempts at healing breaches in the Mideast peace treaty. A rather grainy, overexposed photograph of Clemora House of Friends seemed to suggest an edifice almost like a haunted house. Having seen the institution in person some months back, Jed wondered if the eerie lighting of the photo had been intentionally dramatized.

He scanned the story a second time, then a third, trying to conceive of a reasonable explanation.

He couldn't; he really couldn't. Fifteen retarded students of Clemora, according to the "reliable witness" quotes used in the story, had simply walked into the sunlight and disappeared in a shifting, circular, pale-white light.

> "What's driving me to the brink is not knowing where those poor children are, whether they're alive or dead," Dr. Stacy Bennett told *Star* reporters at the scene. "These are good children. I'd give anything," she added with anguish, "to do more than sit back and wait for word."

She would, eh? mused Jed. A box inserted in the main body of the news report discussed recent UFO sightings throughout Marion County in some detail, emphasizing that two witnesses reported that the "possible alien craft" had alternated from red to white and were "roughly round in shape until they vanished straight up in the evening sky."

Was there a connection between the children's disappearance and UFOs? A bit farfetched, on the surface, Jed felt. He spread the front section of the newspaper on the table and stared thoughtfully down as he circled and underscored with his Papermate pen. Maybe, just maybe, there was something really important here. More so even than the missing children.

He had never fancied the notion of being typed as a certain kind of writer. His first sale was a crime adventure epic, straight fiction, lots of action. The logical way to avoid being unceremoniously crammed into that particular mold was to sell a *non*fiction book before the publication of his novel!

And UFOs were intriguing as hell. Five years ago he'd gone through his "UFO stage," as he regarded it. He'd read everything possible, avidly, concluding at last that there was nothing *to* conclude until some hardware wound up being displayed on Johnny Carson's show, maybe along with birdlike creatures from the stratosphere or lopsided beings from some alternate reality. He was perfectly willing to believe that a UFO *could* have something to do with the kidnapping of the Clemora children, but it seemed inconsistent with most stories concerning such sightings.

Which, he thought happily, left one Jedediah Westphal—he'd finally signed his book that way, instead of J. N. Westphal, on the notion that initials were pompous and someone might think he was "Jane Nancy"—with both an open mind and a rudimentary concept for his next book.

Too many news stories that later became best sellers occurred in more crime-crammed cities than Indianapolis. It was really tough luck, he thought, only half seriously, that there weren't more imaginative criminals in good old Naptown. But *this* freakish yarn was centered just down in old Venus Hill, less than an hour away. He could ask for this Dr. Stacy Bennett, since he or she would "give anything" to avoid waiting for news. It sounded as if that would include a measure of cooperation with a newly published author.

And if nothing came of it, at least he could kill a full day in a reasonably productive way for a change. He'd burst out of the doldrums at last, maybe even drink some champagne when he got back.

Jed got his frayed sports jacket off the doorknob where he'd left it and slipped the uncashed check into his billfold. Never can tell when you might want cash. He'd stop at the bank, maybe even have a nice lunch out somewhere.

At the door Jed picked up his steno-pad notebook from the end table where he'd dropped it five dreadful weeks ago, blew off the dust that had collected, and walked out to begin the story of his lifetime.

9:51 A.M., EST

When Jed approached the Clemora House of Friends, his car having survived the rutted streets and raised railroad tracks, he was momentarily startled to find dozens of cars strewn like immense, shining rocks in puddles in the run-down old street. A number of men were straggling through the front door in the hesitant, half-step manner of people anywhere who are doomed to wait in line. Jed crammed his four-year-old Granada diagonally between a rickety Volkswagen and a new Oldsmobile, gathered his notebook as well as his aplomb, and trotted to join the procession of callers.

By the time he reached the door, he realized that the other visitors were reporters from local newspapers and TV stations, with a smattering from adjacent towns and counties. Since they were getting in, he decided to look like one of their number and sought an expression that was a blend of jaded skepticism and professional curiosity. He fell into line behind a heavyset black fellow and found himself trooping across a marble floor.

The room into which they were led was spacious, a small auditorium crammed with folding chairs. Looking as inconspicuous as possible, the author took a chair, flipped open his notebook, and looked politely around.

Fifty or more reporters faced a stage bare except for a rostrum and an American flag. Jed loosened his collar; it was close in the room, but it was still too early in the year for the air conditioning to be turned on by anyone who was economically minded. Jed had heard rumors that Lionel K. Hartberg, founder of Clemora, squeezed every penny from the operation. Seeing the rough workmanship of the walls and ceiling in the auditorium and the cheaply framed prints on the walls, Jed thought the rumors must be true.

Six people—two men and four women—began filing onstage without announcement, all but one clearly ill at ease and obviously wishing there were enough chairs to go around. A calm, bullet-headed bald man stepped to the rostrum and cleared his throat. The reporters jumped. Feedback from the microphone screeched like a banshee and bounced off the walls. The man backed off. Rather than looking annoyed by the mike's failure, he seemed quite confident of his ability to be heard.

THE BANISHED 35

"My name is Lionel K. Hartberg, ladies and gentlemen," he boomed in a rich baritone. Immediately, the note of authority in his voice was evident. Jed saw that, beneath the penetrating, rock-hard eyes, a red-rimmed sleeplessness sought to undermine the man's assurance. But Hartberg, a man of medium height with massive shoulders, impeccably clad in an expensive three-piece suit, was up to the challenge, unrushed in his remarks. There were no notes in his hand, possibly to suggest that the subject could be easily covered. "I have asked you all here today to answer your queries about the tragic incident at Clemora yesterday morning and to assure you that everything is being thoroughly investigated—by experts on the local police department."

Suddenly the black man beside Jed leaned against his shoulder, head turned slightly. There was a whiff of good cologne. "I wonder what division is assigned to investigate a bunch of kids vanishing in a ball of light."

Jed smiled in return.

"David Van Miler, Indianapolis *Trib*," said a man several rows closer to the stage, standing. About forty, he was chunky, with a dapper theatrical mustache, and glasses that gave him a countering professorial demeanor. "Does it appear that your kids were kidnapped, Mr. Hartberg? And, if so, have you received a ransom note?"

The administrator's small marble eyes gleamed. "I do not at this time know what else could have transpired except an unusually clever mass kidnapping. But, no, to this hour there has been no communication from the kidnappers. I assume they want us to be adequately worried before they contact us—a little psychological ploy to assure our cooperation."

"Julia Outworth, Indianapolis *Sun*." The attractive middle-aged woman arose from a chair in Jed's row. She tapped a pencil thoughtfully against her notebook as she spoke. "In the event that it does prove to be a kidnapping, sir, will Clemora House of Friends stand behind those kids and come up with the money? Or will that be left to the parents of the children?"

Hartberg shuffled his feet before answering. "I've been in communication with our attorneys as well as our insurance company, and I find that we are not specifically liable in this type of, ah, potentially criminal activity." He raised a dark, cautioning eyebrow. "That's the legal position. But that is not to say that Clemora will fail to assist the saddened parents in every other fashion possible."

Neat, Jed thought, very neat. Hartberg's reputation was deserved.

"Bradley Hillman, Southport *Star*," announced a pencil-thin person, of indeterminate sex, with streaming, greasy hair. Jed twisted his head to see the barely concealed outrage on the reporter's sallow face. "Look, there've been suggestions that UFOs—unidentified flying objects—may be at the heart of this thing. From my experience with authoritative types, I can logically expect Clemora and the police both to ignore the possible outer-space origin of the kidnappers. My readers would like a straight answer: *Did* those retarded kids get swallowed up by a ball of round light while you all stood around, hypnotized, or not?"

"I don't think——" Hartberg began, gripping the rostrum tightly.

"Maybe you'd better, sir."

"The question you ask is really out of order, Mr. Hillman," Hartberg answered stiffly. "The assumption it makes——"

"It may well be, Mr. Hartberg," the reporter pressed, "but the public has every right to know if they're in danger from aliens—creatures from another planet."

The heavyset black man beside Jed chuckled. "That sissy sucker doesn't believe in UFOs any more than he believes in heterosexuality," he said in a rough whisper. "He just doesn't want a really *righteous* story to get away!"

"May I answer the gentleman's question?"

Heads swiveled. Hartberg turned to the five people behind him, whom he seemed to have forgotten. He should have known it would be Stacy, sticking her nose where it didn't belong. He released a long-suffering sigh. "If you wish. This is Dr. Stacy Bennett," he informed the press, "our staff psychologist." He paused and made his little advertisement. "A more competent professional cannot be found at any institution in the Midwest." He bowed to her gallantly.

"Thank you, sir," Stacy said sweetly, stepping forward and taking a deep breath. She was a very small woman, Jed observed, the petite kind who didn't age until she put on twenty pounds with motherhood and then passed directly from twenty-eight to fifty. He was masculinely disapproving of her type. Still, he managed the honest afterthought, she *was* lovely. She had shoulder-length, straight brown hair and the bustline of a much taller woman. "The original reports of what transpired here at Clemora were quite true, so far as they go."

The reporters made a collective gasping sound and were galvanized to action. Everything that had happened so far they'd expected. Playing down weirdo incidents was par for the course, and here was this staff member being *honest*. Pencils and pens previously dangling or dropped in laps hovered now above notebooks, and Jed dutifully picked up his own.

"We did indeed—each of the teachers on this stage, plus Mr. Hartberg and myself—we did believe that we saw fifteen children vanish in a ball of pure light. But *believe*, ladies and gentlemen, is the operative word." Dr. Bennett took a deep, cautionary breath enjoyed by most of the men in the auditorium. "Mass hallucination is a subject well known to those in psychiatry, a phenomenon that can disturb anyone. There are numerous examples of it recorded throughout history, even into this century. Stress, atmospheric changes, unexpressed or suppressed problems within a family or sheltered institution such as this"—she managed a private glare at Lionel Hartberg—"are some of the contributing factors to large-scale misinterpretation of facts that ordinarily would be seen in quite a different light." She smiled a small smile. "A light *other* than a mysterious circular one."

Bradley Hillman was again on his feet, positively dancing. "You're saying that all six of you people—experts in your fields—merely *thought* you saw what you described?" His face reddened. "What kind of dodge *is* this?"

Stacy's expression was frosty and condescending. "I am suggesting that mass hypnosis is a distinct possibility," she said, "perhaps one as close to the truth as what we all reported in good faith. It is not impossible that none of us could face the truth of what we really saw and shared a hallucination of globular light, due to the unreasonable amount of coverage afforded UFOs."

"Then, what can we report was factual about

THE BANISHED 39

the disappearances?" asked the reporter named Van Miler, half standing and honestly perturbed.

Stacy's expression was dazzlingly earnest. "That fifteen kids—very nice ones, by the way—are no longer on the premises," she said, "through no known fault of Mr. Hartberg or any member of his staff, and that everything humanly possible is being done to locate them."

When the press conference had ended, two inconspicuous uniformed guards saw that the reporters began filing out. Jed, spotting them ahead of time entering the auditorium to station themselves at the exits, was prepared. While the others were grumbling their way out of the place, he was working his way down to the stage, row by row. There, he quickly approached a door leading elsewhere in Clemora House, found it ajar, and darted unseen into a corridor.

Feeling foolish but determined, he stood in a shadowed corner as the door opened again and Lionel K. Hartberg exited, followed by the four teachers and Dr. Stacy Bennett. She paused when the founder and chief administrator caught her arm.

"You handled a delicate situation beautifully, my dear Stacy," Hartberg told her in rather breathy tones. He towered above the tiny psychologist in a demeanor Jed thought was somewhat lecherous. "You were a pleasant surprise to me, and I appreciate it."

"But I didn't do it for you, Mr. Hartberg," she replied evenly, her fine brows curving in anger above a straight, naturally defiant nose. "I did it because it's the truth, as I see it, and because I don't want those terrified parents to believe even for a moment that little green men snatched their babies away." She cocked her head thoughtfully.

"I do think, sir, that there are a few other possibilities we should discuss—hallucination being only one of them. May I come to your office?"

Hartberg glanced at his wristwatch. "Let's make it tomorrow morning, Stacy." He smoothed his bald, bullet pate with a wide, manicured hand. "I have some other matters to handle at the moment."

Stacy's lips parted in honest amazement. "What other matters could conceivably occupy your time during a crisis like this?"

His smile, Jed thought, was just short of contemptuous. He caught a glimpse of gold at the back of Hartberg's slitted mouth.

"Replacements for the missing students, of course."

"Replacements! Like—like *automobile* replacements? New *parts?"*

"Don't lose your control, my dear. We have a waiting list, after all." The administrator's voice was cool and controlled as he turned. "It's not a difficult task to have fifteen more of our benighted little people attending school within a week, and *that* concerns me. Kindly excuse me."

Jed watched as Lionel K. Hartberg squared his immaculate shoulders and trod off down the marble corridor, footsteps echoing in the newly silent halls like a careful mugger trailing his next victim.

Jed stepped from the shadows, frowning. "Seems like a grade-A bastard," he murmured.

Stacy jumped. "I thought all the r-reporters had left!"

"I'm not——"

"I have said all I have to say for publication just now," Dr. Bennett snapped, her small jaw set, her hazel eyes blazing. "And I do not enjoy being spied upon. That was a private conversation, and if you print it, I shall personally take great pleasure in suing you."

"Look, Doctor, I'm not a reporter——"

But the psychologist had turned, long brown hair swirling, and left him, heading angrily for the nearby stairs. Jed watched a moment, helplessly, thinking how badly he'd handled the matter. He was turning away, when he heard the sharp clatter of heavy footsteps, increasing in sound, drawing nearer.

He was some twenty feet away from the stairs and could not be seen by anyone descending them. Held there by some intuitive warning system, Jed stared as a sizable male body cannoned its way down several bottom steps in a frantic but purposeful leap. Heavy arms shot out, pinning Dr. Stacy Bennett against the light-green wall, like tree trunks on either side of her frail body.

Paralyzed momentarily, Jed caught flashes of a red-and-blue boy's sweater, thrusting jeans-clad hips, and a pawlike hand fumbling at the young psychologist's left breast. It was no match; she was entirely blocked from view by the man-sized body; yet Jed didn't hear a sound other than the huge boy's heavy, hoarse breathing.

Action had always been Jedediah Westphal's long suit—on the typed page. He couldn't remember the last time he'd raised a fist in anger. But at last he hurled himself forward, running unthinkingly the twenty feet or so to the quietly struggling bodies. Unsure what he should do, Jed put out an interfering arm—and received a hard, bony elbow sharply in his stomach.

Instantly doubled over in pain, he saw through the tears in his eyes a manic, drooling young face turned to him in anger, saw two huge hands groping for his throat. Instinctively blocking the move, he thrust his arms up and wrapped them clumsily around the boy, pinning his arms at his waist. Sweat enveloped him, a nasty, sweet stench Jed associated vaguely with locker rooms of his high school days.

"I'll *kill* you!" the boy gasped, his breath vile against Jed's confused face. "You've *had* it, man! *Had* it!"

"C-Calm down," Jed managed to say. "Come on, kid, settle down."

The boy's face was inches from his own. "An' —an' if *I* don't getcha, man, *he* will! *He'll* make you *fry!*" He laughed, a high-pitched giggle, and wriggled to get free.

Jed recoiled, both from the strange threat and the realization that he couldn't hold on much longer. "Get h-help," he gasped at Dr. Stacy Bennett. "I c-can't *hold* him——"

To Jed's astonishment, the youth's heavy body suddenly slipped liquidly through his arms and sagged to the floor in a heap. For a moment the dull, angry eyes flickered over the writer's face, the lips repeating the threat mutely but clearly. Then the eyes closed in unconsciousness.

"How——?" Then Jed saw the empty syringe in Stacy Bennett's hand.

"Thank you," he said, inhaling deeply and trying to smile. His unathletic arms felt weighty, tight. "Thanks a lot."

"Thank *you*," she said, meaning it. She pressed a button on the nearby wall and stepped briskly aside as two aides came running. Surprise shone in their eyes, but they carried the assailant away without comment. Stacy herself provided no explanation.

Jed couldn't help but notice that her brightly patterned blouse had parted, a button torn away.

A rounded, heavy breast was visible to where it disappeared into a concealing white cup. She caught his gaze, blushed, and pulled the blouse together.

"I knew of DeWayne's history, but I really thought he was improving," she remarked.

"That's the kid's name then? DeWayne?"

Stacy abruptly looked displeased. "Yes, Mr. Reporter, his name is DeWayne Johnson. But please don't put this in your newspaper."

"I promise you I won't," Jed replied with a grin. "I tried to tell you before, Dr. Bennett, that my name is Jed Westphal and I'm *not* a reporter. I'm an author."

"What's the significance of the difference?" she asked suspiciously.

"Length," he answered, trying an experimental laugh. "I'm a novelist."

She began walking but slowly enough to indicate he could accompany her. Beside this small woman he felt extraordinarily tall; yet her manner restrained him from any feeling of superiority. Her hazel eyes swept his face. "I don't think I've ever heard of you, Mr. Westphal."

"That's because I've just sold my first novel." He smiled into her intelligent eyes. They were wide, and widely set, the kind a man could lose himself in. "You'll hear a lot of me in six months or so, though."

Her smile was tight. "You don't lack confidence, or gall, do you? Whether it's pretending to be a reporter, hiding in shadows to eavesdrop, or saving ladies in distress from thirteen-year-old kids. Do you have some kind of knight-errant complex, Mr. Westphal?"

With that, she stalked into the Clemora lounge, leaving Jed standing with his mouth open.

"That boy was thirteen? That enormous kid?" he demanded, rushing up beside her in an embarrassed anxiety to defend his own honor. "He was like a Goddamn building!"

Stacy had paused before the coffee machine. A fine brow rose, mocking him. "Now, if he were clinically mad, you could try the strength-of-ten-men fable. *That* might wash," she suggested lightly, relieving some of the sting with a brisk little smile as she groped in her purse for change.

"Allow me," Jed urged hastily, beating her to it. He waited until the paper cup dropped into place and hot liquid gushed. He was conscious of how near to him she was. "May I join you, Doctor?"

"I suppose I owe you that much," she said, accepting the cup he offered.

When his coffee was ready, Jed turned but saw no one. She hadn't waited for him, and it took him a few frantic seconds to locate the tiny woman in a corner of the lounge. He hurried to her, awkwardly splashing hot coffee on his knuckles and trying not to wince. The pain emboldened him.

"What are you, Dr. Bennett—some new kind of women's libber?"

"I don't need any organizations to defend me," she retorted as Jed slipped into the chair across from her. "Some of those missing children were —special to me, Mr. Westphal, kids who might have acquired enough knowledge to make a place for themselves in society. And *all* of them were important simply because they were human beings, and children." She looked pointedly at him. "I don't intend to make a sideshow of them or allow anybody else to do it."

"I don't, either," he swore softly, crossing his heart. "Honestly."

Stacy looked appraisingly at the man opposite her. She saw auburn hair prematurely flecked with gray, sober gray eyes set in a face anyone could overlook in a crowd, a creative person's indolent body just starting to go to pot, and a suggestion of warm sincerity that Stacy felt was genuine.

"OK." She relaxed slightly and loosened her grip on the coffee cup. "What is it that you want from me?"

"Just this." He edged his chair forward. "Help me locate those kids, learn what has happened, and give me your cooperation in writing a factual, even scholarly book on the whole thing. If," he added as reality irritatingly intruded, *"if* there's a book in it at all. Did you really mean what you said about half a dozen people sharing the same hallucination?"

She glared at him and set her coffee down hard. It spilled over, but she didn't seem to notice. "We're going to get nowhere at *all* if you keep challenging everything I say. Don't any of you literary types understand English?"

"All right, so it is a possible explanation. But it isn't necessarily the right one, is it?"

Finally she relented. "My friend, it probably *isn't* the real one." She smiled. "God knows that bastard Hartberg—you used the right word— causes enough tension around here to provide stress for hallucination. And since I spent most of my waking hours at Clemora—or *did,* till now—I could have been sufficiently institutionalized to begin seeing things. But all my psychological profiles indicate that I have an adequate grip on reality."

"Goody," Jed said cryptically. Reality again.

"What?" she asked.

"Never mind." His red leatherette chair squeaked

when he shifted his weight. "I noticed you said you 'spent' most of your time here. Past tense."

"Aha, you *do* speak English, then!" She shrugged, perceptive eyes widening in the remnant of a schoolgirl trick of easy charm. "DeWayne is the only student left, and I am going to recommend, after today, that the boy be hospitalized for deep therapy. And if that monster Hartberg thinks I'll stay on while he callously replaces the lost kids, shunts them aside and forgets them, then he exaggerates my fascination with my salary. I'm not going to get tangled up with a new group of children in this miserable institution, especially when I have no guarantee that they might not vanish as well. Finally, Mr. Westphal," she added, something about the set of her eyes wounded and anxious, "I'm just a little . . . afraid. Not only of DeWayne Johnson, either."

"Hm-m," Jed murmured distantly.

Midway through her last words Stacy had become dimly aware that the thirty-three-year-old writer's attention had wandered badly. Now she wondered how much he had heard at all. "What are you thinking?" she asked, curious at last.

He didn't answer at once. "Two things, primarily," he replied, finally. His gaze was dreamy-eyed, not quite with her. "I have a reporter friend at the *News* named Dick Stryker who can fill me in on the details uncovered by the press, but I'm thinking about taking an entirely different approach to the problem." He was formulating plans aloud as he thought of them. "Possibly I could interview the parents of some of the missing kids." He shrugged. "Y'know, see if there might be some, um, common denominator. If hallucination is at the heart of it, which really seems doubtful"—Jed now appeared to be speaking to a distant corner of the lounge more than to her—"something damned peculiar is going on. They may either have been kidnapped or just taken away at some kind of prearranged signal. You said they all left—from four classrooms—simultaneously, or quite close to that. Now, I have to wonder: How could that happen, mechanically? Why did they leave, and leave that way? And what did they have in common?"

"That's perfectly logical and rather observant, Mr. Westphal," Stacy complimented him, yet with the faint mocking tone still present. He wondered if it was some kind of defense mechanism. "Not bad at all."

"Jed," he told her.

"OK," she said with a sigh that indicated her capitulation to him. "I'm Stacy." Now she looked levelly at him. "I suppose you'd like me to help set up interviews with the parents, since you don't know their names or where they live."

Jed's heart skipped a beat, and he looked her full in the face. "Would you?"

She studied him a moment longer. "Yes, I guess I would, because I have a notion that I can trust you and because you're just weird enough to have the imagination to find out what's happened to my fifteen kids." She paused and began mopping up the spilt coffee with a napkin. "You said there were *two* things you were thinking. What was the other, Jed?"

"I have been accused of being acutely impractical too many times in my life," he stated, beginning with a little preamble, as he often did, "and the sensible conclusion to reach so far is that someone—or something—has literally taken those kids." He leaned forward to her, his gray eyes wide and curious. "So I mean to find out, Stacy, who

—or perhaps *what—is collecting the mentally retarded?*"

"That's a frightening way to put it," she gasped.

"Something else occurs to me," he added grimly, touching her hand. "Will it happen again?"

2

Seven days until April 22, 1984
3:06 P.M., EST

The local press was taking the Clemora story with interest but treating it lightly so far, or as lightly as inquisitive reporters can handle the disappearance of handicapped children. They wanted to avoid any possibility of panic. More attention, not only in Indianapolis but elsewhere, was being given to the new crisis in the Mideast. In the midst of talk of bringing diplomats and expatriates home, the new secretary of state was flying to Israel. Some—not many, but some—spoke of the imminence of war.

Both situations would change.

Her walls were a cavalcade of pictures and posters, not of transient rock wonders but of wonders that celebrated the inherent joys of life. Arranged in three horizontal rows on each wall—four pictures to a row—they beamed warmth and encouragement on fifteen-year-old Debbie Heybeck.

Whether she sat quietly in a straight-backed chair that overlooked the garden she tended so hopefully or at her small, inexpensive vanity table or lay in her bed grandly pretending to be the lady of the house, Debbie could bask in the depicted love of warm kittens and clowns, inspiring sunsets and jolly cherubic infants, of movie stars sprinkled by forever-dust, of a smiling Christ and sunny chrysanthemums and magical cartoons Debbie had posted because they made *her* smile and feel sunny.

She peered now, troubled, into the mirror framed by artificial gold leaf and saw a lovely young Eurasian face folded in frowns, dappled in darkness. Her small fists clenched in her lap, not in anger but in anxiety. From downstairs she could hear her mother and father, bound together by mutual despair, arguing over her "condition," their familiar voices rising strident, outraged, and desperate on the early spring air.

By looking at herself from closer range, Debbie Heybeck could see in the reflection the source of their concern. Because in the white cotton slip that made her lovely tawny skin browner, between the lines of plump budding breasts and the place where her sturdy young legs met—the once-secret place that had been violated at a point in time that calendars said was recent but that Debbie's memory swore occurred in another lifetime—one could detect the slight telltale swelling of her abdomen.

Shouldn't something that everyone said was wrong, evil, inconsiderate, and expensive have seemed more *important* at the time? Shouldn't it have brought her an immense kind of pleasure, of wondrous womanly fulfillment? Debbie-real shook her head wanly at Debbie-reflected. It was hard enough to remember the moment in any kind of detail, and it hadn't been pleasant.

But it had happened, all right; both Debbies nodded. Because in a few moments she had been transformed, altered. Mom and Dad made that

THE BANISHED 51

clear with every wounded glance at her; they were making it clearer now.

"If you say you wish we'd never adopted her, you bastard, I'll kill you!" came Millie Heybeck's voice from below, coming nearer to hysteria than it had since the night she found out.

"I never said that about Fragrant Flower—*never!*" Upstairs Debbie smiled sadly. Her original name had borne that meaning, she was told, and Daddy sometimes called her that or simply "Efef." His voice rose angrily, glad to switch targets, to turn his impotent fury on his wife. "You're wishin' your Goddamn thoughts off onto *me* again!"

Debbie's mind wandered from the argument, returned to the old concerns of her distant childhood. She remembered how strange it had felt when they told her she was adopted. She'd suspected something, of course, for ages. Mom and Daddy didn't *look* like her, regardless of how many times she looked into the mirror and tried to pretend there was a resemblance. Almost nobody she knew looked a thing like her, with her squinty eyes and broad cheekbones and ebony hair and dark-golden skin. "Dear Jesus," she had prayed so often, long ago, *"please* let me look more like Mommy and Daddy. *Please* don't let me grow up ugly like this!"

They had never known she felt that way and tried to shrug off her adoption in a handful of careless remarks three years ago, when she was twelve. "Your own ma and pa couldn't afford to keep you, Fragrant Flower," Daddy had said, holding a beer tight for comfort, "and since we couldn't have kids, we chose you."

Which spoke very well of them, of course, taking such an ugly, unwanted infant and raising her as their very own. They'd always been nice to her; so far as Debbie was concerned, even after she was told, they alone had been her mother and father. The adoptive parents who were willing to show pity on an undernourished, brown-skinned little chimpanzee with tight, un-American eyes.

Now Mom was sobbing loudly. "Oh, Lester," she said, her voice easily rising to Debbie's room, "how could she do this to us!"

"Shit, Millie, she didn't *do* it to anybody—except that snot-nosed Parker brat. Christ, I wish I'd got a gun and castrated the young stud like I wanted to!"

"The filthy, filthy animal!" Mom snarled. "You should have killed him, Lester. A real father would have done it!"

This part of the refrain was painfully familiar, and Debbie's mind wandered. She recalled her first date with Greggie Parker, and her second date. She remembered the first part of the evening of the third date, but the details of the last part —when her parents telephoned to say the car had broken down and they couldn't get home till after two—*that* part was largely blank.

But not entirely. Debbie kept her eyes on those in her reflection, stoically making herself hold her control while she dredged it up again in the hope of understanding what had happened.

"You're beautiful," Greggie had said just as distinctly as if he'd shouted it. "Oh, God, Debbie, you're the most fantastic-looking girl I ever saw!"

And she had lifted her face to him in wonderment, as if he had blessed her, as if he had given her eternal life, and there had been tears in her almond eyes. "Beautiful?" she'd asked, even as his fingers were unbuttoning her clothes. *"Beautiful?"*

She remembered how his hot breath felt on her slender neck as he raised the long black hair that reached to her waist and whispered against her ear, saying things about her face and about her body that seemed a marvelous, impossible contradiction of everything she'd always assumed about herself.

It was so magical then, for a while. How could she push away a person who'd just given her permission to go ahead and live, to live with pride and self-respect?

His hands had been rough on her high, bare breasts. His weight had seemed heavier than she expected as he sprawled on her, all awkward and uncomfortable, and when it happened—when she felt something sharp and hard pierce her—all the magic drained out of her feelings as Greggie drained his boyish impulses in her young, virginal body.

Afterward everything had been OK again. She recalled seeing Greggie lying next to her on her bed, sweaty and skinny and more plucked-looking than nude. She'd thought with amazement and a dawning womanhood that he was just like little Tony Sikma, whom she'd baby-sat for, only longer all over with little patches of funny hair. And then she had thought of how Greggie had said she was gorgeous, and she had tried to think of him as a noble savage at rest after the hunt.

Which hadn't worked too well, even before she'd heard her parents' voices at the front door and watched in shame and dismay as Greggie grabbed his clothes, put on his jeans without shorts, and lowered himself through her bedroom window. She had gone and peered out at the midnight of her youth, while he left deep footprints in her garden and didn't even look back.

And she remembered how very strange she had felt when Dr. Hawes told her, none too gently in his raspy, sixtyish tones, that she was pregnant. She'd wanted to scream, *But how could that be?* Only she knew the jokes that everybody used in answering such a dumb question.

And now she thought again, how *could* it be, when it had all been partly unreal and partly *too* real, and devoid of love and passion and the beauty of shared caresses, shared pledges? When it had just been Greggie and his thing and some hotness and minor pain and then her parents bursting into the room, finding blood on the sheets and the window open?

It was almost impossible to find just the right words, but what Debbie wanted to ask was, How could this happen to a young girl? Even Daddy had told her she was only a child; he'd wept when he said it, before slamming his fist on the wall and breaking one of his knuckles: "My *God*, Efef, you're just a *kid!*"

It was so—so bewildering; that was the word Debbie had found for it, reading. She liked to say new words until she memorized them. It was bewildering.

All she really knew was that she had changed, overnight, from Mom's and Daddy's sweet little funny-faced girl to something else.

Something *what*, then? Gross? Tainted? Malformed? Sinful?

She rested her palm on her expanding tummy, and the gesture reminded her of how she used to do that when she'd hula for her folks' friends. Her dancing hadn't been any better than any other little girl's—she had no memory of Hawaii at all—but they'd cheered and applauded. Now there was something tiny in there, while on the outside she'd grown big overnight, and was getting bigger, getting *grosser*.

THE BANISHED 55

"OK, buster, if you won't consider an abortion," Mom was saying downstairs, a land suddenly grown foreign, "what are we going to do?"

"Don't make me out to be a damned fish eater!" he replied angrily. "I just can't see Efef gettin' cut up like that. But as for *doing,* Millie, it *ain't* gonna be makin' her marry that snot-nosed kid who knocked her up!"

My fate, Debbie thought, and she closed her eyes as the girl in the reflection did the same, in sympathy. *They're deciding my fate right now.*

"Well, do tell me your plans, Professor Fix-it," Mom's voice demanded. "I'm at the end of my rope."

"You ain't alone." He toughened his voice. "Well, then, I've called the Milliken Center."

"What in the world is *that?*"

"It's a home, a home for unwed mothers." Daddy's voice soared higher; it was more decisive somehow, his mind made up. "She'll simply stay there for the time it takes to have the kid. *Naturally,* you know."

"Damn you, Lester, we can't afford to rear another child here! Not now!" The white bone of hysteria curved upstairs.

"We won't have to." He paused. "The—the baby stays right there, at the center. They'll put it out for adoption, the way they did Debbie herself. She'll never even *see* the kid. Then she comes home like nothin' in the world ever happened to her—and I put a fucking chastity belt on her for the next five years!"

Mom's tone was eager; she spoke more quickly, seeing happiness ahead. "Is it a decent place, Lester? Is it safe—clean?"

"Yeah, yeah." Daddy sounded exhausted. "One o' the women at the factory sent her daughter there last year, and it's OK. Hell, it'll be like a vacation for Efef!"

Vacation. She was going by herself on a *vacation.* Debbie suppressed a hysterical giggle. Her arms moved around herself, hugging tight. It had grown very cold in the room. She shivered and stared as the tears ran down the cheeks of her friend in the mirror.

So they'd allow the baby—*her* baby—life. That was nice of them. She thought it without an iota of sarcasm; Mom and Daddy had always seemed to have the power of life and death over her, and it would presumably extend to anything in her belly. They would spare the unborn child's life, and that, she thought, was good. Daddy was always wise. He was like Solomon, in Sunday school.

So why was her reflection crying harder?

So why couldn't they have asked her, just once, what *she* wanted? Maybe she'd never even have chosen them for parents; maybe she'd never even have wanted to come to Indianapolis. Sweet Jesus, had this really happened only to them— this accident, this mistake, this terrible disaster of emerging infant life? Were *they* the sole victims left to hurt so damned badly?

The clowns and kittens and chrysanthemums and cartoons on the walls watched as the fifteen-year-old child went and fell upon her bed, where she cried piteously, in terrible, shaking silence.

Jed Westphal and Stacy Bennett crunched their way up the drive to the Hanzlik home. It didn't resemble that of Mr. and Mrs. Calvin Lucas, their last stop before heading for this Ravenswood section of Indianapolis. The Lucas home had bordered on the palatial; it was one of the mansions on far North Meridian Street that had always

THE BANISHED 57

known the warmth of wealth, the protection of plenty.

At first Jed had been pleased that the Lucases agreed to see them. They were the first family to do so, since all the others were mired in the mystery and loss of what had happened at Clemora, their normal routine drastically modified by the pressing queries of newsmen and TV reporters. But attorney Calvin Lucas, when Stacy phoned his office late in the afternoon, had readily agreed to the interview.

It turned out that Betty Marie Lucas was an ardent fan of UFO literature, while Cal Lucas planned to run for lieutenant governor of Indiana. The thin, aristocratic man had made it clear in various ways that the tragic disappearance of their retarded child, "on whom we've always lavished so much loving care," might provide the springboard Lucas required to win. Publicity, for a politician, was his life's blood.

"I always *knew* that flying saucers would be proved someday," Betty Lucas had squealed, her bag-supported blue eyes gleaming palely beneath an elaborate, heavily lacquered hairdo. "But it's such a *plus* that we're involved! Perhaps the occupants of UFOs really *know* whom they're contacting!"

"Now, darling, we don't want to jump to any conclusions," the attorney had warned, lifting a manicured hand but giving his wife a public glance of condescending adoration. "Let's leave it to the proper authorities, shall we?" He had patted her hand, then inclined his head toward her, cautioning. "They are best equipped to return our poor little Clyde to us."

Betty's eyes had widened in sudden understanding. "Yes, of course. Our *first* concern is poor

Clyde." She thought a moment, as well as she could, and added, "But what I can't possibly figure out is *why* they would take little Clyde."

"Instead of you or Mr. Lucas?" Jed had asked expressionlessly.

"Well, *sure!* I mean, Clyde's a sweet boy, considering his dreadful condition, but what would people of obviously superior intelligence want with him?"

Jed thought of her disdain as he and Dr. Bennett neared the Hanzliks' front door, glad that the Lucases had agreed both to inform him if they received any kind of message and to be available for more questions when Jed was ready to write his book. Their behavior wasn't really surprising, he'd noted to Stacy; politicians didn't usually appear in straight nonfiction, only in satire. Theirs was a more newspaper-oriented, evanescent notoriety.

The writer and the psychologist knocked on the door and waited on a porch that sagged beneath their weight and stank of countless drenchings by nearby White River, where it was at its most boisterous. Most of Ravenswood's homes had been expensively, even beautifully constructed, but that was a long while ago. Many of them had been soaked repeatedly through the years as the obstinate river flooded its banks, rushing toward basements and sometimes finding its way into main rooms and bedrooms. Stacy remembered a photograph she had seen several years earlier of a Ravenswood housewife leaning out a second-story window to shake a rug, while beneath her the front door wore water like a skirt.

Ezra and Catherine Hanzlik, Stacy explained to Jed, were the only parents of Clemora students touched by the chill finger of poverty. She had ob-

THE BANISHED 59

served their obvious devotion to fifteen-year-old Phillip on a recent visiting day; she had seen the way Mrs. Hanzlik's hands hovered like quivering, pale birds over the lad's uncomprehending head, the way Ezra Hanzlik shoved his own work-worn hands deep into his pockets and stared almost beseechingly at the boy. *Learn,* he seemed to be pleading; *learn something, Phillip.* How they managed to keep him at expensive Clemora, Stacy could not guess. It certainly wasn't through the boundless charity of Lionel K. Hartberg, Clemora's founder and chief administrator, who had already assured his staff psychologist that Phillip Hanzlik must leave at year's end, when he would exceed Clemora's age limit. Stacy was sure that only money the Hanzliks didn't have could change his mind.

But Phillip had disappeared, and his parents' difficult investment appeared to have netted them nothing at all.

A creaking sound came as a large hand wrestled the swollen door open.

The bespectacled face looking out at them was full of expectation, marvelously unguarded and unsophisticated, almost welcoming—qualities, Jed felt, that one did not anticipate when one was a stranger.

"You must be the writer and the psychologist from Clemora," the man said in rich, ovoid tones. "Come in, come in!"

Stacy entered quickly; Jed paused to stomp away a surprising quantity of sticky mud adhering to his shoes.

The middle-aged man saw his plight and grinned amiably. "That's perfectly all right, Mr. Westphal," he said. "We're all used to a little mud in Ravenswood."

Jed found it easy to return the smile and, with Stacy, followed the man into a sitting room. The lighting was so subdued that Jed anticipated finding a frail, microscopic woman of age huddled in gloom and decrepitude. Instead, a tall, handsome woman, a brunette of no more than fifty, came forward with a welcoming hand extended to each of them.

"We're so glad you've come," she said affably, "so glad for your interest in our boy and his friends." She glanced over her shoulder at Ezra Hanzlik. "Shame on you, not recognizing this lady right off! She was kind to us when we visited Phillip down at Clemora."

"I am sorry," her husband replied, shuffling his feet in shyness. "I'm afraid I'm not good at faces, and my thoughts have been on the boy all day. Sit down, folks, sit down."

Jed and Stacy settled themselves on a comfortable couch decorated with bright, nearly carefree antimacassars.

"May I get you some coffee?" Catherine Hanzlik inquired, standing over her guests with an air of eagerness.

Jed started to decline, but Stacy nudged him and spoke up. "That would be very nice," she agreed, and Mrs. Hanzlik hustled from the room.

There was a moment of awkward silence, which gave the writer a chance to look curiously around the sitting room. As his eyes adjusted to the relative gloom, he saw that the furniture, overstuffed, was old but quite serviceable. Here and there it had been carefully mended. One spindly floor lamp provided the room's scant illumination. A crucifix gleamed in limited splendor from the opposite wall, Jesus' eyes both sad and disconcertingly observant. It was hard not to look into them.

THE BANISHED

In addition to the door leading out to the kitchen, another led into a narrow hallway that ended in a flight of stairs upward. Although fully carpeted, the floor could be seen peeking through great threadbare patches.

On the coffee table between them, him and Stacy on one side and Ezra Hanzlik, host, on the other, rested a photograph album with a gay red cover.

Hanzlik saw Jed glance at it. His blue eyes twinkled, and a tentative smile played at the corners of his mouth. "Would you like to see some of our family pictures?" he asked, unable to conceal a tone of longing, of imploring. "They might provide you with some background for your book."

Stacy's eyes met Jed's. In such a monetarily deprived home, a photo album could be the centerpiece. Especially when the starring child is missing.

Jed nodded, and Hanzlik quickly joined them on the couch, shoving the large album eagerly into Jed's lap. The weathered hand opening the cover trembled slightly, not with respect alone, and the author risked a closer glimpse of the man. Ezra Hanzlik seemed to be done in shades of off white, skin and hair and brows. Although he couldn't have been much past fifty, there was at once an aged, decorous quality and an agelessness about him. It was as if life had dealt all the worst blows early, Hanzlik absorbing them as best he could, then adopting some unmentioned philosophy that, in its accommodation, suspended him in time.

The photographs themselves, Jed and Stacy realized with surprise, were of no one but Phillip Hanzlik: Phillip at one, as overstuffed as the furniture. Phillip at four, taking form now and all too clearly cursed with the dull and averted gaze of the retarded. Phillip at eight, sitting awkwardly on a new bicycle.

"He couldn't ride it, of course," Hanzlik said as he pointed, "but we wanted him to have it, anyway."

Phillip at eleven, caught beneath a merry Christmas tree, green and forest-grown. The ghost of a smile flitted on his full lips, and he was handsome now but for the telltale eyes.

"He's never gotten very big," Hanzlik said without at all apologizing. "A little more'n five feet, that's about it for Phil."

Phillip at fifteen, this year, the picture obviously taken on their lengthy journey to Clemora. Jed thought he saw, in the dangling hands, the slumped boyish shoulders and, yes, in the slowed eyes, a weariness of continually absorbed defeats which he found troubling, which he thought, oddly, should tell him, somehow, something *more*. . . .

"Are you boring these nice folks with these old pictures?" Catherine Hanzlik set the tray down on the coffee table as they politely demurred. She scooted the album unceremoniously aside, then ignored it. "Help yourself to cream and sugar, as you like it."

On request, Stacy poured a dash of milk into Jed's cup, clearly using her knowledge of psychology to work with these people, to calm them and determine everything they knew. It irritated Jed, recognizing the professional personality at work; it was replacing a softer, friendlier manner he'd experienced gratefully several times that day.

Mrs. Hanzlik was settling herself in a chair. Her voice, when she spoke, rang with clarity: "If you good people can really help Phillip, why, we'll do anything that you ask of us." She paused, and her eyes glittered. "If not, kindly be good enough to finish your coffee and *get the hell out!*"

Stacy and the writer stared at her in astonishment. The words were almost amiable, like all her others, but the fiftyish brunette clearly meant precisely what she said.

"Mrs. Hanzlik, we——"

"Pardon, Dr. Bennett, but we've had reporters here constantly, every moment since our boy vanished. They had the decency to make no pretense that they were here to help. *We,* somehow, were supposed to help *them* with their news stories. *You,* on the other hand, have expressed personal interest on the telephone. That's a different thing." Her eyes were almost black in the dim light. "I want to judge the sincerity of what you told us."

Stacy's aplomb was ruined. She only blinked at the woman.

"I can tell you that Dr. Bennett was enormously fond of all the children, Mrs. Hanzlik, especially your son." Jed set his cup down and perched on the edge of the couch, practicing honesty. "I didn't know them at all, but I hope I'm a decent enough man to care about such a tragedy. However, my intention—the reason *I'm* here—is to chronicle the entire affair, to tell the tale in a truthful, dignified fashion. To do so properly, before I can ever write or submit any kind of manuscript, I must know exactly what happened."

"And we b-believe we have a good chance to —to find Phillip," said Stacy, courageously picking up the thread, "as good a chance as any of the authorities do. As a matter of courtesy, in part, we have begun with the parents."

"That's good enough for me, folks," Ezra Hanzlik put in, giving them a generous smile. Stacy thought warmly, *You old lover, just about anything would please you.* Then he scratched thoughtfully in his white thatch, his glasses sliding unnoticed down his nose. "Seems to me we should prob'ly help these folks all we can. They just might do it."

His wife considered another moment. Then she nodded. "I agree." A plaintive note sounded as she continued, "I don't think we have any o-other offers of assistance."

"All we can do is our best," Jed murmured, the best pledge he could make.

Catherine Hanzlik rose with a sigh and, crossing to them, stooped to the coffee service. "Now I'll have a little, too," she said softly, her great dark eyes luminous. "It can't keep me awake a minute more than I've been since it—it happened."

"Do you know anyone at all who would wish to harm Phillip, any reason for anyone to want him —out of the way?"

"No." She shook her head at Jed. "Only those people, if that is what they can be called, who injure crippled birds and torture puppies. It was impossible, you see, for Phillip to offend anyone, to do anything wrong."

"Phillip was . . . one of my pets," Stacy told her in low tones, staring self-consciously into her coffee cup. "It's true that he had none of the capacity for violence of certain retarded children, and very little of the physical clumsiness."

"Well, now, to be honest," Ezra put in, "he was barely able to recall his own name." Hanzlik spoke startlingly from his chair, the words an angry indictment not of Phillip, but of his own experience with justice. "If we hadn't been obliged to work, both of us, just to keep this property, why, we'd never have sent him off to Clemora. But Catherine . . ." His voice trailed off.

"At the last, he was too much for me." Catherine was apologetic. "And I had held him close too long. I—hoped Clemora might help."

"OK, do you folks have any enemies yourselves?" Jed inquired, finding that hard to imagine.

"Only those you pick up just by bein' alive at the wrong time," Hanzlik replied with a grin. "I don't think, sir, that it's directly connected to us, or even to the boy. I really don't, Mr. Westphal."

The strained conversation began to wind down as Jed and Stacy saw that it was leading nowhere. Jed thought, with some embarrassment for his own talent, it *was* good background material for his book. Indispensable. But as a lead to the whereabouts of the vanished Clemora kids, it was useless talk.

"Please call me at once if you learn anything that might be productive," Jed said, rising. He gave Ezra Hanzlik a slip of paper bearing his telephone number, and he and Stacy moved to the door. The smell of the river permeated the air.

"I'd like to add something before you leave," Catherine remarked. The streetlamp illuminated her face, hollowing the deep sockets of her remarkable eyes. "I've been reading 1 Corinthians, seeking guidance today," she went on, unafraid to be mocked but at the same time not anxious to be, "and I came across these words: 'Beareth all things, believeth all things, hopeth all things, endureth all things.' Well, we try. And it goes on: '. . . whether *there be* tongues, they shall cease; whether *there be* knowledge, it shall vanish away. . . . But when that which is perfect is come, then that which is in part shall be done away.' Poor Phillip—was not perfect."

For an instant Catherine Hanzlik's composure shattered. A little agonized groan sounded from her throat, and tears leaped to her eyes.

Easily, as though he had done it a million times, Ezra slipped his arm around her shoulders and continued for her: " 'When I was a child, I spake as a child, I understood as a child, I thought as a child: but when I became a man, I put away childish things.' " Beside his gentle face, in the background, Jed saw the sad, commanding eyes of Jesus watching them. Ezra finished, more loudly: " 'For now we see through a glass, darkly; but then face to face: now I know in part; but then shall I know even as also I am known.' Phillip always . . . saw through a glass, darkly, Mr. Westphal." Ezra cleared his throat. "I wonder what he knows now that he has been face to face—with the unknown."

As Jed opened the car door and the light flicked on, he saw Stacy's pretty face streaked with tears. He was touched, surprised to see a religious reaction in such a modern-appearing woman. He started to speak, but she caught his expression and murmured briefly, "I guess I believeth all things, Jed."

Jed leaned quickly toward her and kissed her, gently, on the lips. He was further surprised to learn that his own eyes were moist.

3

Six days until April 22, 1984
6:32 P.M., EST

It wasn't exactly a jail, it wasn't quite a hospital or a clinic, and it wasn't quite a college or an institution of any really identifiable nature. Which was entirely appropriate for its inmates, who, similarly, weren't *"quite."*

Weren't *quite* young anymore and surely not *quite* virgins, weren't *quite* women in a psychological sense of immense proportions, weren't *quite* wanted either here or at home. And weren't *quite* mothers—not yet. They weren't *quite* criminals, but they had not abided by the most important, powerful laws of any tribe, great or small: the unwritten ones based upon fundamentals of tradition, social doctrine, and relatively imprecise theological interpretation.

Woe unto those who break such laws as these!

Unlike Clemora House of Friends in dingy, dilapidated Venus Hill, the Milliken Center raised itself phallically from a crotch of land purchased before the city began expanding to the far north side of Indianapolis. Also unlike Clemora, Milliken now stood erect near shopping centers of abundant patronage and private homes of high value. Consequently, it was disliked by those in the neighborhood to a degree similar to the animosity Venus Hill residents showed Clemora. Contrariwise, Milliken was an eyesore.

Its founder, Mrs. Vera Canobly, had been motivated by few of the monetary aspirations of Clemora's Lionel K. Hartberg. Instead of seeking wealth, Mrs. Canobly—who was rumored to have "been in trouble" herself as a girl—sought to provide a relatively profitable, real refuge for unwed mothers—a decent home away from home, a way station on the way back to acceptability.

Years ago, when Milliken was in the planning phase, Vera Canobly knew that this northern section of town would eventually be populated by people of wealth. She had judged wisely, therefore, that such young women as those arriving beneath her wing would come from every kind of American family, and she had no intention of hiding her center away. More than a few people, back then, felt that Mrs. Canobly was utterly brazen to build her womblike edifice in such nice surroundings. Many of those who thought so eventually became nine-month tenants themselves or bore daughters who did.

The lady had recovered from her own early tussle with the vagaries of spermatozoa in time to graduate from Indiana University with honors, and somewhere along the line she acquired and subsequently shed the unremembered Mr. Canobly. In addition to having earned a degree in the social sciences, she had been a versatile student of classical languages, played a tolerable clarinet, and proved to be administrator enough to operate the Milliken Center with a nice balance of gain and charity.

Just who Milliken was, if anybody, was never quite clear to anyone.

The building itself was not, by this time, unfairly considered an eyesore. Although of contemporary construction, it managed to appear stony and ivy-covered, with a wall of huge rock encircling the back quarters and miniature flower gardens—Vera claimed that they were "borrowed," designwise, from the palace at Versailles—dotting the quarter acre at the front. The rock was intended to keep at bay those who were inclined to shout mean things at Mrs. Canobly's girls, and the flowers, largely, were for the romantic aspect of Mrs. Canobly's soul.

Although everything was kept up despite passing recessions and skyrocketing inflation, the building had been the victim of dust clouds kicked up by cars and trucks streaking up U.S. 31. As a consequence, the building and grounds conveyed a rather sad or gloomy quality to the sensitive eye. Some said that Milliken was timorously haunted by the small specters of infants whose gentle spirits had collapsed here in the glare of absolute rejection.

The rumor was untrue. Milliken's only haunts were those women who, respectable years later, passed the center with their unknowing husbands and felt a transient urge to confess.

There was no fencing to keep the unwed mothers confined; it would have been redundant. Unlike the worst anarchist or the bloodiest killer, the maids of Milliken had nowhere to go should they escape. Psychologically, they were bound by commitments of flesh and blood, of the past and of the future. Here they were trapped by their swollen bellies, in a variety of protuberant sizes, and here they all stayed until relieved of their burdens.

This day, sixty females ranging in age from twelve to thirty-one were housed at aging Milliken.

During the daylight hours the young ladies had the option of attending a sort of potpourri scholastic class with lectures from visiting teachers and experts who wished to experiment on a truly captive audience, playing cards and other games in a recreation room that was Mrs. Canobly's pride and joy, reading in a closet-sized room named the "library," praying or meditating in another uncomfortable closet, dining on iron-rich meals in the cafeteria (posted hours: 7:00, 12:00 noon, 6:00), or languishing in their dormitories like so many overfed Camilles.

Of the latter quarters there were four spacious rooms. Large enough to sleep fifteen girls in each, they were carefully laid out like dorms in any middle-class university, with one exception—there were no bunk beds. On the walls, in fact, were multicolored pennants from Indiana, Purdue University, Notre Dame, Indiana State, Butler U., Ball State, and Badler University. Someone interloping on the scene and viewing the dorms' occupants might have thought he'd blundered into the ravages of a *really* big man on campus.

Each dorm had its own name, its own identity, for the purpose of establishing teams. Mrs. Canobly and her echoing staff recommended a number of mildly active sports, at least up to the seventh month. Each dorm was named for a current male celebrity of interest to its occupants, so that a teasing girl, writing home, could say that she was "sleeping with" Erik Estrada or John Travolta.

On the third floor, in a Milliken Land closed to all residents except for a few days of their interminable stay, was the clinic. Here babies were born without names, very often without permanent fathers *or* mothers, the deliverer of the bundle from God and said bundle itself given adequate care until time for their respective departures from Milliken.

Generally, the deliverer went home alone, emptied and drained in more ways than one. The bundles were eventually called for by those on a waiting list or, when economic times were bad, delivered to a state institution, where they would remain until adoption or the age of eighteen, whichever came first. The bundles affixed their signatures on these long-duration contracts in the form of tiny, ink-splotched footprints. Nurses at Milliken sometimes referred with casual cruelty to the third floor as "the baby factory" or "the assembly line."

Debbie Heybeck, age fifteen, was the newest girl in the dormitory named, with simple clarity, Elvis. Through the years a number of unwed mothers, smitten by newly rising stars in the pop firmament, had urged that Elvis be replaced; but they were shouted down by stubbornly loyal fans who were in turn led by Mrs. Vera Canobly, who treasured and revered Mr. Presley's memory.

Debbie, in her first letter home, merely noted that she was "sleeping with a dead guy now, ha-ha." Then she thought better of it and crossed it out.

She had been introduced—first names only—to the other fourteen women in Elvis by Mrs. Canobly herself. Their names had reached her ears so fleetingly that it was impossible now, as she glanced dispiritedly around the dorm from the edge of her bed, to put names with faces. Debbie's glance at them was shy. It always was with new people. Aggressiveness would only make matters worse for her, since her Eurasian ancestry was obvious in her sweet, round face and there were people motivated to dislike her because of the face alone. She had been made painfully aware of this fact several times.

The falsetto wail of the BeeGees came from a phonograph, reminding Debbie that she'd been invited to what Mrs. Canobly called the "music room" to hear Milliken's aging founder play the clarinet. That particular Big Day was tomorrow. In the middle of the musical din, Debbie's attentive ears identified Barry Manilow putting up an outmanned fight.

Cautiously swiveling her head, she saw that several of the younger girls were dancing, although to which phonograph record Debbie could not detect. Their newfound gracelessness was humpish and bumpish enough to make her suppress a giggle.

Two other girls, nearby, sat on a bed in intense concentration, one gesturing pointedly and the other watching through worshipful eyes. Debbie wondered what they were discussing, although she didn't really care.

A trio of females seemed to be sleeping, or working at it, their stomachs pressed up against their sheets like pale molehills.

Suddenly devastated by her isolation from everything familiar, Debbie realized there would be six months of waiting. Although she'd never felt so lonely in her whole life, she tried to find the expressionless mien of her ancestors and reveal nothing important to these strangers.

Inwardly, while her eyes passed over the other girls, she saw instead the posters and pictures of her own room, at home. Behind her, beyond the bed, inexpensive curtains fluttered at an open window through which flies occasionally buzzed, unimpeded. Would Mom keep her promise and tend Debbie's garden? Was it possible that Jan and

THE BANISHED 73

Laura, who *knew,* would keep their big yaps shut for six months? Would Daddy ever really *forgive* her?

"Hi! I'm Marcia."

Startled, Debbie jumped. The girl who had materialized in front of her, clad only in a bra and an enormously protruding maternity slip, might have been no older, but she seemed years ahead in experience. Debbie sensed it at once, recognized Marcia's experience in her level brown eyes and the almost cocky set of her bare shoulders.

"I'm Debbie," she managed to muster. A tentative smile crossed her full lips. "I—just got here."

"I know, the Little Mother introduced us, remember? Look, don't let all this jazz getcha down, huh? It's not worth it."

Debbie took the extended hand and shook it, eyes wide. It had a steady grip, like a man's hand. "I'm fine," she swore, lying.

"Sure you are." Marcia squeezed between the beds to sit beside Debbie. She shrugged elaborately. "I'm sort of in charge of Elvis, y'know? To show the new girls the ropes."

"Great," Debbie replied uneasily. She paused. "What ropes?"

"Oh, how to get extra food—snacks—stuff like that. Privileges. How t'stay up after lights-out and get clean away with it." Marcia grinned knowingly. "You dig?"

Debbie studied her hands in her lap. "I'm fine," she repeated aimlessly.

"Is he a real stud?"

"What? *Who?*"

Marcia licked her lips. "Your guy. The dude who knocked you up." Her wide, knowing eyes evaluated the other girl mercilessly, pried without real interest, searching for one more brief thrill. "Because if he is, I can figure out a way to arrange for him to drop by sometime." Abruptly Marcia giggled harshly and covered Debbie's hand with one of her own. The fingers were very long, almost artistic; blue nail polish gave them a predatory appearance. "They call 'em 'conjugal visits' in jail."

Debbie shifted her weight uncomfortably. "I'm not allowed to see Greggie again, ever," she announced solemnly.

Marcia frowned. Then her brows lifted, and she laughed lightly. "I get it. You're playing the game, all quiet and cooperative, so you'll have a place to stay when y'get out." The hand on Debbie's squeezed. "Well, don't let anybody shit ya, sweetie. And remember, you'll wind up comin' to little Marcia for favors sooner or later." The pause was scarcely discernible. "All kinds."

Swinging her hips, not looking back, Marcia departed.

Debbie thought about washing her hand but looked out the window instead. Clouds of dust from Route 31 reached her nostrils, and she coughed. Seeing the cars speed by only a hundred feet away, she remembered moments of loneliness when she had stood in her own front yard gazing up at the sky, wishing she could be aboard the silver jets flitting past her, wherever they were going. Now, she realized, she was looking at automobiles and feeling the same way, only much worse.

Dinner had been served before she arrived. Fortunately, Mom had prepared a sack of sandwiches and cookies for her, just in case. Debbie reached into the sack and began to munch on a bologna sandwich. She smiled. Mom never could remember

THE BANISHED 75

that she preferred catsup, not mustard. Because Mom dug mustard.

"Can I have a cookie?"

The girl sitting on the opposite bed scarcely seemed pregnant. Slender, perhaps seventeen, she appeared to be all elbows and knees and large, blank eyes. It was as if nature had begun work on her and then gone on a break.

"Sure." Debbie offered the bag. "When are you due?"

"I'm over four months now." The girl had a name tag pinned to her lifeless cotton sweater, Debbie saw, remembering that she'd been given one, too. It was in her purse. The one on this new girl said, HI! I'M RHONDA. "But I'm havin' trouble with the kid," Rhonda added.

"I'm sorry." Debbie spoke softly because she felt guilty about the fact that she'd experienced no pain or morning sickness yet.

"Oh, *that's* OK." Rhonda brightened and brushed a strand of wispy, mouse-colored hair back from her temple. "I might not carry full-term. I might even abort, they say. Then I can just go home again."

"Again?"

Rhonda smiled almost slyly and picked at the sheet on the bed. "Yeah, this place is kind of like my second home, actually. I been here twice before." When she giggled, almost proudly, cookie crumbs gave her a dim blond mustache.

"You must really love your guy," Debbie said slowly, groping her way.

"Yeah, *all* of them." Rhonda bobbed her colorless head with solemnity. "I really do. I guess I just, well, dig guys a lot. And they all *love* me," she boasted happily.

Lights-out came at nine-thirty, after Debbie

Heybeck had watched an hour of TV in the lounge. Then, feeling painfully self-conscious about it, she undressed in a dark corner beside her bed, pulled on a nightie, and slipped between the sheets. They were cool, and she liked the feel of them at first. Then she wondered how many other girls had lain beneath them, and she found a single position that was comfortable and froze into it.

She closed her eyes at last, said the prayer she'd said every night since Mom taught it to her, soon after she was adopted, and she wondered for the hundredth time if God, too, had forsaken her for nine months. Perhaps He went on a vacation now and then, she fantasized, growing sleepy; or perhaps He spent part of the year in *this* continent, part of the year in another. Eventually her nerves were throttled by the weariness that had grown apace over the past few weeks and she slept.

The dormitory seemed to vibrate.

Debbie awakened, frightened, to Elvis's mild gyrations. She stared into the dark, wondering what was happening. Her eyes adjusted quickly, aided by moonlight spilling through the window by her bed, and she decided it must be an earthquake. Not that she had ever heard of such a thing in supersafe, supercommon, supercool Indiana.

It subsided almost at once, and Debbie tentatively shut her eyes.

Although she was barely showing, her abdomen suddenly heaved like a tidal wave, shifted wildly, and brought her eyes open again.

Really scared now, she raised herself up on her elbow and squinted into the gloom.

Throughout the dorm, from corner to corner, a sort of golden haze had begun to drift, languidly, gently. Odorless, it was barely visible, but Debbie could make it out where it hung only inches above the heads of the girls in Elvis.

There were no chimes, no trumpets, nothing loud or showy.

He wants me. Debbie found the thought suddenly in her head, knowing it was true.

She smiled and threw back the covers. Arising, she poked her small feet into fuzzy crimson bedroom slippers, vaguely aware that other girls were also beginning to get up, soundlessly, to stand by their beds in a posture of *waiting.*

Chosen, Debbie realized. *I am chosen.*

Possessing the knowledge filled her head with a rich, peaceful, cozy kind of joy—not a joy of triumph, not an ecstatic joy that led one to lose control, but a certain warm soothingness akin to contentment. And more.

She began walking to the rec room. She knew her destination; it was there she was wanted. Other girls followed, some well into their twenties, all moving in a brisk but unhurried, *decided* kind of way, and with no need for conversation.

Descending the spiral staircase to the first floor, the young women of Milliken passed Mrs. Vera Canobly's quarters, and the founder, hearing their footsteps, opened her door a bit timorously.

Curlers binding her gray hair, she peeped out as her charges, clad in nighties and pajamas and underwear, trooped by. That new one—the Heybeck girl—even gave her a shy, somewhat affectionate smile as she passed.

"Where are you girls going at this hour?" Mrs. Canobly called anxiously. "It's—it's after two."

There was no reply, but it didn't seem rude, somehow. Her girls just looked busy.

Debbie Heybeck and twenty-three other young women strode into the recreation room, formed a silent rough circle between the Ping-Pong table and an old upright piano, and joined hands.

There was no need for them to turn on the light. A circular white light appeared above their heads, near the acoustic tile ceiling, just as they began to sing.

Vera Canobly arrived just in time to see the light appear and, therefore, to hear the singing, as well. The expressions on her girls' faces caused her to refrain from speaking. She listened, instead, not recognizing the song. But its words—mere alien sounds at first—triggered something in a memory that had studied ancient languages years ago. Gripping the doorframe as she began to understand, Mrs. Canobly stood at the entrance to the rec room, lips parted in frank astonishment, looking for words of her own to call out.

The circle of twenty-four young females, apparently quite unaware of the presence of the home's founder, sang with an incredible, midafternoon-in-the-chapel kind of enthusiasm. A certain infectious, spontaneous joy in their voices brought tears to Vera's old eyes. The pretty faces of the young women, lit by the glowing round ball above them, were rapt with attention and happiness.

The ball shifted position, and shadow dappled the women's faces, hid their bodies in darkness—*and the unwed mothers of Milliken, absorbed by the light, slowly began to fade.*

To Mrs. Canobly's shock, the light seemed to *pour* down with utmost gentleness, spreading over her young ladies so that their heads and forms at first shimmered, then dimmed, and finally—*disappeared.* For as the last note of the song ended, so did the girls.

The room darkened at once, because the light, too, had gone. Vera Canobly was left in a frightening kind of darkness, stillness, aloneness. Momentarily she felt bereft—depleted and abandoned.

Staring in the direction of where the girls had been, her logic took over and the founder of the center began to doubt her own mind. But not just because of the disappearance.

It was because the twenty-four pregnant American females, white and black and yellow, had been singing a long-forgotten hymn they could not possibly have known. *And they sang it in Aramaic, the language spoken in Jerusalem at the time of Jesus Christ.*

4

Five days until April 22, 1984
6:24 A.M., EST

When Jed Westphal went to the bank the day before to deposit his advance check, he boldly accepted in cash the full amount remaining after his earlier-written checks were paid: ninety-four dollars and thirty-three cents. He knew that he would need operating capital, for gas and lunches away from home, if a proper investigation of the Clemora incident was to be conducted. Jed hadn't been able to get a credit card anywhere for more than four years; so cash was indispensable.

Then he had worked until after midnight on a short detective story that was intended to become a quick sale to *Ellery Queen's Mystery Magazine*. Once, several years ago, the highly professional editor of that periodical had actually bought a tale of his. Jed often lived in the hope that miracles could happen twice, at least eventually, and that "Mr. Queen" would be impressed by his book sale and even double the usual story price.

But even though the day had been full and he had gone to bed late, Jed had found himself unable to sleep. Part of the problem was the continuing absence of Rosalyn and the important things she had meant to him. Always, in the past, he had been able to talk over his problems with Rosalyn, and even if she failed to come up with a solution, the very airing of them tended to suggest fresh directions, fresh insights, to him.

He'd liked Stacy Bennett, liked her a lot, but they were from such different worlds it was foolish to think of actually dating her. Besides, Rosalyn was a habit of long standing, and Jed had never entirely given up the hope of persuading her to come back to him.

The Vanishment, as the evening *News* was calling Clemora's tragedy, had filled Jed's mind, interfering with his effort to sleep. Inexplicable disappearances had happened before in history, he knew. His imagination still tingled when he thought about what had happened near Suvla Bay in Gallipoli during World War I.

Early on August 28, 1915, the British First Fourth Norfolk intended to mount an assault on what was termed Hill 60, scene of earlier skirmishes and massive losses. More than one thousand men were in the regiment that warm late-summer day, Jed recalled reading, but they were not to see August 29. Not, at any rate, in this dimension.

A low cloud bank had hung over the men despite the fact that the day was generally clear; a breeze was blowing. Observers of the large regiment saw the thousand soldiers climb the hill. And then, to their complete astonishment, the men were seemingly "eaten" by the clouds. For when the cloud bank had moved on, there was no trace of the thousand men from the First Fourth Norfolk.

And so the question formed naturally enough: *Was* there a connection between the clouds of old-time Gallipoli and the shining white circle at Clemora?

Jed had tossed and turned, his imagination working overtime as it often did at night. Some of his best stories had evolved then, presumably as the right hemisphere of his brain, creative and unbound by facts, assumed control. Perhaps the regiment had been somehow teleported—if that was the right word—somewhere else, where they lived out their enigmatic lives, now and then chuckling as they considered the glorious trick played on their fellows.

If so, then it was possible that the children of Clemora *also* lived—somewhere *else*.

The thought had sent shivers along Jed's spine. Where in this world, or in the next, could that "somewhere else" *be*? In what direction was heaven, or, for that matter, hell? Astronauts seemed to have eliminated the immediate solar system.

He remembered standing with Stacy in the front yard of the institution, looking in all four directions, seeking some ground cover into which the students might have fled. But there were only open spaces around the building, leading to the uninviting ramshackle houses of the Venus Hill residents, who did not really need any more children.

Jed finally gave up trying to sleep around six, went downstairs, and turned on his television set as he plugged in coffee from the day before. He'd have to remember to buy some milk and something easy to cook that night. A TV dinner, maybe. The hundred bucks or so he had left would go much further if he ate at home. And, besides, the notion of another meal from McDonald's brought bile into his mouth.

He was slipping the envelope containing his new story for *EQMM* on the table beside his front door, as a reminder to mail it, when the baritone voice of the news reporter on TV caught his attention.

". . . that the Vanishments have apparently spread to the north side of Indianapolis with the disappearance last night of twenty-four young residents of the Milliken Center, a home for unwed mothers on U.S. Thirty-one. Mrs. Vera Canobly, who founded Milliken years ago, reported that the young women filed into their recreation room in the dead of night, began singing, and then somehow vanished in a white light similar to that reported at Clemora House of Friends. . . ."

Stunned, Jed sank into a chair, his coffee forgotten. He had noticed that the customarily disciplined face of the local anchor man was twisted slightly in a mixture of wonder, curiosity, and even worry.

Making a decision, Jed ran quickly to the telephone in the dining room and, glancing at the scrap of paper Stacy had given him bearing her number, dialed the psychologist as quickly as he could. At the other end the phone rang four times, five, six——

"Hello?"

"Stacy, it's Jed." Afterthought. "Jed Westphal."

Her voice was strained with sleepiness and pique. "Do you know what time it is, Jedediah, or do writers eschew clocks and calendars along with reality?"

"As much as possible," he admitted with a grin. "Unless we write s-f, of course. I see you haven't heard the news."

"I can manage to do without horror stories at six in the morning," she grumbled. He could almost see her roughing up her long, lovely light-brown hair.

"You can't do without *this* story," he told her and related what he had just heard on his TV set.

Stacy came instantly awake, scarcely believing her own ears. "That is positively amazing!"

"Yes, it is. Stacy, do you by any chance know the woman in charge of the center—Vera Canobly?"

She paused. Businesslike prudence crept in. "I've attended a few public functions with her, that's all."

"You have to phone her." Jed made a conscious effort to sound firm and persuasive. "Call her and set it up for me to interview her."

"You, ah, said 'us,' did you not?" Stacy demanded after a pause.

"I sure did," he lied cheerfully.

"I guess I can't talk you out of this on the grounds that it's really none of our business what's happened at Milliken?"

"Oh, but it *is!*" Jed exclaimed. "I think it's one hundred percent clear there is some connection with Clemora and Milliken. People are mysteriously disappearing—so far, only at Clemora and Milliken. Who knows what's next?"

"Very well." Stacy sounded a trifle grim now. "You can pick me up in twenty minutes, if you want."

"Gee, lady, you're really a hard sell!"

"Just get here. There might be a new clue to the whereabouts of my kids."

Jed began to dress in his customary rapid fashion. He slipped on a sport shirt before it occurred to him that he should, as an interviewer and an almost-published author, dress more formally. He looked at his two white shirts with their unrelentingly stiff collars and finally settled for carelessly donning a tie. It was a hideous contrast to the patterned sport shirt, and the thickness of its knot left the informal collar wildly askew. There were two practically empty bottles of aftershave on his dresser, and Jed shook what he could from one, dabbing it on his face and neck, then repeated the process with the other bottle.

Stacy Bennett lived in an apartment complex called Wycliffe, which was only a few blocks off the route to Milliken Center. Jed found her waiting for him beside the curb, her long hair ruffled by the spring breeze, her costume a hastily selected sweater and skirt that nearly matched. *We'll never be asked to pose as fashion models,* Jed thought wryly, pulling the car alongside. Approaching it, Stacy looked more like a busty college girl going out on a date than a competent psychologist.

But she changed his impression quickly when she jumped into the front seat of the Granada, carelessly flashing a length of firm thigh. "It's about time," she snapped.

"I'm five minutes early," Jed protested.

She ignored him. "Hit the interstate," she ordered, lighting a cigarette with the lighter from his dashboard. "Vera Canobly is expecting us."

"Aye, aye, ma'am!" he retorted, both annoyed by her commanding ways and pleased by her spirit.

He took the exit off Post Road, merging smoothly with the flow of early morning traffic on 70 and sneaking occasional glances at this extraordinary young woman. In all his nine years of marriage to Rosalyn, he couldn't remember even being alone with another desirable woman. It was an accepted part of his pact with Rosalyn that if he absolutely had to have another girl, he would tell his wife and they would part without rancor. It seemed deeply ironic to him just then that his confirmed loyalty had been given with no better reward for it than being walked out on.

He rolled his window down, shaking his head in the breeze to dislodge the reproachful face of Rosalyn Westphal from his mind's eye, and glanced again at Stacy. "I guess we don't know much about each other," he began.

"That isn't important," she said flatly. She faced front, a fine-lined profile with her eyelids half-lowered. Smoke issued from her nostrils almost threateningly.

But Jed wasn't to be put off today. "I think it is," he contradicted. "If we're working together now, a dash of friendliness might make it more pleasant."

"I'm sorry." She turned to him at last, and the surprising warmth of her gaze was genuine, and without an iota of scorn, for the first time. "Look, I really *am*. I suppose I'm a pretty single-minded lady when something this important is at stake. Maybe I stuff too much into the old computer."

"I sympathize with your concern for the kids."

"What do you want to know about me?" she asked, exhaling smoke. There seemed to be something of a wary, hard screen erected, as if Stacy wanted to be careful about what she said.

"Well, is there a Mr. Bennett—or even a Professor Bennett—somewhere in the background?"

"You have a nice linear mind," she teased. "Very straight line. Lots of people find that dull and claim it represents a type of thinking that is closed, narrow, leading only to preconceived conclusions."

"I'm just an honest, candid guy," he murmured, hoping to avoid a complete psychological profile. "I tend to say or ask what's on my mind. For example, Doctor, you are very, very pretty—and you didn't answer my question at all."

She shifted on the front seat, crossing her short, well-proportioned legs. Why, Jed wondered, did he find her so attractive, when he really preferred taller women? "Thank you for the compliment, Jed, and 'no' to Mr. Bennett. And in answer to your *next* question, no—I've never been married. And you?"

It was the first time since Rosalyn left him that he'd been asked, and it made him feel rattled. "Yes." Slowly. "Yes, I was married, until just a few weeks ago."

Stacy considered the remark and kept her expression noncommittal. "How long did the marriage last?"

"Forever. There was nothing at all before Rosalyn and Darren." A lump in his throat, he stared straight ahead. Dimly, he felt disloyal talking about the situation. "I miss Darren very much."

"And your ex-wife?" Stacy watched his face with interest. "What of her?"

He frowned. "Really, I'm not sure——"

"*You* started this Hour of Confidence program, Jed, not me."

His shoulders made light of it. "Well, I simply don't know yet whether I'm missing Rosalyn or missing being married. It's one of the two."

They were silent several moments. "I was thinking while I was waiting," Stacy began anew, "that this horrible thing at the Milliken Center ruins the theory of a mysterious fleet of UFOs."

"Why, particularly?" he asked, curious.

"Because I've never heard of any vehicles that pass through *walls*." She smiled, proud of her deduction. "And the unwed mothers vanished from their recreation room in the center."

"It's possible that your Mrs. Canobly imagined it, isn't it?" he asked, dodging into a lane to his right to escape from a semi cannonballing up to his rear bumper. "Your hallucination theory again, maybe that applies. She could have heard of the thing at Clemora, and she might have been ready to pin a weirdo explanation on anything that transpired."

Stacy laughed. It was a midrange tinkling sound of real merriment, and it automatically made Jed smile. "Now who's playing shrink?" she demanded. "No, Mr. W., I do not think that would be true of Vera Canobly. Milliken isn't an institution at all to her, but a precious home. Any pressure there she'd have had to apply to herself. She is a very open person, a woman with a good mixture of business sense and genuine interest in her girls. Everyone I know speaks well of the lady, even businessmen who hate women owning their own place."

He nodded as they turned off on North Meridian Street, and they drove the remaining mile or so in thoughtful silence.

Jed parked on the center grounds, surprised to find only a handful of other cars already there. Apparently seven in the morning was too early for the city's press.

They found a smile face stuck on the front door. Pushing the door open, they saw five or six young pregnant women milling about in the large room beyond the foyer. The two visitors stood quietly, unsure of where they should go.

"Hi! I'm Marcia."

The girl had broken away from her group and drawn swiftly near, intently evaluating Jed with her steady gaze.

"We're looking for Mrs. Vera Canobly," the author told her. Like many men, he felt distinctly ill at ease around pregnant children. "Would it be possible for you to take us to her?"

"Why not?" Marcia said breezily, turning. "I'm almost sixteen," she called over her shoulder, "since you're wondering, but I know the score."

Stacy took mercy on Jed. "How long do you have to go?" she asked, following the girl.

"Three or four months, I guess," Marcia answered, shrugging as she walked. "I waited too long to abort the little son of a bitch. Ol' Ralph, he outsmarted me."

Stacy exchanged a quick glance with Jed.

"Couple of reporters t'see ya," Marcia announced casually as she leaned in through glass partitions, giving Jed a final, coolly appraising stare before bouncing off down the hallway.

"Oh, dear," said the voice within. "Dear me. The press conference isn't until nine."

Stacy walked in with a smile. "It's Dr. Bennett, Mrs. Canobly. How are you?"

The elderly woman blinked behind thick lenses. "Forgive me, but Marcia said you were from the press, and I'm afraid my sight has never been exactly twenty-twenty."

"This is the author I mentioned," Stacy said, indicating Jed, who stepped nearer. "Jedediah N. Westphal. We hope not to take too much of your time."

Jed found a firm, dry, pillowy palm in his. The woman who leaned across the desk to shake hands was around sixty, give or take a decade, gray-haired, her eyes like shiny quarters behind the heavy spectacles. There was a girlish roundness to her face, her bosom, and her arms that gave her the aura of an aging Rubens cherub. She wore a blue business suit over which she had donned, startlingly enough, what appeared to be a bandsman's jacket.

The founder caught Jed's surprise and blushed prettily. "It's for this," she explained swiftly, pulling something up on the desk from the floor at her feet. It was a black leather case. When she opened it, something with a high polish glittered. "My old clarinet," she said. "I must confess, music is one of my most prized hobbies. I had promised the girls I'd be entertaining them today. Now this awful thing has happened!"

"That's what we're here about," Jed remarked, pushing the conversation forward.

Vera Canobly had tears in her huge, almost colorless eyes. "Perhaps you should simply put me through a series of tests, Dr. Bennett. Maybe I've imagined it all."

Stacy, seated in front of the desk, reached out to pat the older woman's plump hand. "The girls clearly have gone. I'm sure you're every bit as bright as you ever were. There's an explanation somewhere, Mrs. Canobly."

The founder sighed her relief. "It's positively beneficial having you here, my dear. I guess you'll want me to tell my terrible tale."

"If you wouldn't mind, please."

Jed listened attentively at first, then realized he was hearing only what he'd heard on TV earlier in the day. That in itself was somewhat surprising. As a rule, reporters in their haste were inclined to make little inaccuracies, which multiplied until someone at last cried "distortion" or "taken out of context."

Here, though, it was as if everyone involved in the Clemora and Milliken "Vanishments" had striven to get all the facts straight—perhaps in a superstitious hope that good, hard facts would dispel the shade of unreason.

As the two women conversed, occasionally going off on tangents about particular girls, the exhaustion Jed felt from loss of sleep caused him to tune them out. Keeping his face politely masked, he suddenly began to wonder why only twenty-four of the sixty girls at Milliken had disappeared. Why not the *other* thirty-six? Who was being so selective, and why?

Surreptitiously, he checked his notes from the interviews at Clemora and reminded himself that, while all but one of the retarded children had been . . . removed, a single violent and angry student had been left behind. The bright, circular light hadn't taken—apparently *didn't* take—all.

But what was the common denominator? What could be the connection between Clemora and Milliken?

When the idea struck him, it was with such force that he burst back into the conversation as if he hadn't left it, interrupting Stacy Bennett in midremark.

"Tell me, Mrs. Canobly," Jed asked earnestly, "what kind of girls were taken?"

The older woman blinked owlishly, a plump hand tidying her gray hair at the nape of her neck. "I'm sure I don't know what you *mean*, Mr. Westphal. They were all—pregnant ones!"

"No." He shook his head and waggled a hand negatively. "Aside from that. I'll rephrase the question: Would you say that the girls who were —who have *gone*—were the good girls or the bad ones?"

Before she could answer him, Stacy frowned at Jed. "That's a qualitative judgment that isn't really fair to Mrs. Canobly," she pointed out. "I'm sure that——"

"It's all right, Dr. Bennett," Mrs. Canobly interposed. She was very serious now, the cherubic image replaced by that of someone who was dedicated and personally concerned. Very much so. "Perhaps you're onto something, Mr. Westphal, because I was wondering the very same thing." But then she hesitated, fat fingers toying absently with the reed of her clarinet. "The girls who vanished, to be honest about it, were the cream of the crop, the absolute cream of the crop. Girls who *fell* into trouble—not those who *looked* for it."

Jed pursed his lips as he held the woman's gaze in agreement. "I thought as much. It makes sense."

"Why?" Stacy demanded. "What made you wonder such a thing?"

"A random notion," he replied, tapping his fingers on the desk. "Stacy, how would you characterize the missing students at Clemora? Other than their mental condition, IQs, and so on."

"Why, they were *lovely* children, really. I had begun to reach them all, I think—Phillip Hanzlik, Susan Renick, Elizabeth, even little Clyde Lucas. I really felt that I was getting——" Stacy stopped talking. She gaped at Jed, her lips parted in surprise. "I see what you mean. The one who was left behind at Clemora—DeWayne Johnson—is quite uncontrollable, disinterested in himself and everything and everyone around him."

"Yeah. A bad kid." Jed nodded, recalling the brash pregnant child named Marcia who had brought them to the Milliken founder's office. "I'll say it for both you ladies quite candidly, then: The ones who *were not taken* are bad kids."

"Which means," Stacy said soberly, "the—the *force* wants only decent, good kids. What kind of ghastly ... *experiments* can the kidnappers have in mind for all those nice children?" A look of sheer revulsion and horror transfigured her pretty face.

"I don't know just what is going on," Jed responded, intense now, "but whatever this power is, whether it's man-made or mass-hypnotic—a warp in time and space or someone from another planet acquiring specimens—it seems to choose the most decent children from those who are available. Somehow, it *knows* who each of these kids is."

Caught up in the conjecture, Stacy said, "Speaking of DeWayne, do you think now that there was anything to that threat he gave you? Jed—isn't it just possible that—well, that *we* might be in danger, too?"

Jed took her hand and squeezed it lightly, looking from her to Vera Canobly. "At this point, ladies, I'd say that almost anything has become possible in this crazy world—anything at all."

12:06 P.M., EST

The noon news on television seemed to have been seen by, or repeated to, everyone in Indianapolis and all Marion County. By midafternoon the second Vanishment had become a favorite topic of conversation, temporarily overshadowing the events in the Mideast.

Shortly after noon, however, a man in India who had hinted for years that he was the returning Messiah was assassinated. Attention quickly veered to the world scene.

For the time being.

* * *

Vera Canobly had led Stacy and Jed around the Milliken Center, introducing them to pockets of pregnant young women, most of whom seemed to confirm the writer's theory. Their attitudes and qualities seemed coarse, self-serving. A few were rude or boastful. He was shocked by some of the stories Mrs. Canobly told him and Stacy in hushed tones, tales ranging from stolen food to boyfriends who were smuggled in to acts of lesbianism. Stacy, experienced in the perils of institutional life, was somewhat amused by Jed's obvious astonishment.

They examined each of the four dormitories, where the temporary tenants, witnesses to the strange exodus of their sisters, described what had happened.

"Did they appear, well, *hypnotized* in any way?" Stacy probed in dorm Elvis.

The wide-eyed, slender blonde girl shook her head. "No, ma'am. They jest moved quietlike, got up and plain left the dorm. I followed 'em partway and heard 'em singin' after they went into the rec room. But they scared me, sort of."

Jed had a sudden idea. "Was there anything they said, or anything in what they sang, to indicate that the girls might have joined some kind of religious cult?" he asked. Stacy's heartbeat quickened when she heard the query. "Is it possible that they may simply have left the center to join Hare Krishna or the Moonies—one of those offbeat religious groups?"

Again Rhonda shook her head, a tornado of blond hair, immediately dashing their hopes. "I've knowed some of those girls for absolutely *a-ges*," she averred, "and I know they woulda asked me t'join up, too. No, I don't think they was especially religious, 'cept maybe two or three girls who read the Good Book or went to the prayer room on Sunday." Suddenly she shuddered, her thin body shaking and jerking. Rhonda's drab eyes had a faraway, remembering glint. "But I got to tell you, that *song* they sang gave me the creeps!"

"Why?" Stacy pressed.

"Because I didn't unnerstand a word they sang," she replied as if that explained everything. "Why, the song was *foreign*."

Jed became aware that Vera Canobly was trying to get his eye. He turned, and she nervously cleared her throat. "May I speak with you two privately?"

She led the writer and the psychologist away from Rhonda, almost wringing her hands. "I'm afraid, well, I hadn't mentioned *that* part to you —about the song. But Rhonda confirmed it; so I guess it wasn't my imagination after all."

"Confirmed what, Mrs. Canobly?" Jed inquired.

Clearly, she didn't want to go on. "Well, the words of the—the hymn were definitely foreign, just as poor little Rhonda told you." Vera Canobly flushed beneath her gray hair. "I'm a student of ancient languages, you see, from many years ago. And—well, I began to recognize some of the words that my girls sang just before the light got them. It was my impression"—she stoutly drew her little body erect—"that they were singing in Aramaic."

"Aramaic!" exclaimed Stacy.

Mrs. Canobly nodded firmly. "Yes, that's right. The language spoken in biblical times."

"Did you teach them the hymn?" Stacy asked.

The founder shook her head.

"What about a member of your staff, someone very religious?" Jed inquired.

"Oh, no. I know my people, and they don't know the language. And I had never heard the hymn before. But the words were—moving."

"Well, could there be a book in Aramaic around

here?" Jed asked, adding with a face, "Perhaps an English-Aramaic dictionary?"

Mrs. Canobly shook her head again.

"Curiouser and curiouser," he mumbled.

"It's becoming a Lewis Carroll world," Stacy agreed.

Hurrying to complete their unhappy tour of the Milliken Center before the press conference was scheduled to begin, the trio wound its way downstairs to the recreation room.

The founder stopped at the door, gesturing. Her tone was low. "This is where my girls vanished."

It was by no means a mysterious place. Everything one could place in a rec room to make it enjoyable for young women seemed to be there, Jed noticed. In addition to a table tennis set and a pool table, each immaculate and almost newlooking, there were card tables bearing stacks of new playing cards, a large cabinet stuffed with boxed games ranging from Scrabble to Monopoly to Uno to Parcheesi to backgammon, plus an upright piano standing on a small makeshift bandstand.

A snack bar with a variety of soft drinks stood against the far wall, adjacent to it an area for writing letters or perhaps doing some light reading.

"Could you show us exactly where the girls were at the moment they vanished?"

Jed turned to look with some surprise at Stacy.

"Certainly," the founder replied, hip-wriggling around to an area between the Ping-Pong table and the piano. "Exactly here, Doctor."

Jed watched Stacy with growing wonderment. Her fine little features were both determined and, he concluded, slightly glazed. She drew nearer the area very slowly, senses alerted, and then stood there with an uncertain attitude, almost as if she expected something to happen there again.

As the others stared, Stacy shut her eyes. Her arms were raised slightly from her sides, the palms open in a groping motion, then closing slightly—as if *on* something.

"Why, Mr. Westphal," Mrs. Canobly whispered hoarsely, amazed, "Dr. Bennett is standing *precisely* the way the girls were standing—because they were *holding hands!*"

"And you didn't talk about that to us, did you?" he asked in a hushed tone. Suddenly he was afraid the young woman might follow the others and disappear. "Stacy, what's going on?"

The psychologist's hazel eyes snapped open, blinking and dazed. For a moment she could not seem to reply. The back of her hand touched her forehead, then her lips.

At last she moved away from the area of the disappearance in a shuddering, abrupt motion, as if leaving one frightening room for another, and took the writer's arm. She gripped it hard but avoided his anxious eyes. "I th-think we're through here," she managed.

"What's going on, Stacy, damn it? What did you—*feel*—over there?" He looked intently down at her, concerned. "Tell me!"

Stacy looked up at Jed with her lovely eyes intense, lost and almost fearful. "Awe, Jed," she replied. "I felt . . . *awe. Respect and wonderment.*"

They had stayed for the press conference, finding the questions similar to those asked at Clemora. Jed saw a few familiar faces. Some of the reporters were becoming nastily persistent in seeking an explanation for what was happening. All of them eagerly tied the Milliken incident to what had transpired at Clemora, and Mrs. Canobly and her staff made no effort to dissuade them. Interviewed by one of the reporters, the immense black man who'd been Jed's seating companion at Clemora, Stacy told them that, from a scientific viewpoint, the conclusion of a connection was vastly premature.

Jed took her to lunch at the Steak and Ale near Broad Ripple, and for a while they dropped the discussion of disappearances in preference to enjoying each other's company.

It was after one when they were served, and Stacy's joke led the way to lighter topics. "They call a late breakfast a brunch," she said, "so is a late lunch a linner or a lupper?"

It was the first glimpse Jed had had of Stacy's humor, and he found himself drawing closer to the young professional woman. He began opening up, saying things to her one normally saved for an old friend.

To his astonishment, Jed realized he had been under enormous tension during the closing days of his marriage to Rosalyn. When he spoke now, it was a nervous chattering, as if a dam had burst inside and he was trying to retain some control. Things he had bottled up for months sprang out —plans and hopes, ideals and dreams.

Stacy listened with growing interest. It was hard to describe, she thought, but there were several areas of Jed's life that coincided nicely with her own, opinions and needs he expressed that appeared to be a masculine version of her own. She listened attentively while he described his first novel, how it came to be purchased, and what he hoped to achieve in the future. Now, it was not so much that Jed was echoing her own ambitions as it was that she found his hopes and plans agreeable, the kind with which she could sympathize or identify. Besides, while he was not precisely handsome, she found his manner of speaking—sometimes making a little explanatory speech before getting to the heart of the matter, a sign of insecurity she found engaging—enjoyable and charming.

It was nearly four by the time Jed drove Stacy back to Wycliffe, her apartment complex, and he found himself quite naturally following her into her apartment, borne there on a flood of amiable chitchat and revelation.

He even followed her around the place as she went into the kitchenette to fetch Cokes, helping her crack ice and slip cubes into two glasses. The apartment itself was strikingly spare, he saw, in terms of furnishings. He had the impression that Stacy had planned it with two concepts in mind: to provide enough furniture to be minimally functional and to provide enough decoration to allow one to relax.

In the latter category, Stacy had leaned heavily toward a graphic approach, hanging inexpensive prints of the masters—mostly Rembrandt and Van Gogh, Jed noticed, finding the combination less clashing than he'd have thought—on every wall.

Carrying the Cokes into the sitting area of the small apartment, they went to a long sectional couch and sat a couple of polite, just-friends feet apart. Across from them, Jed saw a small stereo and a handful of records, plus a single recliner. Otherwise, the room was bare.

For some time, in his outpouring of bottled-up views, he was not aware that Stacy's own conversation had seriously lagged. When he noticed, at last, he asked why.

She shrugged a little and gave him a nervous smile. "I've never had a man up here before," she replied, sipping her Coke. "The Clemora House of Friends has been my life since college. And before that, grad school." She hesitated. "I don't think I've had a date for the last four years."

Jed turned instantly to her, seeing that this was a confession tinged with a tentative tone of apology. Perhaps, too, he thought, it was something of a plea—a plea to be patient and understanding. For the first time he began to perceive that her caustic manner was used for a purpose.

"Being married to one person for nearly ten years," he told her slowly, carefully, allowing his hand to rest on her shoulder, "develops a kind of —new virginity. Artificial, of course; wouldn't hold up in court. But the loyal husband doesn't even touch other women; so, with everyone but his wife, he's as much a neophyte as someone who's *never* had sexual relations." He was abruptly, hotly embarrassed and shook his head in self-derision. "I guess that doesn't make a lick of sense."

"Probably not," she began in her usual snappish way. Then she startled him by inclining her head slightly to kiss his hand. "Oh, yes, Jed, it does *so* make sense. I don't want to be a hypocrite. With your wife you might be practiced, experienced, expert, even mechanical, but every other woman is still a fresh challenge in every respect, isn't she? You might prove to be as loutish and as fresh to a strange woman as a schoolboy." She laughed and held his gaze with a sudden swift turn to severity. "I'm not just a—a new kind of virgin, Jed. I'm the old-fashioned kind."

His smile was tender, as were his feelings. "For some reason, I'm not surprised."

"Thank you, I *think*," Stacy replied, her brows

curved querulously. "Not that I make a fetish of it or brandish my virginity like a Goddamn weapon. At least, I *hope* I don't do that. I've just had—other interests."

"Don't apologize," he urged her.

Suddenly she sat up, embarrassed by the topic, and freed herself from his arm. "Those are the last Cokes I have in the place." She studied him silently, and he had no idea what she was thinking. "Could I possibly persuade you to go get us another carton?" Stacy paused. "I'd like you to stay awhile, Jed—to talk."

He stood, grinning almost boyishly again. "There's nowhere I'd rather be. Would you prefer something stronger? Wine, perhaps?"

She shook her head, averting her gaze as the idea that had crossed her mind produced her customary shyness. "Cokes will be fine."

When Jed went out to the car, it had begun to drizzle rain, the kind that seems to be spitting at one in total derision; but by the time he returned from Haag's with a new carton of soft drinks, the rain's insults were full-blown and wildly impudent. He was obliged to run through a downpour, his shoes splashing at the new puddles, and he was fully drenched when he finally slammed the apartment door behind him.

Stacy looked at the writer and giggled, one hand across her lips. "You look like a drowned rat. Worse, with your hair washed flat that way you remind me of some villain in a thirties gangster film."

He gave her an imitation frown. "The least you could do is help me off with my shirt."

She jumped up and did as he asked, and when his bare, damp back was to her, she found herself wrapping her arms around his waist, briefly holding him against her suddenly maternal warmth.

Jed was surprised, even delighted, but when he turned to her, Stacy had already resumed her position on the couch.

"Jed, you were seeking some common denominator for the Vanishments, as the papers are calling them. Well, I think it's obvious, what you said at Milliken—obviously *true*. And—something else."

"What?" Puzzled by Stacy's about-face, Jed sat down on the floor and began removing his wet shoes.

"Well, all those who've been taken are *young*. No one much over thirty has been taken."

"You're quite right," he said solemnly, thinking about it. "*Yet*," he added, his eyes warning her.

"You think there'll be more, don't you?"

"My mom was a trifle superstitious. She read some strange things. Believed some, too." He reached for his wet shirt and coaxed a damp Camel pack out of the pocket. When he offered Stacy one, she declined. "Mother always said things of this kind—*and* deaths—comes in threes."

"Do you believe that?"

He lit up, inhaled. "I believe you were virtually terrified back at the center, in the rec room," he responded. "What the hell was going on?"

"No, not so much terrified as awed." She paused, evasive momentarily. Her long hair swung forward as she reached down to toy with her small shoe. "It's—hard to say. A just *knew* how the girls had been standing. At—the end. Their end. And I was, well, *drawn* to stand there, too."

"Did you have any kind of, um, premonition?"

"No, not really." Her hazel eyes had forgotten his naked chest for a moment and seemed faraway. "I was meant to experience something of what those girls experienced, I think. Although you shouldn't ask me what I mean by 'meant.' That and, well, I had a distinct—apprehension."

"Apprehension of what?"

Stacy shook her head, impatient with herself. "I don't know. DeWayne, maybe. Really, Jed, I've no idea. It was probably nothing but nerves after the scary happenings at Clemora."

He squinted at the scarlet tip of his Camel. "When I couldn't sleep last night, and again while I was at Haag's, I remembered something that Mom told me or that I read somewhere, about a vanishing British regiment during World War I."

Her head shot up. She seemed enormously surprised and delighted. "You, sire, are drawing things out of me I haven't discussed since I was a child. Jed, I had a very proper religious upbringing. Once, I was Catholic. Perhaps that's a part of why I'm still a virgin: the Mr. Right syndrome, to be wed in a church, all that." Her eyes flickered quickly to his bare torso. "I guess I'll never know what I've missed. . . . Well, in school I became interested in —in *outré* things, bizarre events—the kind they usually call supernatural or paranormal events these days—but *factually* based." She shrugged, rubbed her hands along her arms. "I'm still inclined to read things like that, to believe in God but *because* of Him to believe in a much more marvelous, complex, even incomprehensible universe than the one nice fundamental folks accept."

"And?" He looked up at her, lightly holding her ankle.

"And I know that there are *more* modern examples of inexplicable disappearances. I just didn't have the nerve to cite them before."

"I wonder: Are you referring to the Philadelphia experiment?" he inquired, smiling. "The old rumor that the navy experimented with invisibility in 1943?"

"I *could* have been," she replied, taking a drag from his cigarette. This time she held his gaze. "There are strange supportive strains of evidence about that disappearing ship and a good book on the subject. But it wasn't what I had in mind." She turned her Coke glass between her hands. "Back in December of 1937, Japan and China had been fighting for half a year when a Chinese colonel, Li Fu Sien, took three thousand reinforcements in an advance along a two-mile line. It was near the bridge over the Yangtze River, as a matter of fact. And it was kind of a last-ditch stand."

"What happened?"

"Well, as the sun rose, the colonel was informed that all contact had been lost with his army, all reinforcements. He went off to investigate but discovered only a tiny residue of soldiers. They were encamped, confused, by the bridge. Jed, all the other positions were *deserted*. The men remaining there hadn't heard a sound, and the sentries swore that no one—absolutely *no one*—had crossed the bridge."

Jed blinked. "Well," he began, not unreasonably, "where the hell did the rest of the three thousand troops *go*?"

Stacy shook her head. "No one knows, to this day." Her eyes were wide. "They vanished forever, I guess, never appearing on a casualty list or any lists of captured personnel. They simply stood beside their weapons, obediently ready to fight to the death, and then presumably—*vanished*."

"Stacy, you're a beautiful woman," he said romantically, kissing her calf.

She ignored him. "There are many more strange disappearances than the average person knows.

The *Mary Celeste,* for example. Or those in the Bermuda Triangle. Or that great band leader of the forties, Glenn Miller, who tried to fly to France during World War II after heroically prerecording more than a hundred and twenty-five shows. He did them all for the fighting men between July and mid-December, 1944. There were all kinds of wild rumors about what happened to him, but some of the strangest involved why *his own band* wasn't notified until it arrived at Orly, and why Orly didn't ask about him when he failed to arrive there, and why Miller had insisted on going up in a plane the day he did—against *all* advice. Again, no one has ever answered these questions."

His eyes looked back to her lovely, intent face. Her deep bosom was rising and falling more quickly than before, he thought. "Stacy, I think I'm falling in love with you."

She seemed frozen where she sat; her voice was taut. "It's not necessary for you to say that!" she snapped. "It's so—so damned characteristic of a man whose wife has walked out on him! So doggone trite, so expectedly, miserably *characteristic!*"

As Jed clambered to his feet, damp shirt in one hand, embarrassed and angry, Stacy began to regret her outburst. He wasn't a big man and he wasn't in the peak of condition, but there was something warm and comfortable about him, she thought, something good and open and reliable.

"Pardon me for being honest and for liking you too much," he retorted as he looked heatedly around for his notebook. His own chest was rising and falling now. Several absurd little blond hairs grew around his nipples, Stacy saw; his shoulders, when he turned to seek the notebook, were amply broad and sloped into distinctly masculine arms, the hair reaching only to above the wrists. "I'll get the hell out of here as soon as I find my stuff."

"Don't go, Jed. It's easy to pardon you." Her voice was different somehow. "Because in addition to those other things, which aren't all bad, you're also sweetly lovable and maybe the only tamable man I've ever met."

The fresh tone of her voice was like a scent, and he turned to it. When he looked down at her on the couch, Stacy had unbuttoned her blouse and was slipping out of it. For a moment she wouldn't let him look; she held his gaze with her own as she reached behind her slender back to unhook her bra.

Then she let it slip to the couch and raised her arms to him, her smile at once loving and brave. The arms lifted her full breasts in the oldest invitation, and he accepted it, and them, allowing her to draw his face down between them, where he eagerly snuggled and nuzzled, faintly moaning.

"I *like* your honesty, you fool," she told him softly, kissing the top of his auburn head and holding him against her. His hands stopped gripping her breasts, and she felt them in her lap, where it was warm, and growing still warmer. "I like the fact that you are open—what you are and no more." She raised her finely chiseled young face in something like first ecstasy as his lips worked alternately on her erect, elongated pink nipples. His fingers, beneath her skirt, caressed the incredible softness of her inner thighs, then, as she parted her legs, searched deeper and found. Stacy drew in her breath sharply. "And, ohhh, God, Jed, I *like* what you're *doing* to me!"

The study in Lionel K. Hartberg's home was in many ways a duplicate of his office at Clemora

House of Friends. The furniture, as a matter of fact, was absolutely identical, since it had been possible to get a discount by buying everything in twos.

In the few ways that it was not quite a duplicate of Clemora, the study was an extension of his institutional quarters. Because Mr. Hartberg's profession was the business of making money, he considered it both prudent and pleasurable to bring his work home with him. One never knew when opportunity might ring on his residence phone instead of rapping at his office door.

This particular spring evening, Mr. Hartberg was in an especially industrious frame of mind. He had things to do, profitable things, things that would maintain and perhaps increase profit. He had been so occupied with interruptions concerning the tribe of morons who had been kidnapped from Clemora that he'd never quite squared away all the precious paper work necessary to replace the little dim bulbs with a fresh crop.

There had been phone calls from two or three of the lost children's parents, begging his help, when he had already assured everyone publicly of his intention to stand behind them one hundred percent. In all but a monetary manner, of course. Then there had been the veiled accusations, from two members of the always nosy press, that Lionel K. Hartberg knew more than he was telling.

Which might be entirely true in *other* matters, certain sideline operations that brought in a little nontaxable, under-the-counter cash, but was absurd and maddening in connection with Clemora. As if he would ever do anything to jeopardize the good name of his House of Friends, let alone interfere with the brisk influx of hard cash for the little retardos' care. Understandably, he had bristled, even told them off in no uncertain terms. He made it perfectly clear that whatever else he might do, Lionel K. Hartberg was honest about Clemora.

Now he sat before his walnut home desk, a discreet cognac ready to be sipped, the folders containing the files of new prospects for Clemora residency carefully lined up for his final inspection. As always, there had been more applicants than space. But that was before the Vanishment, before adverse publicity. Mr. Hartberg knew, as he smoothed a large hand over his great bald head, that there was the possibility that a few timorous souls who actually loved their loonies might withdraw the offsprings' names from consideration.

True, those who were genuinely desperate, who'd reached the final straw in striving to care for their backward children, would still be eager to enroll at Clemora. The task at hand was to locate those who remained that anxious, in order to be certain that there would be no loss of income at all— either for Clemora as an institution or for Lionel K. Hartberg.

He screened the folder of a boy named Andrew Sautherus with considerable care and interest. He had already given the boy's father a tentative verbal agreement. The damned foreigner had pleaded with him off and on for weeks to take his miserable spawn.

At age ten, Andrew was in many respects "ideal" —docile and too small to cause a great deal of physical difficulty, toilet-trained, and with a Standard Achievement Test result indicating that he could learn a few fundamentals but wasn't bright enough to depart from Clemora before the mandatory discharge age of sixteen.

The question was whether Dimitri Sautherus

had enough money for those little refinements, the added touches, that would make Andrew's stay happier—and Mr. Hartberg's bottom line more advantageous. The obese Greek lived out of town, and it would be hard to reach him whenever Hartberg deemed it wise to propose little extras for Andrew's benefit. A tasteful bill could be sent, after the fact, of course. Besides, Sautherus had made his arrangements to cover the initial cost, still wished Andrew to be enrolled, and Lionel had voiced his approval of the boy.

Beneath the Sautherus folder lay another, that of Patrick Hugh Winston.

Patrick was fourteen and had grown enormously, almost abnormally, in the past year. Patrick had "little accidents," according to the mother, Viola Winston, who said she could no longer care properly for him. That, of course, meant an added responsibility and burden for Lionel K. Hartberg and his staff. Hartberg did not give a hang how much extra work his people had to do—they were all richly overpaid, he felt—but he despised listening to their complaints.

Frowning, he was about to close the folder and lay it aside, when he perceived the white envelope gleaming pristinely beneath Patrick's top sheet. Mr. Hartberg remembered that the envelope had been hand-delivered to him earlier in the day, while he was quarreling with a reporter from Muncie. His heavy brows raised in fresh curiosity and expectation, the Clemora founder inserted an ornate gold opener and slit the envelope.

A check fluttered, featherlike, to his polished desk.

Delicately, Mr. Hartberg averted his gaze and withdrew the note from inside the envelope. On the letterhead of Klase, Winston and Bernwell,

Attorneys at Law, it read, simply, "When you can find room for my son, Patrick, feel free to accept this donation as a *personal* bonus for your consideration." The note, tastefully, was not signed.

Hartberg cleared his throat. With care, he lifted the check by its crisp turquoise corners and stared almost obliquely at the printed figures.

The check was made out to him—personally —in the affable amount of five thousand dollars.

Well! He inhaled. Well, it was easy to see that Mr. Winston was a fine attorney; he had such a persuasive manner! And Stacy Bennett always found these little problem cases an intriguing challenge.

Mr. Hartberg permitted himself a wispy, pleased smile. Tenderly, he laid the check prominently atop his IN basket and beamed on it. Certainly, the founder had a duty to help those who expressed their urgency, their desperation, with such outstanding clarity.

He secured an admittance form from a box inside his desk, then began printing the name of the new student: PATRICK HUGH WINSTON. His great bald head was inclined, in careful tidiness, as he worked. He hummed. His businesslike gaze was fixed on the form; he felt as cheerful as he would ever get.

He did not see the check when it exploded into flame.

Nor did Mr. Hartberg see the fingers of flame that simultaneously began nipping at the edges of his suit jacket and at the cuffs of his trousers like thousands of tiny, red-lipped puppies.

It was all quite spontaneous. The creeping fingers worked sinuously for a few seconds, unobserved, until he noticed the acrid, sharply unpleasant reek of burning cloth.

When at last he was conscious of it, Mr. Hartberg spun his chair entirely around without arising, slapping penguinlike at his dark jacket and inhaling painfully when the fire scorched his fingers, then went out. He breathed a sigh of relief when it stopped, unaware that his glass of cognac had exploded in a syrupy-sweet little burst of flame, and unaware that Patrick's admittance form had burst into fire and disappeared from view as if it had been created from a magician's specially treated paper.

He was too busy discovering the hundred and one tiny infernos appearing all over his heavy person, absolutely from *nowhere*.

The amazing thing, he saw as his practical, unimaginative mind still labored, still functioned adequately, was that the fires burned only briefly and left no mark when they were gone, except those upon his person—as if in some terrible warning or announcement.

But he did not perceive the nature of the warning or announcement in time. Not by a long shot. As he started to rise, to run until he found a blanket in which to curl or to summon help, Lionel K. Hartberg's body burst into an explosion of yellow-orange flame that began from nothing but ate his large body hungrily. He became a human bonfire, a living torch. While he yet lived, while he could still think, while his lungs still grudgingly accepted air, Clemora's self-serving founder saw with terror and pain *a glowing white light*.

It was shaped like a ball, had a shimmering aura, and hovered scant, watchful inches above his burning, blackening bald pate.

He *knew* then, in that instant. And then he was

only an incandescent, quickly charring hunk of human meat.

The round, pale light quickly vanished. The fire went with it, as swiftly as it had come. It was quiet in the study.

The body of Lionel K. Hartberg, still seated at his desk, was a horrid manikin of tarry cinders. But the chair in which he perched, the desk and all the papers upon it—with the sole exception of the vanished check and admittance form—the very clothes on Mr. Hartberg's ebon corpse, were as spotlessly immaculate as the day he'd acquired them. At a discount, of course.

5

Four days until April 22, 1984
8:51 A.M., EST

He absolutely, positively could not remember when he had last felt so richly, gloriously wonderful. God, the effect of the human mind upon the body through its feelings of ecstasy was *profound!* (His imagination was racing, while part of his mind chided him for analyzing it at all.) Jed felt so exultant that his body seemed in fantastic trim, ready for the summer Olympics in Los Angeles. Except that he somehow didn't think this particular event would be covered by the networks!

He wriggled his toes and beamed happily up at the ceiling, thinking, suddenly, *Or is it the other way around?* Perhaps it was more that his body had been released from tension, leaving his thoughts crystal-clear and restored! He fought a silly impulse to giggle at his own schoolboy impressions and turned, relaxed, on his side.

The strange sheets in this unfamiliar apartment contained Stacy's special fragrance, and he inhaled, remembering when they had awakened simultaneously in the night and reached for each other. It was different that time, but in some respects better since they were both more patient. Unlike Rosalyn, she had permitted him to turn on the light and explore the magical universe that was Stacy Bennett's small, rounded body.

He remembered the way her breasts, large and heavy for such a petite woman, had continued tilting upward even when she was on her back. He remembered looking down to see the way her sweeping mane of tawny hair had covered his lower body, and the acute sensations her generous mouth produced in every inch of him. And he remembered how he had almost been frightened by the first full release of her pent-up frenzy during the half hour or more he had sweetly kissed and tongued her everywhere—and how dear she had been when she clung to him, before going to sleep, telling him that she really *wanted* to love him, too, if only she dared do it.

Suddenly he was eager to see Stacy on this fine, new day and vaulted from bed. Soon he was poking around in her unfamiliar bathroom, bemused by its many feminine touches, dismayed by the miniature towel he found. With hot water cascading over his indolent writer's body, Jed lifted head and voice in song, giving anyone in the world who wanted to listen his special version of Rodgers and Hammerstein's "Soliloquy." Until, that is, the brave high notes at the three-quarter mark outmanned him and left him, wetly happy, hanging musically out to dry.

He dressed, switching to the more manageable "One for the Road," deciding that the sentiment was never more suitable than now.

But his good spirits fled within seconds after encountering Stacy in the living room. Her pretty, intelligent face, set in a glum expression that somehow indicated a strain of desperation, stopped Jed in his tracks. "What's wrong?" he whispered.

Wordlessly, she held the morning paper up to

him, and he read the headline: LATEST IN BIZARRE EVENTS. CLEMORA HEAD BURNED TO DEATH.

He sagged to the floor beside Stacy, who sat on the couch, to read the entire story with growing astonishment. Lionel K. Hartberg hadn't been one of his all-time favorite people, but he hadn't known the man well. Maybe with time he could have learned just to despise him. Nevertheless, it was a terrible death for anybody.

"You seem extremely upset," he said softly to her, resting his palm on one round knee. "More so, I believe, than you probably should be, considering what a thoughtless bastard Hartberg was."

She turned her head to gaze thoughtfully down at him, trailing her short fingers through his auburn hair. "I hate the waste of human life," she replied in low tones, "any human life. But you're right. Jed. It isn't just Mr. Hartberg dying that terrible way. It's the idea of—of burning to death with no apparent cause or source. I'm becoming very, very afraid of what is happening here in Indianapolis."

"Well, I can understand that, darling," he said sympathetically, kissing her fingers.

"It's starting to—*duplicate,* Jed, what's happened elsewhere."

He scratched his head, looking perplexed. "I must confess I don't know what you mean," he said. *"What* is being duplicated?"

"First one disappearance duplicating another, and now—a burning. Come sit by me." She patted the seat next to her, and he hipped his way upward until he could recline on the couch with his head in her lap. Instantly, her yielding belly against his face, he felt a renewed need for her. He kissed her there, but when he glanced up, he saw that the psychologist was lost in troubled thought.

"There was a real-life spontaneous burning in New Jersey back in 1916," she told him slowly. "And again, more recently, in St. Petersburg, Florida—1951. An old lady's body was found there, charred to death. Normally, during life, the poor soul had been a little heavy—more than a hundred and sixty pounds—but when they found her, Jed, in death—there was nothing left of her body but a sh-shrunken skull and one small foot."

"Dear God," he murmured.

Tears sparkled in Stacy's eyes, and she felt Jed's tremor. "Her remains—all of them—weighed only ten pounds." Suddenly she looked down at his concerned face, almost fierce in her manner. "Jed, that happened in *real life!* It's not some thrice-told story from three hundred years of illiteracy ago! It actually *happened* that a mature woman simply shut her door one night and burned away t-to *nothingness!* With *no* explanation for it!"

"There *must* be some explanation for it," he began awkwardly, trying not to incense her. "Perhaps——"

"According to the Bible," Stacy said, staring across the room, "we're to burn to death this time. Us, the world. No more water." Her eyes were distant and frightened. "Perhaps it was never meant to be a bomb; perhaps atomic power is just a smoke screen. Perhaps it's all j-just God—playing with matches."

"You're taking this much too hard," he told her brusquely. "It could have been lightning in either case—Hartberg or your old lady."

She shook her head, awed and terrified. "I checked it out, Jed. It takes heat in a concentration of more than twenty-five hundred degrees to cremate a human body. We're pretty durable." She swallowed hard. "A man at an undertaker's told me so."

"OK. Different atmospheric conditions, then." He shrugged, worried for Stacy's balance. "Or a special condition of the body—some *unique* characteristic a handful of people have."

Stacy sat up straight, erect and imperative. Her lap nearly disappeared, and Jed had to sit up. "Don't you *dare* patronize me, Jed Westphal! I'm *not* making any of these things up. If you don't think the true stories I told you are frightening enough or convincing enough, I'll try one more."

"Honey, I——"

"In 1930, Jed, a woman named Mrs. Lake was found burned to death, hideously."

"What's different about that case?"

"Jedediah," she replied hotly, "Mrs. Lake's clothing was *not even scorched!* That's right." Stacy nodded. "She was fully dressed, but the clothes on her burnt-up body were *untouched*, without a *mark!*"

He glared at her. "That's impossible," he said bluntly.

"Yes, I suppose it is, but it's also *true*. Please, Jed, *please* don't be like all the close-minded scientists who just laugh off terrible things like this. No one in the world would consider it funny if it happened to them or to a loved one."

He gave her an encouraging nod. "Yes, that's certainly true." He caught the sound of coffee starting to perk again and leaned forward, ready to go to the kitchen. "And you're pretty certain there's some kind of close connection? You think there's a tie-in not only between the fire at Hartberg's place and the Vanishments but also between the terrible historic fires you cited and your late, unlamented boss?"

She caught his hand and held it against her wide mouth, making him feel ten feet tall. "I don't know what to b-believe," she sobbed, clinging to him a moment longer. "But don't forget something else, Jed."

"What's that?" Something in her tone of voice worried him.

"*I* worked at Clemora, too, remember? Jed, it could happen to *me!*"

It was one of the hardest things he'd ever done, but he produced a relaxed smile. "There's no reason to believe that for a moment, honey."

"It could happen to *both* of us—if we're getting too close to things that aren't our business, things *beyond our ken.*"

He sat down on a chair, startled and more than a little worried. "You honestly think it could happen to you and me? That *we're* in danger?"

"Perhaps. Jed, I j-just don't know anymore." She shivered as she stared intently into his eyes, the tension in her body so immense it amounted to passion. "But I'm terrified now. For God's sake, darling—*who's next?*"

8:42 P.M., EST

The newspapers throughout the United States and elsewhere on the planet Earth carried the reports, as did TV and radio, of the experimental atomic device that had been used in the Mideast. Its use was bad enough, but it hadn't been set off or dropped: it had been sent. All of which was highly disturbing, to say the very least, and the White House issued a formal protest. Indeed, the entire government of the United States, including both houses of Congress, expressed "deep disapproval and our united, serious concern for such carefree and apparently reckless experimentation, which is capable of affecting the lives of all the world's citizens."

The reply was taciturn of tone and basically meaningless, but everybody got the message. Simply stated, it was: We don't give a damn what you or the rest of the world happen to think. The Ayatollah has shown us the way.

In Indianapolis, however, ordinary people were more intrigued with their own lives and the unfathomable local occurrences of late. It was not that the Indiana capital was more insular or less cosmopolitan than other cities: it was just that the Mideast was so far away, its mores and interests surpassing the definition of *foreign*—so long as Americans weren't taken hostage—that an atomic bomb exploding over there might as well have been exploded on the moon.

Or so, at least, it seemed to Hoosiers at the time....

It was an aging middle-class two-story building on the north side of town, and it had a few pleasant bedrooms, in one of which resided—for the time being—one Gus Bliss.

Gus was in his seventies these days and obliged to live with his lanky son, Ted, and Ted's wife, Louise.

And just as he was obliged to live with them, they—for a while—were obliged to live with Gus.

The old man had been tall once, too, but strange things had happened to his spine or his neck, and he seemed to have shrunk more or less overnight. And, for all intents and purposes, invisibility had come along with the shrinkage. "The incredible shrinking grandpa," Gus had called himself once, looking for humor in it and not finding any. "Come one, come all—but look sharp!"

The invisibility attacks came on Gus almost anywhere he went. At the drugstore, for example, when he tried to buy a baseball magazine annual to keep up on the new pennant races (He'd never get used to all these doggone *divisions*, though! Whatever happened to just two *leagues*?), there were always burly teen-age boys and buxom, startlingly tall teen-age girls who crowded in front of him. They squeezed up by the counter with their remarkably slender, seemingly boneless bodies without so much as a "pardon me" or a "thank you" and threatened to run through him on their way out if he didn't step lively.

Generally, but not always, the man behind the counter spotted him ("Hi, there, little fella. Wanna ride my shoulder?") just in time to collect his money. Gus figured it had something to do with the size of his purchase.

On the rare occasions when Gus dined out, it was worse. If he went to a fast-food dump, the place was bound to be crammed to bursting with skinny teen-agers, and the girls at the counter knew they'd eat three times as much as one old man. And if he went to a nice restaurant, why, the waitress would come to the tables of sizable families, drink-guzzling middle-aged businessmen, or even young newlyweds before she'd notice Gus. After all, she seemed to say when she sighed and got her pad out at last, the old son of a bitch was on social security—how much of a tip could she possibly expect from him?

Customarily, the kids—*his* kids: Ted and wife, Louise—weren't *quite* as determined to treat him as if he had terminal invisibility. But if today was only an exception, it was one Gus Bliss would never be able to forget.

He had paused on his way downstairs, wanting to fish around in his pocket to see how much change he had left from the current government check. His palm sprinkled with shining coin of the realm, Gus overheard Ted arriving home and then the conversation that ensued—just enough, at any rate, to get the message very clearly indeed.

He'd listened—eavesdropped, he'd have to admit—because the tone in Ted's voice was extraordinary. Like most of the young fellows these days, appearing "cool" was important to Ted. If somebody'd said, "Ted, the White House is yours," he'd have smiled politely and murmured, "Thank you." But tonight his son had been ebullient, all self-discipline stricken from his tone. It was obvious the boy had exciting news.

Gus didn't have to wait long to hear it: "Louise, it's going to happen!" Ted exclaimed. "Tomorrow, in fact! Dad's going to the home *tomorrow!*"

Louise's reply was a small whoop of feminine joy that made Gus shuffle a step on the stairs, feeling his heart skip a beat, and balance himself against the wall. "Where?" she demanded enthusiastically. "Where are we sending the old boy?"

"Logan Memorial for the Retired," Ted answered, his tone that of a man who knows he's just correctly answered the $64,000 question and is off for a trip around the world. "And don't worry, babe, it's nice enough—you know, relatively new and perfectly clean—to help keep your nosy women's club off your back."

"How'd you manage it so *fast?*" Louise enthused, wanting to know all the juicy details.

"Well, generally there's a waiting list to get the aged into the joint. But I made it clear that Dad was positively *ruining* our life together, and after I talked to them for an hour, they made an exception." Ted paused, unseen, shifting tactics. "You get your own way again, Louise. I'm putting my father out of his misery. If this was Iceland, we could just stick him on a cake of ice and let it float away until the old bastard drowned."

"You hypocrite!" came the soaring contralto of Gus's daughter-in-law. Gus felt his fingers tremble on the banister. "You just want to blame it on me, don't you—to keep it off your *own* pathetic conscience! Well, don't dump it on *me*, buster! I could remind you of a hundred times you've said how much you wished he was gone. Once you even wanted him *dead,* for Christ's sake!"

"Maybe . . ." Ted's reply was muffled; Gus couldn't understand the words, as if the boy had come up close against his woman and was nuzzling his long, pointed nose in her neck. Then he backed off. "Once Dad is gone, by God, we can make it anywhere we want—*anywhere!* In the living room, the dining room, even right *here* in the kitchen!"

"Get your hands out of my skirt!" she replied, her words barely intelligible. "He's not gone yet. The old fool might walk in on us anytime."

That was quite enough. Gus nodded silently. Old fool, he. Wished him dead once, eh? Well. Well, well.

He shuffled slowly, unsteadily back upstairs to his quiet, pleasant, tidy room with the good light and sat down at the window with the fifteen-year-old photograph of his wife clutched in one veined and arthritic hand. The hand that once, he recalled, threw a no-hitter in the Triple A and on another occasion struck out, by God, fourteen men!

But now, Gus thought, wasn't the time to remember what an athlete he'd been. It was a time to be practical, to figure out just what a man *did* in this situation. Sure, he'd known friends who had this kind of problem befall them. But Gus never really thought it would happen to him, since he loved his son.

They'd told him, back when he was young, about death and taxes, how inevitable they were. But he hadn't known that having his son turn against him or discovering that he no longer had a place to live nor any voice in it were part of the big picture, too.

He looked down at the much-beloved face in the old photograph, trying to memorize every shadow, every line or crinkle, every hollow of that face, in case it, too, might be taken away from him. Again.

Anguished and bereft, obliged to deal with absolute surprise and to confront sharpened aloneness and abject hopelessness at a time when no man or woman is less equipped to handle any of these, old Gus Bliss aged a little more and cried deep inside.

He wondered with dulled curiosity and not much interest which one of the strangers on the first floor would get up enough nerve to tell him they were doing what he'd once had to do to an old dog —put him away.

The Hanzliks were sunk deep in their customary chairs, their faces carefully arranged in patterns of affable, comfortable relaxation in an effort to hide from each other a very simple fact: neither of them had been able to get their son, Phillip, out of the mind's eye for so much as ten waking minutes. He was a mote of memory, and not even the eye-winking spasms of tears could dislodge the boy.

It had been a rather muggy day for the season, and Ezra supposed that it was all right to immerse themselves in TV's banalities, although they'd tacitly agreed not to turn on the most promising adult entertainment indicated by the newspaper TV log: watching that might lead to disloyal genuine interest.

The TV set across the room beamed back at them with the sullen and dim face of the mentally shortchanged. From time to time Ezra would vaguely recognize a situation meant to be comic and laugh rather too loudly. And occasionally during the evening Catherine would sigh and arouse herself to the sort of pithy, critically amusing comment with which she had pleasured Ezra prior to Phillip's vanishment. Then Ezra would remember to smile, an imitation of contentment or amusement, and so move on to the next comic scene in an endless procession of the absurd.

It's exactly like being haunted, Catherine noted. *You can't talk much about that, either. You just pretend nobody's died.*

For the life of her she didn't know where those notions came from and was a little surprised at herself. She rarely gave a thought to dying or to the dead she'd once known in life. And besides, please God, Phillip was *alive* somewhere, even now as she stared at the TV. Her boy was alive and bound to come home to her sooner or later.

She trembled faintly in her chair and glanced at Ezra to see if he felt the chill, too. His soft gaze was so swiftly upon hers that she was almost embarrassed and quite unable to ask him. Peculiarly, this disconcerting feeling of being haunted—or, possibly, of something on the verge of happening that would make her *feel* haunted—would not be banished.

She tried to identify the source of the discomfort. Partly, it was because it seemed darker in the house this evening. Not exactly the darkness of light's *absence* but in terms of the *presence* of something else—some latent Thing, subtly stirring on cockroach feet in the room's turgid shadows, swirling below the streams of the subconscious like a surly and unremitting nightmare. There, the odd Thing tickled, oozing silently across the floor of her mind, always just out of reach.

Catherine had heard tales of how the world, this very world in which she and Ezra Hanzlik and their son, Phillip, and that nice Mr. Westphal and sweet Dr. Bennett lived and breathed and usually tried hard to do the right things, meant to *end itself* someday. She hated the topic, turned from it with the psychic hope that her quick rebuff would smash it underfoot.

But on the rare occasions when she contemplated the possibility of a final handful of lines being recorded and mankind's venture on a somehow unfamiliar planet twinkling away like the light of long-dead stars, Catherine was inclined to think of it in just those terms—the planet Earth *ending itself,* consciously and entitylike taking a final suicidal breath—both because she *would not* allow herself to think of man doing it to himself and because she *could not* blame it on God. For someone who believed in Him the way Catherine did, it was a fierce, cold, and hard thing to consider God wiping out all the decent people along with the bad, like an indiscriminate eraser scrubbing away a formula for immortality along with childish graffiti.

And in any case, deep inside her sober, decent

soul, Catherine felt that somehow the people were not right who expected a terrifying nightmare evening with the twilight sky filled with falling bombs, like an upside-down garden, dozens of plants leaping in deadly bursts of spontaneous growth, as if doctored by some lunatic virago or a madman whose green thumb had turned crimson with gore.

No, that wouldn't be God's way to end it, if He decided to do it—nor would He give permission to man for him to do it that way. Everybody, Catherine believed to the soles of her feet, would never be scrubbed away at once. Possibly forced to stop and think—*that* could happen—about all the missing others and to face up finally to the guilt that belonged to the remnant. But not absolute annihilation.

That, she always concluded, simply would not be fair to Ezra.

She loved her husband that way, believed in his protection of her in just that way. No tornado or earthquake could kill her or ruin her things, because a just god would never attack such a man. And a sane god would treasure him.

She glanced across the room to her white-haired husband and saw how dutifully he worked at pretending to watch the dreadful TV sitcoms. She thought about the way he had journeyed all through the house this afternoon, trying to do something useful about the holes in their ceiling and then placing containers beneath the leaks with a mathematical precision that was absorbing to watch. When rainwater began to trickle musically through the holes, Ezra removed each cup or pan as it filled, making a bit of a game with her, pouring wet ballads into the opera of the kitchen sink, where they soon reached a crescendo in that stopped-up artifact and finally swept out to sea.

He'd told her jokes today, too, terrible and outrageous puns. He'd asked riddles yanked from God knew where in his ancient, premarital memory. He'd done his level best to cheer her up, and once or twice she'd let the sorrow subside and laughed as long as she could. Even though their evening meal was again helplessly, impotently subpar and Catherine knew how much Ezra hated liver, he smothered it with globs of catsup and ate nearly three helpings with gusto, raving about the magical way Catherine's cooking got better year after year.

Such a dear, silly man. God would have to do something different if He meant to wipe the planet Earth clean of its Ezra Hanzliks, and she knew it. It would be an example of absolute injustice for anything but gentle moments to befall this tired and decent man. *Liver sandwiches with tomato!* Catherine recalled with a shudder. *Lord, that man could eat anything!*

Once more she froze in her chair. Outside, at a distance that seemed unreal, a cat meowed. She shivered and considered fetching her shawl. It was not only haunted in this old house tonight, it was cold. While she knew the sound had only been that of Alex, the avaricious and lustful neighborhood tom, there was something plaintive, even enigmatic, in his wail this evening. As if little yellow Alex *saw* or *knew* things that the human Catherine Hanzlik could not even begin to suspect.

Ezra heard it clearly, too, and had different thoughts. A part of his mind always urged him to believe in the dictum that all things happened for the best in God's green world. And another part insisted, as his mind turned from the mewling feline to his beloved son, that Phillip's disappearance was only a small cog in some terrifying machine powered by Planned Events, Scheduled Incidents—some kind of fantastic *contest* of cosmic nature, with rules and prizes quite unguessable by mortal men such as Ezra Hanzlik.

A clap of thunder sounded, and he moved his hips uncomfortably in his chair, too weary to think about playing with the rain-splattered pans again just yet. For a moment he had the impression that there had never been an event in his life before this one, that he and Catherine had always sat just where they were, pretending to watch TV, that time—their time, anyway—was hopelessly caught in the cogs of repetition. Through the front window he could see a zigzag streak of lightning trimming the flannel edges of the dark, and he realized, as he often had since getting started on middle age, how fundamentally *helpless* he was. Helpless, when you got down to the honest core, to deal with much of anything at all. Why, in an instant or less—should unfeeling Nature turn over the card bearing his name, rank, and serial number—he could be eliminated as if he had never existed.

And what was so damned scary and made a man feel so damned solitary was that his lack of existence would be noted by so *few,* or cared about so *slightly,* that there was no better reason in the universe for man to believe in God. Because if someone who dealt the fatal cards *did* care, it was the one thing that made it all right.

The sharp knock at the front door made Ezra and Catherine jump.

Their wondering, staring eyes met across the shadowed room, and neither breathed.

Who could it possibly be, in such a storm, on such a night? *Who?*

The awful fears each Hanzlik had kept barely

THE BANISHED 131

at bay until then began to gather, like specters at some convention in hell, clutching and knotting together like fists squeezing their hearts. For a moment longer man and wife shared their gaze.

Then, "I'll get it, dear," said Ezra, more mildly than he had ever spoken in his married life.

"Be careful!" Catherine gasped, watching his back grow smaller as he moved toward the front door. *"Turn on the porch light first!"*

"Darn thing's burned out," he called casually back to her, his tone of voice that of a sports announcer absently observing a passed ball or a called second strike.

Belatedly, Catherine leaped to her feet and flew after him. Light from outside the old house crawled through as Ezra opened the door slowly. He could make out nothing and paused for a moment, listening.

Finally, with a determined, quick breath, he threw the door wide.

A figure of no great height stood there, just outside, turned momentarily black by the drenching rain. His face was abruptly illumined by a jagged crack of lightning, and, rather than the face of Satan, the aging Hanzliks felt they might have been staring into something quite divine.

"Dad, Mom," the small figure began slowly, lifting his arms and wearing a joyful smile that spread from ear to ear. *"I'm home!"*

6

Three days until April 22, 1984
9:51 A.M., EST

There was absolutely nothing about the Logan Memorial Home for the Retired that was worse than any other old people's institution, but not a great deal that was better, either.

True, the structure—a converted mansion far out on Keystone Avenue, finished as a residence when large families and incomes to pay the enormous heating bills began to decline in tandem—was somewhat less aged and was better maintained than many of its kind. None of its residents were likely to be injured because of its flooring or wiring or to suffer because they were cold. Because it had been a private home in its heyday, the old house had an outer ambience that was less hospitallike and hopeless than most of its fellows. Those facts, combined with handleable rates, provided the main attractions. It had become in recent years a fairly popular place for impatient young people to store their unnecessary parents.

Very few of the elderly themselves, however, had chosen to spend the rest of their days at Logan Memorial. Not that they were asked, except in the artificial squeal of joy that usually went, "Isn't it just like *home*, Daddy?" or "Don't you just *love* the dining room?" Rhetorical questions asked of a generation too polite to answer truthfully.

Whenever the elderly were given a preliminary tour of the facility, they generally saw at once the awful, tottering array of the aged seated in the lounge at the front or lined like sticks of dry firewood along the hall leading to the rooms. Most of the senior citizens who were merely dropping by were immediately appalled, especially if they still fancied themselves capable of doing more than staring absently into space. Such a tour was rather like a man recently ill with cancer being exposed to a dozen bleeding terminal cases the moment he entered the ward.

While some of the thirty-two retired people at Logan were forcibly retired and healthy enough, "considering," there was something utterly shocking about the extensive display of unrelieved white hair, deep-lined faces, watery, forgetful eyes, and shaking or spastic limbs that turned the average visitor away with a feeling of horror and revulsion. This is the way *you'll* be someday soon, came the inevitable message. It was like when Mama left you alone at school for the first day and you saw all the other children as distinct but unknown threats.

It was, after all, one thing to be getting along in years; it was quite another to be obliged to see one's future self mirrored in a descending sequence of deterioration.

Gus Bliss hadn't even been given the benediction of a preview. His first examination of Logan Memorial's residents was meant to be his ongoing *last,* and he made no effort at all to socialize or even introduce himself as he trudged slowly down the corridor to his room.

There would be plenty of time for the amenities

later, Gus felt; the old are bitterly familiar with the nature of time, or at least with an approximation of its inexorable realities. Gus already knew that minutes and hours are inefficient tools of measurement, entirely unacceptable guesswork. It was quite plenty for old Gus to know that he'd be spending achingly endless segments of time in the lap of longevity, the den of decrepitude. He approached his room slowly not because he was unable to hurry, but rather because he viewed it, much as a condemned man on death row, as walking his last mile.

Ted and Louise trailed along after him, fussing over the old fellow and smiling a great deal. When they arrived, Louise began unpacking one of his bags, fully unasked. She put some of his clothes away in a dresser, smoothing and patting them repeatedly until Gus asked, rather testily, if she'd like a hammer.

Both his son and daughter-in-law assured and reassured him of how happy he was going to be here, and the incongruity, the absolute absurdity, of what they were saying brought an honest grin to his seamed face. Encouraged, they patted his shoulders and kissed his cheek and forehead a good deal, reinforcing his general view that there was something about this of a doomed child being left in a boarding school where he was to be shot.

After his one crack, Gus tried to be nice about it, but he couldn't help noticing the way their guilt and private joy battled for supremacy. Tolerantly, he heard their pledges to be frequent visitors, "after you get settled in." "How soon?" he'd asked, more to be polite than anything. "Certainly in just a few weeks," Ted had told him.

No hurry, Gus thought without rancor. No hurry. When they finally departed, exceedingly anxious to be through with the place, Gus didn't blame them. In fact, he was relieved that they were gone. He began immediately planning ways to be on sick call when they showed up.

With a sigh, he sat in a dismal pea-green chair and switched the television on. It took half of forever to warm up, and then the picture trickled onto the screen with simpleminded reluctance. For a while he stared bleakly at a commercial depicting suntanned teen-agers gulping soft drinks and frolicking in aimless abandon, completely unaware of time, so many half-naked children on a beach. He tried another channel, and a mean-faced ex-athlete assured him of how much more comfortable he would be if he switched to her brand of tampon.

"Shit fire," Gus muttered and switched off the set.

"Is there anything we'll be wanting?" inquired the heavyset black aide, her immense tree-stump arms crossing the valley of her vast bosom perilously. There was an incongruity about her that told him he'd come to like her, but right this moment he didn't want to like anyone.

"I can't speak for you, lady," Gus replied tersely, "but I'd just like a little time t'get used to the place."

Still she didn't go away. It occurred to him that he was probably breaking some sort of regulation, simply sitting there, doing nothing. When he gave her an open glare, she started plumping his pillows, peeping out of the corner of huge black eyes to see what he was up to. Sighing, he took a seat by the window and hoped that would be enough for her.

When he glanced back, she had waddled away, and he heard her tray clinking down the corridor.

Gus looked around appraisingly. The room was perhaps twelve feet square, cheaply carpeted, with thin spots here and there. There were two lifeless, rather apologetic watercolor prints blending into the wallpaper. A tiny square of window framed by stringy curtains looked out upon the back of the building. Gus could make out an enormous trash burner standing like a crematorium against the cement wall, on which some passerby had thoughtfully printed, in glaring green chalk, the legend AGE SUCKS. Gus grinned; he couldn't argue with that. Two fat, dented gray garbage cans trailed some sickly yellowish residue along the serrations of their groaning sides.

And he could just make out a narrow inch or two of Keystone Avenue and points of freedom.

Now and then a car flashed by the space, but it was so small from Gus's room that the car was gone almost before it registered on the eyes. He frowned slightly and wondered how long it would be before he was making up games about the destinations of the fleetingly glimpsed vehicles. He supposed he would eventually hope ardently that one of the cars would brake in front of Logan Memorial and expel his son and daughter-in-law.

And he wished fervently that he would be long dead before those dreadful things transpired.

Rooms. Gus turned back to his new one, sighing and licking frightened dry lips. A man spent his life in such a remarkable variety of rooms—rarely outside, where it was real—sitting and eating and sleeping and making plans or love in a series of imaginary quadrants of space carved clean from infinity, assigned arbitrary purposes, and then colored with life by those who occupied them.

He thought about the room in which he had been born and had spent six years of his life, until his alcoholic father lost the house and young Gus was obliged to become acquainted with a different, smaller room. He'd grown quite a bit then and suffered his first nightmares.

He thought about a hotel room he'd liked a lot when he was a pitcher with Evansville in Triple-A baseball and remembered that he liked it because a girl came to it with him one night. He'd pitched a one-hitter, striking out eleven, and she'd liked his style. Later, he liked hers, too. She'd made him feel triumphant, clean and young, not dirty. Sometimes he could still see her bright button eyes, and sometimes, like now, he could remember what they'd called her: Sunny. Gus nodded, tasted his lips again. Yes, her name was Sunny. He sighed.

Funny thing was, he decided with a frown, even if he'd made the big leagues and posted a few twenty-game seasons, he might have ended up right where he was. In a way they hated to see athletes get old, the public did; better that they be dead instead of having the nerve to look old and ordinary.

Gus thought about the room in which he'd consummated his marriage, left that one swiftly because it was too precious for bitter times, then remembered the room in which he had greeted his wife, the new mother, and newborn Ted. He'd been a skinny, helpless-looking thing with an Indian mug and strange dark hair, almost like they hadn't the time to give him a decent cut before they sent him on to his new parents. Gus grinned. And he thought about the room in which his wife had breathed her last and how he hadn't known that that was almost the end of *his* life, too.

Finally, he thought about this room, here, in which it was clearly intended that he expire. Where was it written down, he wondered, that of all the rooms he'd been in and all the rooms he hadn't, *this* particular drab, imprisoning, impersonal, boring, frightening room was where he was supposed to take his final breath? He thought of such things and tried to find the meaning and purpose in them—and failed.

It's just a crapshoot, Gus thought, *and everyone has loaded dice; so everybody loses, lookin' stupid in the process.*

He raised his bony wrist and, waiting till his vision cleared of angry tears, checked the time. Barely after 10:00 A.M. He'd been there, sweet Jesus, twenty-seven—no, twenty-*eight* minutes. Not a second more. *Adapt, old man,* he commanded himself. *When fighting is no longer possible, a sane man adapts.*

He worked on seeing his surroundings with a less jaundiced eye, and it helped. They weren't really too bad: clean, fairly bright and airy (although those garbage cans at the back could be trouble, come summer), and there'd be people in the other rooms with whom he could make friends.

Try was the operative word. Once, Gus had been open, amiable, quickly accepting half the folks he met and calling them friends. But as the years passed and he jumped over into the decade of his seventies, Gus came to feel deserted—by friends. Christ, he no sooner made one than the guy died! From sixty on, it had been a Goddamn parade of death rooms, a tour of Indianapolis's finest mortuaries. Now he found it harder to get friendly. He just wasn't sure he could take another funeral.

Besides, these folks were, well, *old* in this place. Obviously older than he. Average age must be close to eighty-five. Yeah, they were old and not very tough or clever about seeing the way death snuck up on a guy; they were clearly unreliable about themselves, apt to die on you without one blessed warning.

Ten after ten. Gus sighed. Less than two hours till lunch. He remembered how delicious were Esther's meals, and how adequate, even, were Louise's. It revolted him to think he might wind up longing for Louise's damned cooking. But the few times he'd been in a hospital—there was that appendicitis attack in Houston, in the ballplaying days, and a gallbladder surgery ten years ago—he'd learned that institutional food suffered because the cook was making it for a bunch of strangers. A cook needed to *love* the person she cooked for.

He steeled himself anew. If he got to longing for Louise's food, that was OK, too. He'd just tough it out, the way he'd toughed out a thousand other miserable things during his lifetime. He'd eat their damned food and not complain about it. He'd learn to like it.

The old rebellious feeling arose: Eat it, *yes*—but, by God, he didn't have to *like* it!

Squinted at the watch again. Not quite, but almost ten-thirty.

Uh-huh. Phony relaxed sigh. Long day.

He cleared his throat cautiously with the kind of attention to detail, to the quality of rasp and rumble of phlegm, of a man who has all the time in the world. Damned funny, the way it'd worked out, he mused. He could recall being a boy on a farm at his uncle's, lying in the hay, bored to his toes, so doggoned *full* of time he was choking on it. Then the many years between, all those swift and hectic years of struggle; and *bingo,* here he was back again, too full of throttling time—but not full enough of it to go home.

THE BANISHED 141

Outside, Gus saw through half-parted lids, a sliver of bright light—not as garish or show-offish as lightning, brighter than sixty-watt bulbs—just a flash of it, glimmered, dipped past the window, snapped his picture.

He *knew*.

Gus *knew* at that moment what he wished to know, without even having realized there was anything he really wanted to know. He smiled to himself and nodded, agreeing eagerly with what he'd seen in his head. By the Lord Harry, it *did* make sense—it was fitting, *proper*—it was what he'd *earned,* to be frank about it, and what he certainly *wanted!*

The old man arose and walked to his door with more alacrity than usual, peering out into the corridor to see that others, too, had received the message. Already, he noticed, they were beginning to leave their rooms, slowly and arthritically in some cases. Some pushed others in wheelchairs; still others dragged themselves from beds of nausea to totter along unsteadily, legs careening them into the Logan Memorial hallway, where they joined the march.

Some of the aged smiled at Gus, sharing: they knew, too. He found himself smiling warmly back at them. When a lady in her eighties appeared to be having difficulty with her frame walker, Gus moved to her side with gallant haste, helped her to half lean on his strong arm as he guided the contraption forward, foot by struggling foot.

It was like Bataan, like Corregidor, he thought.

Most of them had reached the cafeteria before the nurses discovered what was going on. One of them, a Ms. Gallo, had the presence of mind to duck back into her office to summon the doctor, who was at the restaurant on the corner. By the time the officials of Logan Memorial were bunched together, all thirty-three residents of the old folks' home were safely ensconced in the cafeteria.

Gus Bliss's immense black nurse was bustling forward to see what was happening, when Dr. Clyde Harvester came rushing in. She paused at his arrival. A pencil-thin young man with a little rat of a mustache, Dr. Harvester was one of two physicians hired by Logan's board of directors to come in twice a week—whether anybody died or not.

Harvester paused just inside the entrance to the cafeteria and saw his aged charges sitting crowded together at the large table usually commandeered by staff and at two other tables shoved together. With this arrangement, the older people were able to join hands, and although there was no breakfast nor the usual watery supper before them, they bowed their heads in prayer.

Dr. Harvester was shocked. Who had begun this idiocy? What had made these people so cocksure, so independent? He took a brisk pace forward, about to gesture, readying the officious words he'd use to reprimand them.

And found that he had somehow stepped into a furnace of enormous heat.

Although far short of burning, it was distinctly uncomfortable, and he looked around to see what had captured him.

But there was nothing to see except his own suited body bursting into waves of perspiration that dampened the expensive suit material and began flooding off his youthful forehead and temples. Suddenly he felt weak. What was going on here? "Nerves," Dr. Harvester said forcibly to himself but aloud, and he took yet another brisk step forward.

THE BANISHED 143

The wall of heat resisted with force, energetically, effectively. It stiffened, intensified almost to burning level, and—pushed.

Face and hands lobster-red from proximity to the heat, Dr. Clyde Harvester made a yelping sound and jumped daintily back two steps. Immediately his body began to cool to normal temperature. He was unharmed.

But before Harvester could conceive a new plan of attack, he and his nurses spied the circular, shifting, pure-white ball of light as it materialized. Then it hung, suspended, above the seated and subdued, waiting old people.

"Oh, my *God!*" someone cried. Heads turned at the alarmed tone. It was a dyed-blonde nurse, seemingly about to pass out. "It's happening *here!*" she gasped.

A black aide pointed, moaning low in his throat. Another aide took a step away from the scene, crossing himself; a nurse followed suit. Dr. Clyde Harvester inhaled sharply. "Now, then," he said aloud, importantly, as if ready to say more. He did not do so, however. He could not find anything to say. He settled, instead, for rapid blinking.

Slowly, the thirty-three residents of the Logan Memorial Home for the Retired began to chant in unison. Their voices were low, indistinguishable at first.

Then the obese black nurse whispered loudly, "Why, it's the Lord's Prayer they're sayin'!"

Dr. Harvester nodded blankly and thought that he said, "Quite so," aloud, but he wasn't sure. His blinking eyelids seemed to be trying to fan out the heat and the lights before him.

The circular white globe descended at last; it almost appeared to be *breathing* in and out. Close to sentient life, it settled smoothly over the waiting heads of the nearly three dozen aging human beings, shielding them from view in a manner that seemed protective. Not a one of the oldsters was frightened, nor did they cease praying. Gus's face, like *all* their faces, was calm, resigned, close to contented.

And when the light disappeared, the fluorescents overhead, throbbing dully from the cafeteria ceiling, bathed a tiny assemblage of ignored wheelchairs, needless walkers, and forgotten crutches, all revealed in an eerie aura of complete and abject abandonment.

Jed strode down to the corner mailbox to post his half-forgotten submission to Ellery Queen's periodical. As he returned, he had the feeling or impression that the neighbors' eyes were upon him. In fact, he imagined a dozen pairs of them staring, gaping, from the two-story and trilevel frame houses: prying eyes that *knew* he had slept with a woman other than his wife. Or rather, his *ex*-wife.

But the fact of his separation wasn't making it any easier to cast aside the habitual ways and the memories of nearly a decade. It seemed strikingly unreal to Jed that Darren would not be playing out in the front yard on a nice day or rushing to the door to greet him as he returned. Rosalyn herself should be working on one of her interminable jigsaw puzzles on the card table in the living room, not looking up when he entered but lifting the fingers of one hand in a salute, muttering, " 'Lo."

Besides, he thought as he reached out for the front door knob, he was starting to *feel* different as a consequence of spending one warmly sexual night with lovely little Stacy Bennett. Silly, he knew, but it was as if his skin itself had altered, taken on a layer of *her*—or merely her sweet, innocent fragrance—before he had quite shed the fragrance and skin smell of Rosalyn Westphal.

He closed the door behind himself, stepping into the quiet he'd known would be here instead of wife and son. *You, sir,* he told himself, *are behaving like an idiot. And possibly a bit of a hypocrite, since you can scarcely wait for another night with Stacy!*

The impolite phone jangled its jeer from the dining room, beckoning him with its childishly insistent wail. He went quickly to it, hoping it would be Stacy.

"Hello?"

"Mr. Westphal, it's Ezra Hanzlik, this end."

A pang of new guilt wound its way through Jed's chest like negative adrenaline. Here he was, reveling in his newfound role as a lover, completely neglecting the promises he'd made so earnestly to the pleasant Hanzliks. He wasn't much further along toward an understanding of the disappearances than when he and Stacy had called upon them. He didn't know quite what to say.

"Oh, yes, Mr. Hanzlik! What can I do for you?" It was hearty and stone-phony. Jed hoped it projected a note of interest and concern. "I'm afraid I haven't been able to learn anything useful yet."

There was no reply for a moment. When he did speak, Ezra appeared to be barely in control of his own voice. Was it bad news? For an instant Jed couldn't tell whether the man was laughing or crying.

"Well, *I* have learned a few things, Mr. Westphal!" Hanzlik told the writer. It became clear then that he was, indeed, chuckling—that he was almost hilarious with joy, in fact! "Phillip *came back* to us last night. Mr. Westphal, *our Phillip came home!*"

Jed was stunned but happy. "Why, that's fantastic, sir," he said as his pleasure built. "Absolutely marvelous!"

"It's even more than marvelous, Mr. Westphal." Ezra giggled. "Phillip is all right!"

"Well, I'm sure glad he wasn't harmed."

"No, you don't understand what I'm saying." Hanzlik was clearly groping for the right words. "What I *mean*, Mr. Westphal, is that Phillip is *really* all right. That—that he's *normal!*" Ezra paused, chuckling with joy that he scarcely bothered to control. *"He's just as normal as you or I!"*

1:15 P.M., EST

Jed replaced the phone in its cradle and stared at it as if he expected it to leap up of its own accord, waggling its sinuous and corded tail, to provide him with further revelations.

He'd expected a number of things to develop, but Phillip's merely showing up at his parents' front door was never one of them.

He fixed a glass of iced tea in the kitchen and brought it into the dining room, where he just sat by the phone and tried to figure things out. His nerves sang to him along the full length of his arms and legs, and a pulse throbbed annoyingly in his forehead. After several more moments of seeking to gather his thoughts, trying to see precisely what the enthralled Ezra Hanzlik had meant by describing his retarded son as newly "normal," Jed lit a Camel and then searched through his pockets for Stacy's phone number. This called for a conference, if anything did.

Never the most organized man in the world, he

was narrowing down the search to his left hip pocket when the phone bell shrilled again, startling him so that he dropped his cigarette on the floor. Groping for it and rubbing his toe over the spilled ash and grinding it into the carpet, he snatched up the phone with an angry gesture.

"Yeah? he snapped. "What is it?"

"Not *what*, honey, it's *who*. My name is Stacy Bennett, and I'm working my way through life." She was taken aback a little by his tone of voice. "Are you OK over there?"

"I was just going to call you," he half explained.

"For what reason? To tell me you hated my guts and never wanted to sleep with me again?"

His laugh was richly apologetic. "That'll be the day. I'm sorry I yelled at you, darlin'. Listen, I have very important news."

"So do I."

"Mine has yours topped," he crowed with rude excitement, plowing ahead. "Ezra Hanzlik just phoned to tell me that their son, Phillip, has come home!"

"You're kidding!" Stacy exclaimed with clear delight. "That's really wonderful. How did it happen?"

Jed scratched his head with his free hand. "Evidently the boy just appeared at the front door." He paused to consider whether to tell the psychologist the rest of it now. On the spur of the moment he decided to allow her to draw her own, professional conclusions about Phillip's so-called normality when they got to the Hanzlik home. "I told him I'd pick you up and we'd be out there as soon as possible to talk with the boy."

"Of course." With two words she was the solid pro again, retreating at once into a businesslike precision of tone, eager both to see Phillip and to resume her role as his psychologist. "You did the right thing. I'll be outside waiting for you."

"You said that you had some interesting news, too," Jed prompted her.

"But it isn't good news like yours, not at all," she answered. "Jed, I'm afraid there's been another Vanishment, at Logan Memorial."

"The old folks' home?" He hesitated, grimly assimilating the news. The Camel in his fingers almost scorched them before he could grind it out. "My God, that's terrible," he breathed at last. "How did you learn about it?"

When she replied, he could almost see her making a face. "Once, sweet first lover, I had a date with Dr. Clyde Harvester of Logan. He turned out to be all eager hands and prickly mustache, but we parted friends, anyway. Or at least colleagues. Well, Clyde telephoned me, knowing of my involvement with Clemora. He—thought I'd want to know."

"He did, did he?"

"You sound jealous."

He cleared his throat. "Was it the same pattern as the others?"

"Exactly the same. The residents were all over sixty-five years old. They left their beds and their rooms and a front lounge, then gathered in the cafeteria—all as if they'd heard the same kind of internal signal. Clyde said that when he tried to approach them, he encountered a strange blast of positively withering heat that—that seemed *consciously* to prevent him from getting near his patients. He hated to put it that way, of course. But it very nearly burned him."

Jed thought of some mustached lech with his hands on Stacy's round breasts and glared at the phone. "Too bad it didn't. Did the light show up again?"

"Yes." Her voice sounded baffled and newly frightened. "He described it the same awful way it's been right along: white, pale, circular, descending over the people until both they and the light *disappeared.*"

"So when do we see your old boyfriend?" he demanded, fighting jealousy the best he could.

"We don't, and he never was my boyfriend."

"What? Why can't we see him? He knows the particulars."

"Jed, when I mentioned I was coming out to see him, he was sorry that he'd called at all. The board of directors at Logan Memorial will make all the statements directly from the offices downtown, at the Market Square Center building—the one with the gold ball on top. And they aren't allowing anyone on the premises at the home. Clyde was very worried."

"Can't we interview the lech away from there, then?" he inquired impatiently. "Maybe at his own office?"

"Perhaps we could, Jed, but I think he's already told me everything he knows about it." She paused. "Look, I'd like to get out to the Hanzliks' and check on Phillip's condition. It must have been trying for him, whatever occurred, and I'm sure he can use my professional guidance."

"I'm not sure of that," Jed murmured.

"What does *that* mean?" she asked, startled. "Is that a crack?"

"I'll be there in fifteen or twenty," he said by way of reply. He started to hang up, then caught himself. "Oh, Stacy, one more thing."

"Yes?"

"How many old folks did the mysterious light claim?"

"All of them. Everyone on the premises."

"How *many*?" Jed persisted.

She was puzzled. "Dr. Harvester said there were thirty-three residents at the time. Why do you want to know?"

He shook his head. "Never mind for now. Look, I'll see you shortly."

He touched his jaw with his fingertips, discovering a fringe of bristly hair cropping out. It reminded him of his old habit of putting off shaving until it was absolutely necessary. Rosalyn had really hated that trait of his; she said it made him a perfect slob, and he'd told her it was nice that he was perfect in some area. Well, after what little Phillip Hanzlik had been through—*whatever* it proved to be!—a two-day growth of beard wasn't likely to frighten the kid. And Phillip's folks were so glad to have him home that Jed could have shown up stark-naked and not even been noticed.

He grabbed his aged sports jacket and notebook, then hurried out to the faithful Granada.

After the downpour of the day before, the weather was obligingly dry, the sun still smirking from behind cloud cover yet dispensing enough warmth so that Jed could make do with his heater turned to low.

Hoping to enjoy musical accompaniment enroute to Stacy's, he switched on the car radio. He learned quickly that the disappearances were becoming a topic of fascination to the people of Indianapolis. Instead of the usual recorded claptrap of thundering rock or even the jazz played by the more civilized stations, Jed encountered considerable commentary and discussion about what was going on in town. Or, as one solemn voice put it, "what's happening to Indianapolis." Commentary was all over the dial, a series of sonorous voices representing a complete spectrum of civic concern.

The chief of police was quoted by a newsman as saying that "the perpetrators of these kidnappings will be swiftly brought to justice if interested citizens will only begin getting on top of this, notifying their police about any suspicious characters with electronic equipment, floodlights, spotlights, or flares." The chief hinted that he suspected someone who had acquired sophisticated spying devices.

Jed switched the dial and heard a Reverend Miley Bashescu suggesting that, just as God works in mysterious ways, so does Satan. Mr. Bashescu expressed his abundant confidence that there had never been a time when worship was so necessary, not only in churches but in the home, during family gatherings. "This world of ours is ill," he claimed, "but this time the patients—America's people—must heal the institution of a whole world. What is transpiring in our city," he continued, "may well prove to be a symptom of what is happening with a blaze of machine-gun fire in other parts of the world. A person can vanish in a puff of smoke as easily as a ball of light."

Between panel discussions, one unrepentant local disc jockey began reminiscing about the radio heyday of Yehudi, comic Jerry Colonna's creation, "the little man who wasn't there—you know, that invisible guy who turned off the light in your refrigerator whenever you closed the door." The deejay chose to play a range of "mystery music," as he called it—bizarre, ultramod sounds with a lot of rerecorded sound effects, flutes, oboes, and

Moog synthesizers. Jed winced at the racket and turned the dial again.

On the new spot on the dial he caught the tail end of a broadcast in which His Honor, the mayor of Indianapolis, was assuring a persistent reporter that the city was doing everything in its power "to apprehend the obviously warped soul behind these monstrosities" and intended to "stand solidly behind each and every citizen who has suffered grievous personal loss." He pledged to declare the city a disaster area, as numerous people telephoning his office had demanded, "if and when the Vanishments cease to occur in only isolated pockets of our fair city."

Jed tried to determine whether it was good or bad that the authorities of his city had become actively engaged in trying to solve the disappearances, intrigued enough to begin making semiofficial and official pronouncements. Deep inside, he couldn't help but wonder if the explanation or source behind the mystery wasn't entirely beyond the reach of hard-nosed cops, quipping deejays, SWAT squads, socially conscious religions, and mayoral pledges of action or government intervention.

Certainly it was clear that Ezra Hanzlik hadn't notified anyone, as yet, about Phillip's unexpected return. Obviously, it was quite enough for Mr. and Mrs. Hanzlik—at least for the time being, in the moments of initial relief—that their son had come back to them safe and sound. But what this revelation might mean to other persons throughout Indianapolis Jed couldn't calculate. Phillip, he was sure, would be in for a great amount of questioning. The boy might be better off if he'd remained retarded!

The Vanishments and the disappearance by spontaneous fire of Lionel K. Hartberg were everywhere on the radio, constantly, doubtlessly mirroring the concerns of ordinary folks in the city, possibly the entire nation. One report, Jed noted with mild annoyance, did come from a network announcer whose dignified and oblique similes clearly indicated that he thought the matter had been blown out of proportion by the yokels of America's heartland. This city, after all, became important to the insular Gothamites only once a year, when the 500-Mile Race was run at the Speedway. The rest of the time New Yorkers believed the town was overrun by Indians and descendants of Al Capone.

When Jed heard another deejay remark that the source was probably the Internal Revenue Service, collecting people "since there's more of us these days than there is money," he switched the radio off and sank lower into his car seat. *Americans!* he thought with asperity, a mixture of pride and disgust. *We'd make a joke out of Judgment Day!*

But what was really troubling, he realized, was whether or not people were adequately alarmed by what was transpiring. Was this massive response founded on nothing more than curiosity? Did people really understand that no one knew, as Stacy Bennett had aptly expressed the risks, who might be *next* to go?

He peered out the window at people strolling the streets, shopping in a supermarket, apparently going about their business, and thought that the number of persons up and around was approximately the same as any other day. Then Jed's mind turned to the peculiar numbers that appeared to be involved, and he wondered if he was the only one growing aware of the simple *addition factor*.

Years ago, his superstitious and sporadically religious mother had told him that "six sixty-six" was the number of the beast. She had meant Satan. Jed had no idea whether there was any significance to such figures, since his interest in prophecy, biblical or otherwise, was never more than a passing thing. But somehow Mom had succeeded in alerting his mind to the *strangeness* of numbers—the way the elementary numerology seemed to play a weird role, tangentially, in the activities of mankind. With some reluctance he observed that fifteen children had been removed, somehow, from Clemora House of Friends; and one plus five equaled *six*. Twenty-four pregnant girls had been seized from the Milliken Center; and, again, two plus four was—*six*. Now thirty-three persons had vanished peculiarly and identically from the Logan Memorial Home for the Retired—three plus three equaled *six!*

Which, it occurred suddenly to Jed, was *his own age*—thirty-three! Christ's age when He was crucified!

Despite the warmth of the early spring day, Jed shuddered. His shivering spine sought to resist the inexplicable, stomach-turning suggestions of the unknown as it had impinged on his normal daily life.

He turned onto Doyle Boulevard, then onto 42nd Street, added the four plus two of the street itself, and came close to sideswiping a catercornered mail truck. You could go absolutely *nuts* playing games like this!

He had to cut this out. Stacy's brand of superstition—and his late mother's—were starting to get to him. He had to get control of his own vivid imagination if he was going to be of productive use to anybody and write a decent book on the subject. His imagination was lurid and unrealistic enough without allowing silly superstitions to make it worse! Rosalyn's pragmatic, earthbound turn of mind was required now, her knack for believing in what she saw or touched and virtually nothing more. It might be a limited scope his ex-wife had, but it was also probably safer.

But his mind wouldn't let go of the numerological aspect. He knew that six, according to the great mathematician Pythagoras, stood for harmony and domesticity, because it was, as a perfect number, equal to the sum of its divisors—one plus two plus three equaled six—and because it was divisible by both an odd number (three) and an even number (two). Six, therefore, involved love, harmony, the home, union, honesty, and dependability, and since it had the power of three doubled, it could be creative if it avoided fussiness about detail.

Well, Jed mused with a smile, *homes* had been attacked, he seemed himself to be falling in *love* and establishing a new *union,* and Stacy was the soul of *dependability*. But right now he was getting pretty silly about *details!*

He lost his smile when he remembered his mother pointing out that the Battle of Waterloo took place on a six day, from Napoleon's standpoint, when he should have sought tranquillity and avoided conflict—while Wellington's numerology called for decisive action, since for him it was a one day!

Jed was drawing close to Wycliffe Village and Stacy's apartment when it occurred to him that the common denominator of youth, in the Vanishments, could now be discarded. In fact, it *had* to be. After raiding an institution full of mentally retarded children and another place housing young unwed mothers, that enigmatic white light had kidnapped—if that was the right word—nearly three dozen old persons, some very old indeed.

Jed's hands began to perspire. He gripped the steering wheel more tightly, his knuckles whitening.

It was true—the angle of youth would not work after all. But there *was* a common denominator— one that he could not perceive until now.

He was so excited when he saw the answer clearly for the first time that, when he turned the corner, the right side of the car bounced high off the curb. Jed had just realized that the people who were being taken were those *whom nobody wanted.* They were the expendables, the sidelined and cast-out, the *discards* of society: the people who were, for various reasons, effectively *banished* from the uncaring bosom of society.

Ahead, he saw Stacy waiting in front of her apartment building, and his thoughts raced feverishly. That was a good start, he felt—but it got him absolutely no closer, to be realistic about it, to an understanding of *who* was causing the people to vanish or *what* the source might be or *why* it would want them.

He began to slow the car. Phillip, yes, Phillip Hanzlik should be able to tell them. If the boy could really speak normally now, if he could reason to an extent and remember even a *little* of where he had been and what had happened there, Phillip would be able to enlighten them.

Filled with curiosity, seeing how lovely Stacy looked in a crisp peach-colored dress with matching handbag, her sweet and intelligent face smiling at his arrival, Jed slid the Granada to a stop, threw the door open for her, but raced the motor.

Stacy saw the fevered, intense expression on his face and got in quickly. She was scarcely seated before the car squealed away from the curb.

7

2:24 P.M., EST

"Come in, my friends, come *in!*" Ezra Hanzlik chuckled as he threw wide the front door of his old Ravenswood home. He seemed to be overflowing with the unused laughter of a lifetime, as if —rather than never having experienced merriment—he had carefully saved it all up for this happy time. The man appeared years younger somehow, revitalized. He took Jed and Stacy warmly by their hands and pulled them gently inside. It reminded Jed of a moment when an old friend with his first child did the same. In a way, he supposed, this was also a birth—or a rebirth. Joy overriding manners, Ezra preceded them down the short hallway, virtually dancing. "Afraid I forgot to warn them you were coming," he bubbled. "I was just too busy *talking* with my boy! Really *conversing!* But come, see for yourself what a remarkable thing has happened to us all!"

The middle-aged man's words bespoke not only the boy's startling return but the pain Ezra had silently suffered through the years because of his son's impaired mentality. Jed felt oddly confused; he tried to stay detached and logical, to evaluate Phillip's condition for himself. He thought it possible that the boy's new normality might be enormously exaggerated by parents who *yearned* for it so badly. And in his writer's imagination, too, Jed wondered if he might see something dark or evil in the lad—if there might possibly be, in this extraordinary return, a sinister cast visible in Phillip's eyes.

But he saw Catherine Hanzlik first and thought he'd remember the image of the lady for a long while. She was seated as lightly as a feather beside Phillip on the couch, and if she was aware of company, she did not show it. It was as if every nerve, muscle, cell, and fiber of the darkhaired woman's body and spirit had been captured by her magnetic son so there wasn't enough left for anything else to impinge on her consciousness. She was so absolutely rapt, without touching him, that Jed had the notion he was seeing a oneness she had shared with the boy symbiotically a decade and a half ago. His thoughts, feelings, and needs were, at that instant, truly his mother's as well.

Phillip had obviously been looking through the photograph album before him—the one that was a pictorial life story of someone sweet but hopelessly dull and half-finished, someone he had once been—and the expression on his sunny face was one of surprise and, Jed thought, possibly reverence. Or gratitude.

To *whom*? Jed wondered. To *what*?

Spotting them in the doorway, Phillip responded like a normal teen-age boy, jumping to his feet and grinning engagingly at Stacy even before Ezra could announce them. "Hi, Dr. Bennett," Phillip said softly, a trace of shyness or respect in his high voice. "It's great to see you again."

Impulsively, Stacy dropped her professional ways

and hugged the boy. "God, I'm glad that you're all right!"

"Me, too," he answered, seeming to mean more than what was implied.

Jed sought to appraise him in his own way as Stacy chatted. Just as photographs had indicated, Phillip was very short, no more than five feet in height. He wore a tank top, revealing arms that were thin, just better than frail, and patched blue jeans. He had a thatch of blond, unruly but soft hair that framed an affable, intelligent face. *Yeah*, Jed chided, *that's the truth: he looks like a bright kid.*

A normal teen-age American boy—who, along with his retarded classmates, had quite literally vanished.

"This is Jed Westphal, Phillip, a new but very dear friend of mine." Stacy made the introduction carefully. Jed noticed that she had an I'm-making-this-as-simple-for-you-to-understand-as-I-can note in her voice. "He's an author, hon. He writes books."

"I think most authors do, don't they?" Phillip said, his grin impish. He put out his hand, and it was warm and soft but had a decent masculine grip. "Nice to meet you, sir."

"To be honest, Phil," Jed remarked with a reflective smile, "I never really thought I'd have a chance to meet you. Where've you been?"

The question was intentionally cool and casual, meant to throw the boy off guard if he was hiding anything. But Jed saw instantly that it hadn't deceived or disturbed Phillip, not at all. Something rather astute and also amused flickered in the boy's eyes. "With my friends from Clemora," he said simply, then turned back to his parents. "It sure is great to be home."

Catherine Hanzlik watched every movement of her son, as if filming each of them, determined that *this* time she would record every nuance of word or motion in case he vanished again. "The Lord has blessed us," she said, her striking black eyes barely, reluctantly moving from Phillip to Stacy and Jed and back. "He has shown us how much He loves us and that He truly cares for His flock. Isn't that right, son?"

Jed stared intently at the boy, whose head bobbed in quick agreement. "God is always showing us those things," he replied softly in his high-pitched voice, "if we can only remember to look and listen to what He says."

None of these remarks, Jed mused, were the thoughts of a retarded child. The Hanzliks were obviously correct about that. But this was also not the normal speech of an early teen-ager. Jed felt almost compelled to converse with this kid, try to probe his thoughts. "Why is it that we *don't* look and listen to God, Phil?" he asked mildly.

The boy took an easy seat again beside his mother. Ezra moved behind the couch, possessively resting a large palm on his wife's and son's shoulders. It was almost as though he tried to hold them there lovingly.

"Because we're so involved with the *here* and *now* of our lives, Mr. Westphal," Phillip replied, looking directly at Jed. His face was serious. A string of blackheads—what children these days call "zits"—showed beneath the yellowish hair on his forehead. "Most of our illness on earth, both physical and mental—even my own retardation— could be healed if we were *truly* willing to stop what we're doing long enough to hear what God's saying to us. But you see, sir, we're more creatures of habit than anybody realizes. Once we get an idea, or a way of doing things, stuck in our heads, it's very hard to shake it loose."

Jed was astonished by this lecture he was getting from the boy. "I don't understand how——"

"Let me explain," Phillip interrupted, continuing his thoughts. There was a trace of the talented youth here, Jed felt, the boy asked to produce his clarinet or saxophone who plays it perfectly for his parents' friends. "We stick everything in *categories*. So-and-so is fat, so-and-so is a women's libber, so-and-so is gay, so-and-so is Jewish or a Methodist or a basketball player. Now *that* can be bad enough," Phillip said, leaning forward on the couch and glancing at Stacy to see if she was following his remarks, "but what's really bad is that we *accept* these categories, these assignments— as if other people had the right to give them to us. We say something like 'Yes, that's right. I'm retarded' or 'Yes, I'm a terrible student' or 'Yes, I'm old now,' and in doing this—well, we've bought the whole ball of wax! We've accepted all the *rest* of what society believes about the particular category we fit into! And the funny thing *is*, we're none of us that category *alone*, however much we try to cooperate with the assignment we're given! We're lots and lots of things, all in the process of *becoming*, becoming a new reality."

"And you say we do that with health, mentally and physically?" Stacy probed. By now, Jed could see, she was virtually devouring the boy from the standpoint of her own professional training in psychology. "But that it isn't *limited* to our health?"

"No, it's with *everything*." Phillip shrugged. "But a doctor will make his diagnosis and say to someone, 'You have this or that incurable disease,'" and the person accepts it completely—*assumes the role expected* of him or her. And since it's incurable and perhaps fatal as well"—the boy lifted his thin shoulders—"he or she cooperates by dying."

"That sounds almost like Christian Science," Jed grunted, wanting to keep Phillip talking. "Is it?"

"No, it's just the truth. Which almost all religions and a lot of philosophies have a piece of," the boy replied with a smile. "Trouble is, they take that one little chunk of truth and make their followers try to buy *only* that piece. So all the other, equally important pieces of truth held by the other religions, philosophies, sciences, and so on, are ignored."

Light from the picture window gave the impression of stage lighting, Jed thought, with Phillip, who was the focus, his parents, and Stacy all haloed by the emerging sunshine.

Stacy lifted her pencil. "Can you tell us more about the—the categories you were discussing?" she prompted him.

"Well, what I was saying was that each of us accepts the category we've become stuck in. That's the way all *new reality* is born, and it's the secret behind evolution, which is neither accidental nor selective but self-determined. *You,* Mr. Westphal, somehow 'bought' the idea completely that you are an author. Authors write books; so you wrote one. Your conception of yourself was that you were a *published* author; so you sold your book." His grin was ingenuous, boyish. "Now you're doing what authors do after that: you're researching your next book. But way back when—a long while ago—you weren't an author, and you hadn't planned to be one. At that point in your life, sir, you might have been anything, anything at all. But then something happened, and you've been creating new realities ever since. So you see, Mr. Westphal," the boy concluded, "it isn't just a case of *believing* or *having faith* that such-and-such is true. It's a matter of *knowing* something, the way you know, totally, that black is black, songs are music, pain hurts, or—or the way your *fingers* know how to type, but your mind itself, consciously, *doesn't* know. It's a case of *knowing* something mentally, or with *perfect* faith, knowing it's a fact, and then all the rest of the reality falls right into line."

"Until a few days ago," Stacy said in a low tone, "you didn't always know that songs were music. You confused your fingers with your toes."

"Just who are you?" Jed asked suddenly.

Ezra Hanzlik turned to Jed with surprise and indignation. Catherine Hanzlik's black eyes flared in fury, and she started to speak.

But Phillip lifted his hand and grinned. "Let me think how to explain," he said and paused thoughtfully. "For some of us it's impossible to experience that moment when we *know* the new reality. In fact, if we let other people *tell* us long enough who we are, we lose our own chances. Well, I was just too ignorant even to know that I was retarded, dull. For people like us sometimes there must be help from outside."

"Like prayer?" his mother asked him softly.

He glanced at her with love. "Like prayer. Or the source of answered prayer." He sighed and scratched at the blackheads on his forehead. "I'm still Phillip Hanzlik, Mr. Westphal, but I'm the way I would have been if I'd ever had an opportunity to form my own realities, if I'd been able to *know* that I wanted to be normal, even bright. I —well, I got that help I was talking about."

"Where, Phillip?" Stacy asked soberly, gently,

touching his hand. "Where did you get that outside help? Honey, where have you *been*?"

When he answered, for the first time Jed wasn't convinced the boy was telling the truth. Perhaps it wasn't actually a lie, but Jed had the impression of certain elements of the truth being . . . withheld. "I've been in a place of much beauty and light and comfort, with people who were nice, who were very kind to me. But I can't really remember exactly what anybody *said* or *did*." He shrugged fleshless shoulders slightly. "I just—*know*—the sort of thing I've been telling you all."

Stacy folded her hands patiently. "Was it still in Indianapolis?" she inquired. "Were you in Indiana, still in the Midwest? Where?"

"I don't think so," he answered slowly. "But I don't know that it was a—a *'where.'* It was more like—like my body had to be taken where the people here in Indianapolis and at Clemora would let it alone, so that my *brain* could be reached without interference."

Do you remember what happened?" Stacy asked.

He nodded. "Yeah, we got outside Clemora, and then—*zap!*—like magic, we were all somewhere else entirely." He smiled. "I don't know what else to call it but 'somewhere else.' "

"Was the place *real*, Phillip?" Jed demanded. He was thinking about hallucinogenic drugs. "Could you *touch* things, *feel* them? Did it *look* real to you?"

"Oh, yes, sir." The expression on the boy's face now was intent and serious. "I've never known reality like that. It was—sort of—*all* realities. Or at least all the good ones. It was *warm*, not like heat from a furnace but like—like my mom's arms when I hurt. And I liked it there." Some wistful strand of memory drifted over his face. "I—didn't really want to leave."

"Your captors," Jed pressed, unwilling to give it up. He leaned forward with determination. "What did your kidnappers or captors *look* like? Could you provide the authorities with a description of them?"

There was a moment's silence. Then, *"I wouldn't do that for anything in the world,"* Phillip whispered. He paused again. "But I'll tell you this, Mr. Westphal: They weren't ever captors or kidnappers. *Never*."

"And that's quite enough for us, Mr. Westphal," said Catherine Hanzlik, standing with dignity and an air of finality. "We promised to cooperate with you and Dr. Bennett, and we have. You have a little more of the story, for what you can make of it, and we've fulfilled our obligation. Now I think it is time for you to go."

Stacy stood, too, approaching the mother with concern. "Mrs. Hanzlik, it simply *isn't* enough. For now, of course, you want to visit with Phillip and enjoy having him home. But it's simply mandatory that I test your boy fully, that we learn precisely what has happened to his brain and——"

"No," Catherine said, shaking her handsome head. "No."

"Just a moment, Mother," Phillip said, a note of boyish pleading in his voice. "Dr. Bennett, *when* do you want to test me?"

She patted his hand. "As soon as possible. What about early next week?"

"Sure." He glanced at his mother. "I don't see what's wrong with that. It might be fun."

"I don't want you to do it, Phillip," Catherine said with a frown. "I'm still your mother, son, and I say no."

"Mrs. Hanzlik," Stacy said softly, "how else can you know that this change that's come over your son—is *permanent*?"

Catherine's lips parted in surprise and consternation. Jed, watching, saw Phillip hug his mother, adding, "Dr. Bennett's right, Mom. How *else* can you know?"

"It won't hurt," Ezra said from behind the couch in his amiable, proud baritone. He looked lovingly at his son. "I'm sure we'll be thrilled with the results of any IQ tests, Catherine. Thrilled!"

She sighed, outvoted and overwhelmed. "Oh, very well."

"Monday, then," Stacy said quickly, glancing at Jed to indicate they should leave now. "Monday at Clemora, as early as possible."

"Sure, Dr. Bennett," Phillip agreed brightly, his eyes gleaming. "Monday next week."

At the door Jed hesitated and turned back to the short teen-age boy. "Knowing the way the official mind tends to think, Phillip," he murmured, "you could be in some trouble. Sooner or later your return will get out, and since you're the only one who's come back, the police might conclude that you're somehow responsible for all the others' being gone."

The expression Phillip turned to the author was bland yet somehow studied. "Oh, but I won't be the only one who's returned, sir. Not for long."

"What are you saying?" Jed asked, startled.

"The others, they're coming back, too. Why, they'll *all* be back—when it's *time*."

Jed paused, Stacy already on the porch, wanting to ask Phillip what he meant by his remark. When *would* it be time? Time for *what*?

But he was rushed by the impatience on Ezra's face and the open resentment on Catherine's, as well as Stacy's ladylike, properly timed exit. Still full of questions, he looked speechlessly at each of them in turn. The little boy—he was still that, physically at least—was as open-faced and honest of manner as the kid who delivered his daily newspaper. But the last time Jed had felt this uncomfortable was at the Cincinnati zoo when they went into the cage to feed the lions.

"We've intruded upon this family reunion too long," Stacy said lightly to him, tugging his sleeve gently but firmly.

"Look, Mr. Hanzlik," Jed began in desperation, "may I return for further interviews as my book demands it?"

Catherine frowned and started to speak negatively, but Ezra replied first in his eagerness for them to be gone. "Of course. Sure, Mr. Westphal. But please telephone first."

And find you busy or gone, the author thought with admiration for the slick move. He and Stacy had reached the aging Granada, and he was holding the door for her when little Phillip Hanzlik came running down the driveway to them. Jed looked around, startled. The boy's chest panted a little beneath the tank top.

"The scribe, Mr. Westphal, is a special soul," Phillip intoned in his high-pitched voice. "The Gospels would not exist—nor any of the Bible— had writers not put them down for others to read." His mop of yellow hair caught the sun's reflection, almost creating an aura. "But you must be very *careful* from now on. Discreet. Do the right thing, always, so you won't leave yourself open to attack. And you, too. Dr. Bennett." The boy's eyes gleamed. "There is the Opposition—you know, who *oppose* what must happen. Very, very soon."

Then the boy turned and dashed up the drive,

gravel flying along with little puffs of dust. At the front door he glanced back and waved in a boyishly comical manner.

When they had pulled away from the curb, Jed found that his nerves were shrieking and askew, that he was glad to be gone from the Hanzlik residence. Reaching Westfield Boulevard, he accelerated to forty-plus and sped quickly along White River and past the huge Haag Drug Store at 56th Street. His hands trembled on the steering wheel; he had the disconcerting feeling that he had just witnessed something even more extraordinary than what he thought he had seen. Certain —problems—had caught his attention; they troubled Jed.

Stacy broke the silence at last. "Honey, I get the impression that Phillip is *more* than merely returned to normal intelligence. That a person of *inferior* intellect has vanished and a person of, well, *superior* intellect has returned."

"Yeah, I know what you mean," Jed grunted, unwilling quite yet to say what he was thinking. "So that makes the question arise, *is* that the same person who was taken? The same person you had in class at Clemora?"

"I can't answer that question until I test him," she replied thoughtfully. "But I'll find out next week, I'm sure of that."

"That's something else." Jed turned onto Kessler Boulevard, watching the street suddenly narrow from four to three lanes. At the stop sign he glanced at Stacy with concern. "I watched Phillip when you asked to test him. Stace, he said it would be fine with him—*but not until you made it Monday, of next week.*"

Frightened, she looked at him. "Meaning what?"

"Meaning," Jed replied, "I had the absurd notion

that Phillip thought that would be OK because—because there won't *be* a next week!"

"Oh, my God, that's ridiculous!" she snapped, turning forward and frowning at some schoolchildren being picked up by a bus. She didn't even see them. She began nervously tapping her peach purse with the fingers of her right hand. "That's positively absurd. It—*has to be*."

"Stacy, I know you've been fond of him, but that boy isn't quite—right," he said softly, touching her knee. "I don't understand it, I don't pretend to know where he's been or what he is now, but he's . . . *something else*."

"What the hell does *that* mean?" she asked, coloring. "I know you're not scientifically inclined, but that remark is meaningless. Honey, you're getting sillier by the moment!"

"I am?" He kicked the accelerator viciously. His lips were tight-pressed before he spoke. "Then, tell me this, Stace: Ezra said he hadn't even told his son or his wife we were coming today, which means Phillip had never heard of me. You're the one who told him I was an author; but, my lovely darling, how could Phillip possibly *know* I'd already written *and* sold a book?" Jed's gaze was hard, demanding, on her troubled, fine features. "Go on, sweetheart, tell me that! How could Phillip *know*?"

5:33 P.M., EST

The house of old Gus Bliss's son and daughter-in-law was quickly becoming something it had never been before. No, not a home. Not exactly. A one-woman seraglio might come closer to the truth.

It had been an exciting, even extraordinary couple of days for both Ted and Louise. From his standpoint it might even have been idyllic had he been able to relax into the new role expected of him by Louise. Although they'd actually been joined only twice in copulation since Dad's banishment, Louise's sudden abandonment of her customary nervousness had aroused some deeply hidden memory in Ted—not a memory of how marvelous sex had been, but the older one of a young boy who hoped one day to be thrilled by an eager and deft woman. Sex wasn't yet what that young Ted had desired, but he had to admit that his hopes were resurrected.

Tonight Ted had come home from work at the usual time, punctually, hungry for dinner. While he was hanging up his coat and loosening his necktie, he noticed how Louise had closed all the drapes in the living room and dining room, how she had sprayed some kind of room deodorizer and possibly something sexier as well. Even the pillows thrown on the sofa looked plumped and waiting.

He meandered out to the kitchen and found dinner cooking, all right—but dinner wasn't the only thing getting hot.

Louise was wearing nothing but lacy crimson panties, her generous, late-thirties breasts bobbling as she hoisted a bottle of Ted's best wine. It was a bottle he'd been saving for the rare occasion when his boss came to dinner, and Ted watched, a bit undone, as Louise dribbled some of it into a pan on the stove. Clearly, he thought, Louise had already poured more of that expensive bottle into her throat than she had into the pan.

"Welcome to the new Bliss household, Home of Delights," she called by way of greeting, fluffing her costly dyed-blond hair. She held out the bottle to him. "Once the old man's away, the young people play. And play 'n' play!" She giggled and, when he didn't quickly accept the bottle, shoved it into his hand. "Blissful bliss for the Blisses," she added, stumbling against him.

Ted put his arms around her naked back a trifle awkwardly. He was surprised when her tongue parted his lips, probed at his teeth and on through to his tongue. Her hand cupped him between his legs; then she removed it and replaced it with herself, pressing and grinding until he began to respond.

"I th-thought we'd already had, uh, our little celebration," he said mildly, stepping back and looking for a wineglass. It was hard with Louise's hot fragrances rising to him, and he settled, with his hand trembling faintly, for a regular tumbler. "How long does the celebration go on?"

She smiled lecherously at him and to his astonishment lifted the band of her panties and slid her hand inside. "Forever!" she exclaimed. "We got years 'n' years 'n' years t'make up for that crazy old fool being in our way!"

"As a point of fact," Ted argued, trying not to look at her as he sipped his wine, "Dad wasn't actually here all that long. It was only——"

"What am I," Louise interrupted, nothing dampening her spirits as she came close again and worked first at his tie, then his shirt, "married to a Goddamn *computer*?"

As a point of fact, their sex life hadn't been so wonderful before Gus Bliss came to live with them. Ted knew that, but as his wife continued to undress him, he felt a surge of fresh hope. Maybe she was using Dad as a scapegoat, the way she always did, but maybe—just *maybe*—it could still be great between them. The way his friends at the office always said sex was, tremendously exciting and fulfilling. "Even when it isn't very good," one of the cronies was always telling Ted, "it's better than anything else."

That would be nice, he thought, stripped now to his shorts, socks, and shoes. He looked storklike, a tall, very thin man with only slight fringes of body hair here and there. It would be lovely if it could be that marvelous just once.,

Now Louise was sitting on the counter by the sink, leaning back. He could see the dark patch through the panties; her tilted breasts were exciting, oddly new, downstairs where they never made love. Ted wanted to take her there, right then, the way she wanted him to—but he paused, knowing that he was almost unfailingly premature if he entered her at the height of his passion.

"Let's have some more wine," he told her, pouring his own and then handing her the bottle.

Louise was somewhat surprised but sat up willingly enough. She grinned lewdly at him, thinking she understood his motives: Ol' Ted wanted to tease her, to make her wait until she *really* wanted it! She put out her hand and snapped the elastic of his shorts. "You rascally son of a bitch," she muttered affectionately. She looked down at him. "But don't try t'hide the truth from *me,* buddy. *I* can tell when you want it."

It was hard to shuck all his dignity, Ted found. He'd spent years building up a good supply of it as a defense mechanism, and now he felt more idiotic than he felt sexy. "Let's go in the living room," he suggested, thinking it might make him less nervous than the kitchen.

"Yeah." Louise licked her lips. "On the rug."

She preceded him through the kitchen door, elaborately waggling her silk-shrouded hips. Experimentally, Ted patted a buttock and was rewarded by a manic whoop and a twisting lurch into the front room.

She sank down on the rug in front of the fireplace and beckoned to him. *"This* is somethin' we'd never'a dared do with your poopy pappy around."

"I don't really want to talk about him," Ted replied, awkwardly getting to the floor. "It makes me uneasy."

She pressed her hand in his bulging lap. "Same old hypocritical Theodore Bliss, my skinny fink husband," she teased him. "Try to learn a little honesty from Mama. You never gave a flying shit about Dad Bliss, and you know it."

He stared down at her, at first resting his hands on her breasts, enjoying her closeness and the way he surged inside. Then he noticed that her latest blond dye job hadn't been as effective or thorough as usual. There were great swatches of gray, even one or two that were prematurely white. But more than that, while her body still excited him in this unorthodox place to be naked, the muscles of her face looked a trifle lax, as if they had slipped.

"You don't really look too well to me, Louise," he said.

"Helluva thing t'say to a naked lady," she protested, but she laughed. "Come on and admit it, Ted. C'mon—*admit* that you don't care what happens to your old man any more'n I do."

A part of his mind clicked the thought off, *She doesn't want to carry all the guilt herself*. And another part answered, *She's right, in a way. You were only trying to do the right thing, but Dad hasn't meant anything since you got married*. He cleared his throat. "I could never admit a terrible thing like that," he protested stiffly.

Louise turned over on her stomach. "Sure you

could," she whispered, kissing what was available. "Sure you could. Say it, Teddy. Say, 'I couldn't care less what happens to my old man.'"

The shorts were now lying off to one side, but Louise's head was still in his lap. He wriggled slightly, pressured. "I won't, Louise," he replied with his absolute last ounce of dignity. "It just wouldn't be right to say a thing like that."

"It'll be *right*, all right," she whispered as she paused for a moment, the tip of her tongue between her lips. She held him upright in her hand. "But not unless you *say* it!"

Moments later he couldn't resist. The up-and-down rhythm had begun, and he didn't want it interrupted for the world. "I couldn't care *less* what happens to my dad," Ted groaned, arching.

"*Again*," Louise managed to whisper.

He repeated it, shouted it, finally, into the living room: "*I couldn't care less what happens to Dad!*"

When another hour or so had passed and each of them had been satisfied, the wine bottle drained and lying empty against a chair in the living room, dinner on the stove turned to a simmer, Ted arose stiffly from the living room floor and awkwardly began replacing his clothes. "I have to get a nap before we eat," he announced, moving like an automaton. He was conscious of a terrific pounding between his ears. "Right here on the sofa."

"See how many uses this room has with the old fart out of it?" Louise laughed. "Well, I'm not the only one who doesn't look so hot." She saw how Ted's shoulders and chest muscles had gone slack; he looked pale as she patted him on the back. "Maybe we'll slip up on it next time, give ourselves a little more time. You'll see, baby. It's gonna be a second honeymoon for good."

He nodded, hurting too much to reply. Even his teeth ached, felt like they were coming out; he had a terrible taste in his mouth. Ted stretched out on the sofa, the bristly material making marks on his face. He frowned. "Dizzy," he stated to no one in particular, "dizzy." He laid his wrist over his closed eyes to make the room darker. "Gotta sleep."

It turned out to be the kind of sleep that retains a faint awareness of passing time but renders it unimportant—of negligible value in the presence of one's need to rest. Eventually Ted even dreamed: something silly about his father when Ted was still a boy, something about fine, enjoyable moments playing catch together, and cards; and then something Ted had forgotten—how sweet his dad and mom were together, when Mom was still around. He groaned audibly then, as if at loss. Several times, too, his lips curled in a grin. For a while Ted was home again and not at all careful of his dignity.

He thought he had awakened to a shout—his mind told him he'd had almost two hours of sleep —but when he sat upright on the sofa, Ted heard nothing except small noises from the kitchen, Louise finishing up, he decided, barely noticing several tiny white things sprinkled where his face had lain. His eyes were sandy, grainy. He rubbed them with his knuckles and yawned. Maybe Louise had called him for dinner.

Barefoot, although he'd dressed before lying down, Ted stood up. His whole body ached and protested motion. His arms and left knee felt stiff; they pained him. He was vaguely aware he wasn't quite standing up straight as he began to shuffle toward the kitchen, in need of companionship.

When he walked in and glanced toward the stove, Ted couldn't believe his eyes.

A strange woman stood there, her thin back to him, shoulders rounded, longish snow-white hair streaming between her narrow shoulder blades. He got one audible word out: *"Who . . . ?"*

And then the stranger turned to him questioningly, and he stared back at her in open horror.

This was a terribly old female, a crone deep into retirement age, deep into the so-called golden years. They'd been tarnished for her. This ancient, ugly hag who had curiously materialized in Louise's kitchen had a long-handled fork in her blue-veined hands. She had been testing the roast, he saw. A strand of reddish meat protruded disgustingly from between the hoary, slackened lips, and the aroma from her decrepit body was a mixture of wine and the graveyard.

He couldn't speak; he just stared. She had deep-set eyes that were red-rimmed, feebly and dimly focused on him in surprise. Her skin was coarse, yellow, and leathery, with the appearance of a detailed road map. Worse, she was absolutely nude, and Ted gaped in revulsion at her pendulous breasts, empty sacks sagging past her sunken navel, at her dank white pubic hair and unbelievably wrinkled legs covered with a network of angry veins. When the crone smiled at him, as if to offer an explanation, several golden kernels of human teeth dribbled from her mouth and mixed with the stinking drool on her double chin.

Before he fainted, Ted heard the hag speak. "You silly fool," she said quite distinctly but in good humor, the voice a shrill cackle of amusement, "take that white powder out of your hair and quit holding your stupid mouth that way. You look like you haven't a tooth left in your head."

Also before he fainted, Ted saw the clear truth of the matter: *This awful and aged crone was his wife, Louise.*

8:06 P.M., EST

Jed had driven Stacy Bennett down to Venus Hill, where she had an early afternoon appointment with the late Lionel K. Hartberg's attorney. She had asked Jed to sit in for the meeting as she tried to sort out the founder's affairs and arrangements.

Unfortunately, Hartberg had been such a totally solitary man, self-involved and close-minded, that the continuation of Clemora as an institution was now very much up in the air. In addition, as the corporate attorney explained in his dapper, precise fashion, certain papers were missing, presumably destroyed in the inexplicable fire that had destroyed Mr. Hartberg.

For Stacy, of course, that meant that her job was in doubt as well. She was owed almost a month in back wages, which, the attorney smoothly reassured her, would be paid to her in full— "eventually. The litigation, of course, will tie those funds up for a period of time." She asked him to estimate how long that would be, and he peered thoughtfully into space for a moment before answering, without an iota of appreciation for her situation, "For at least six months, but no longer than two years."

And that, in the most businesslike, oblique way, was how she realized that Clemora would be closed. Almost none of the underpaid employees on the late Mr. Hartberg's staff could conceivably afford to wait for their salaries such an indefinite period of time.

Now Jed looked across his living room, holding

a hot cup against his forehead and appraising the worried psychologist. "How long can you wait before you'll desperately need money?" he asked quietly.

Stacy had collapsed into the chair Rosalyn used to call her own and, when she returned, presumably would continue to prefer. She gave Jed a feeble smile. "How does a week from Wednesday strike you?"

"Is it really that bad?" he wondered. "I thought professional people—doctors, psychiatrists, and psychologists—made wonderful money."

Stacy glared at him with a trace of her old sharpness. "Never confuse doctors, if you mean GPs, with surgeons, or surgeons with psychiatrists, or psychiatrists with psychologists. That's the worst apples-and-oranges mixing you can possibly do." She drummed her fingertips on the chair arm. "Now, surgeons and corporate psychologists or even private-practicing psychiatrists can go together, if you like jam, but my position is on the low rung of the ladder."

"What are you going to do?" he inquired, concerned for her. "How can I help?"

"You can't, except by being you," she said with a faint smile. "But, actually, I'm exaggerating my poverty. I'm a pretty frugal sort of person, as you could detect from the lack of sumptuousness of my apartment. I have a few thousand socked away for a rainy day—or a day when the head of my institution is killed by spontaneous combustion."

"You look tired," Jed observed in a kind tone. "Sleepy?"

"I can't remember when I've ever been so sleepy," she replied with a yawn, holding her hand over her lips. "I feel as if I could sleep for a year."

Jed felt his heartbeat accelerate even before he

found the right words. "Stacy, I don't want to take you home tonight. I don't really believe that we're in any danger, but I'd feel better if you were near me." He paused, and his voice sounded hoarse when he continued. "Stay with me tonight. Don't make me take you home."

"All right."

She had replied so quickly, so easily, he was surprised. "I had no idea I was so persuasive," he remarked with a grin.

She got up from Rosalyn's chair and came over to sit on the arm of his chair, giving him a brief kiss on the temple. "I've already lost my virginity to you, Jedediah; so I might just as well make sure you stay faithful to me." She ran her hand through his hair and studied his suddenly quiet profile. "What's the matter? Is something bothering you?"

Jed sighed. "Do you remember when you were in conference with Hartberg's attorney and I slipped away to use the phone?" She nodded. "Well, I called my ex-wife. I asked her to let my son, Darren, visit me for a day or two, and she refused, point-blank. I could probably force her to let him go, if I wanted to get into all that with my lawyer, but I despise the idea of using Darren as a soccer ball."

"I'm so sorry." Stacy slipped down into his lap. "I don't know how women can be such bitches."

Jed looked into space a moment longer. "In a way," he said at last, "the child—*my* child—has also disappeared. And I'm beginning to realize that, unlike Phillip, he isn't ever returning to me."

Stacy kissed him on the lips and, before he could reply, slithered to her feet. "Everything'll seem much better when you get something in your stomach. What do you have in the fridge?"

Jed's expression was one of bewilderment. "I haven't the foggiest notion."

"Men!" Stacy exclaimed, wrinkling her nose and heading for the kitchen. She stifled a yawn. "You're utterly helpless without us."

"Only when we get used to having you around," he argued, standing and following her. "You're just a habit, that's all—like following the Pacers or reading bad mystery stories or watching soaps on TV."

She glanced sharply over her shoulder at him. "But the withdrawal symptoms are real doozies," she observed, giving him a frosty smile.

He responded by slapping her rounded buttocks. Then, together, they raided his refrigerator, finding four somewhat world-weary eggs, a few strips of exhausted bacon, and a chunk of Colby cheese. After he'd succeeded in breaking a plate and putting bread in the toaster too soon, Stacy managed to kick him out and take over. Jed sat in his chair in the living room, listening to her hum a Cole Porter song, enjoying the splendor of being a helpless male.

The scrambled eggs Stacy fixed for them were a culinary triumph which Jed slightly marred for the psychologist turned cook by insisting on a healthy dollop of catsup. "Didn't Rosalyn ever succeed in getting you properly housebroken, man?" she demanded, staring with open repugnance at the mess on his fork.

"As I told that dubious lady, you just don't know what's good." He dipped the bacon in another pool of catsup and munched contentedly. Then his manner changed, becoming more serious. "In answer to your question, *only* in the ways that don't really count."

He deeply enjoyed the small but decent meal,

but he enjoyed Stacy Bennett more. She made coffee for them, and it was the first decent cup he'd had in weeks. While they were having a second cup apiece, conversation naturally wended its way back to the Vanishments.

"Aside from my economic problems," Stacy began, "there are so *many* unanswered questions about Phillip Hanzlik, the most important of which, of course, is—where in the world has he *been?*"

"He claimed that he didn't really know, himself," Jed replied over the lip of his cup, "but I suspect that he knows, that he—somehow can't tell us." He sipped. "I have a theory on why he alone has returned—a partial theory."

"Tell me," she said, leaning on her elbows.

He shrugged. "It's just a notion, but I think Phillip is a—forerunner, someone whose job it is to pave the way. Call him an advance scout, if you will—the point man on a reconnaissance team."

"But an advance scout for what?" she asked, puzzled. "Someone to pave the way *for what?*"

He shook his auburn head. "I honestly don't know, sweetheart. But I don't believe he was kidnapped, not in any meaningful or exact sense of the word. Brainwashing, well, clearly he's undergone that—but for the good. Tell me this, from your professional point of view." He set his cup down firmly. "As a psychologist, do you think that Phillip Hanzlik is a different person now?"

"I should think that's perfectly obvious."

"No, no, you aren't following me." He paused, ordering his thoughts. "Has an *entirely different* individual come back—that's part one—or the same *body* with a wholly different brain—that's part two. Or, part three, do you believe that Phillip is *exactly the same human being* except that some—obstructions to his ability to think rationally and maturely have been removed?"

"I can't say definitely until I've done my tests on the boy next week," she replied steadily. Then she saw Jed's face cloud in irritated protest. "OK, OK—I know it's not for the official record, so I needn't be coy with you. Honey, I have to tell you that I feel strongly your answer is part three, but they—whoever 'they' happen to be—haven't merely removed an obstruction. Oh, no." Her eyes were intense with concentration as they locked with Jed's. "They've done that, yes, but they have also succeeded in enabling Phillip to become *the very best Phillip* he is capable of being. Somehow, in a very limited space of time, those people who took the children have freed Phillip from his intellectual limitation of birth, educated him better than school could manage it for years, and given him some strange, all-new sense of *purpose*. Because, my darling Jedediah, I sense about that boy some *mysterious intentions* that are unknown to us but *entirely clear* to Phillip Hanzlik."

"I agree fully," Jed said with a brisk nod. "He's up to something."

"Not very scientific, but I have the same feeling. But"—Stacy placed her hand on his—"something good or something *bad?*"

"I don't know, really I don't." He shook his head again, wearily. "The appearance, of course, tends to be that of good. He's obviously delighted to be back with his parents. He's polite; he says things that may be preposterous but have the ring of good intentions."

"Even when he was retarded—and we still don't know if his improvement is permanent—he was a decent kid."

"Look, hon, you mentioned the 'people' who've taken him." Jed hesitated. "I *told* you I'm always candid about what I think," he warned, then continued, "but how can we even be certain it *was* 'people' who took him?"

Stacy frowned and withdrew her hand. She began tapping her fingers nervously once more. "Come on, writer man! This is real life, not a science fiction film. What else could have taken those kids except people? 'Jaws'? Bug-eyed monsters? Zombies? UFO occupants? Aliens from another dimension?"

"All sound possibilities," he said with near solemnity. "Just maybe you're right about one of those."

"Hogwash," she jeered, her vital face marked in good-humored scoffing. "In fact, my friend, bullshit! Stacks of chips and moose pie!"

"Don't be indelicate," he answered with a grin. "My beloved wife used to sit in that same chair. But I *am* serious about this. Take UFOs—unidentified flying objects—for a moment. Whether anybody likes hearing it or not, there is a lot of hard evidence that occupants from UFOs have literally *abducted* earth people—not just once, as in the famous Hill case, but in others." He ticked them off on his fingers. "There's the Andreasson kidnapping, which Ray Fowler described so entertainingly; Travis Walton, who appears to have spent several *days* on a UFO; Sergeant Charles Moody, a fourteen-year member of the air force; Charles Hickson and Pascagoula; and, more recently, the Tujunga Canyon incidents of *multiple* contacts, even seizures!"

"Are you telling me all those people were kidnapped and taken aboard UFOs?" Stacy asked incredulously.

"No, but under hypnosis *they seem to have been*. They *believe* it happened; so maybe it did, at least once." Jed's jaw was set grimly. "But if it happened only *once*—if all the sightings of UFOs since 1947, when the first flap began, are phonies but one—and that *single case* is genuine, then mankind has a serious problem. And, more to the point, Phillip may have been seized by UFO people for experimental purposes."

"And if there *is* that one, true case," Stacy said, surprised by what he'd told her and thinking of what it implied, "then the abductions we discussed before—the vanishing army troops, for example—may have been the work of beings from another planet."

"And we may not be alone in the universe after all. However, what you said doesn't necessarily follow." He lit a cigarette thoughtfully. "We don't know what UFOs are. There are a dozen theories, at least, to account for them, *in addition* to the outer-space possibility. Some are ingenious, and some are pretty persuasive. But, yes, all of the famous snatchings throughout history may have been the work of whatever motivates unidentified flying objects. Even some of the great missing-person cases, like Judge Crater or Glenn Miller or Amelia Earhart"—he grinned impishly—"they may live right now on Regulus, Amelia dancing to Miller's 'String of Pearls,' while the old judge applauds along with the little green people."

"Even in theory, I find it hard to accept," Stacy said deliberately, trying to assimilate what Jed had suggested.

"OK. Do you know of a *single* psychiatric or educational theory that would explain such a miraculous change in Phillip?"

To her consternation, Stacy again found herself

yawning. She covered her mouth as her throat constricted. "No, I haven't," she confessed, "but who knows what the government knows and isn't telling? Maybe the people who have vanished were taken by the CIA or—or some unnamed, unspecified branch of government or——"

Jed comically put his head back and, to the tune of "California, Here I Come," caroled hideously, *"Par-a-noi-a, here she comes!"*

"You, sir, are a terrible human being." She made a mock frown, then smiled at him as she stood and gathered up their few dishes before her on the table. Scarcely needing to bend, she kissed the tip of his nose. "Would you mind terribly if we did these in the morning, and if we just went to bed now?"

He looked at the pretty, petite woman beside him and impulsively hugged her with affection. His arms went easily around her waist. "That has to be the nicest invitation I've received this year," he told her happily.

Then, as naturally and comfortably as any husband and wife, requiring few words, their arms locked around each other, they climbed the stairs. Jed yawned, too, but he knew that he was holding out a little extra energy.

However, he paused at the room across the hall from the master bedroom, his glance at it guilty and regretful.

"The boy's room?" asked Stacy. "Darren's?"

He nodded. Then, together, they entered the room where he had spent so many nights with Rosalyn Westphal, where, in fact, Darren had been conceived.

Sensing his feelings, knowing he wanted her and knowing that he still experienced traces of guilt, Stacy closed the door behind them and, in the dark, came into his arms. She had to rise slightly on tiptoe to kiss his mouth, although he wasn't a tall man. When he began to respond, she put his palms on her hips and came against him in a hard little rush.

"She chose to leave you, darling," Stacy said softly in his face, and he could make out her wide, intelligent, caring eyes. "She threw you away like an old shoe. I'll *never* hurt you that way, Jedediah," she swore to him, whispering intensely now. "I promise you, my love—*never!*"

His lips formed the words, "I know," and there were tears in his eyes.

"Wait there!" she commanded him. "Don't move!"

He stood beside the bed as she located hangers in the closet and began to undress. It would have been beyond Stacy Bennett's power to turn herself into a sex object, to remove her clothes stripper style, teasingly. Instead, she removed them as quickly as possible, except for her panties, and, barefoot, padded back to him. He had watched her every move, and when her hand reached out, below the waist, she giggled slightly. "You moved," she said.

To Jed's infinite surprise, Stacy came into his arms and raised his hands until they were holding her large, heavy breasts. A little shudder ran through her small, delicately curving body. Then she began to undress him—slowly, tantalizingly, kissing where he was newly left naked.

Then their hands met without a word, and they moved lazily, languorously, to the bed. Somehow, with the affection and the renewed passion he felt for this petite woman with the bright eyes and light-brown hair, it did not seem to Jed that they were violating the bed of his marriage. Some-

THE BANISHED 189

how, he thought with gladness and expectation as they lay down and their arms enfolded one another, it seemed all right—and quite wonderful.

"Let me," she said, pleading with him when his anxious hands began to push her over on her back.

For a moment Jed didn't understand. Then he obeyed her own gently pushing hands and turned on his back. In a moment, as though she had done it a hundred times, Stacy lifted herself across him and, with incredible slowness, with a delicious sensation that turned his body to hot liquid, she lowered herself onto him. "My man," she said in the darkness, leaning forward to kiss his mouth, her breasts pressing against his upper chest. "My man."

He had an indelible, unforgettable image of Stacy riding him, her head thrown back in ecstasy, his own hands reaching up to grip her raised, warm breasts, and then, to keep from hurting her, throwing his hands like claws on the sheets of the bed as her rhythm accelerated. Astonishingly, time vanished and what followed seemed endless, a magical period apart from time and apart from all else that either of them had known. At the very end, his explosion was massive, missilelike, as her body impaled itself on him—hard, *wrenchingly*—and then they were panting together, just as everything else was truly shared.

Later, when they were apart but somehow yet locked as lovers on an emotional chain of shared adoration, Jed raised himself above her panting breasts in order to peer seriously down at her happy face.

"I want you to know something," he said softly to her, his lips inches away from hers. "Whatever may happen now, for good or bad, whether anyone has truly blessed us or given us permission, I want you to understand that you are now my wife, Stacy Bennett." He paused to kiss her uptilted, full lips and briefly run his fingers through her mane of tawny hair. "You are mine—as of tonight, this moment—and I am yours. I"—Jed hesitated, groped for words—"I cleave unto you, my darling. *Only* you."

"What a strange, sweet thing to say," she murmured in delight, closing her eyes for a moment. "And I love you, Jedediah. We are . . . each other's."

Smiling, tired now, he leaned down and pulled the tangled sheets up from the corner of the bed. Despite those features which were marvelously womanly about her, Stacy had, he thought, knees like a six-year-old girl. He lay back contentedly.

"Jed, why did you put it that way, darling?" she asked, turning on her side toward him. "Why is it important to you that we be—married now?"

He curled his arms behind his head, under the pillow, and looked at the ceiling without seeing it. "I suppose it *was* strange, but I—I have a sensation of events spinning past, of time starting to rush by—perhaps to run *out*. And I suppose I wanted the Creator to know that we're together for always, that we *belong* together through eternity. Of course, I'm just being silly." He tried to shrug it off.

"Then, you felt it, too," she said with concern. "About Phillip Hanzlik."

"What about him?" Jed asked, largely stalling.

"That there was something . . . *ominous* about his return. Something possibly . . . *fatal*."

Jed shrugged lightly. "Oh, I thought he was a nice enough kid."

"I think he still is," she agreed. "I meant that we both sense that what Phillip's doing is somehow—threatening. You don't really believe for a moment that UFOs are involved, do you?"

"No, but I didn't want you to be frightened again," he said. "I don't like you to be afraid."

"I'm not afraid anymore," she answered, almost talking to herself, "not of burning, anyway, like Hartberg." She yawned, suddenly very sleepy again. "I think I've convinced myself that the worst things are happening, for the most part, to the bad guys, like Hartberg—and we're white-hats, Jed." Suddenly her voice grew agitated. "But it isn't just the incidents that have occurred. Jed, what *is* it that must *happen* when the other banished people begin returning? For God's sake, what is planned—and *by whom?*"

"I just don't know," he confessed, trying to think of a way to soothe her. He saw how sleepy she'd become and encouraged it, stroking her mane of hair.

Outside the bedroom window the moon seemed swollen and huge, a purposive and alien eye that watched them through the thin curtains. "I seem to be forming some opinions," Stacy said in a tired little-girl voice. He had to strain to hear her. "I believe that there's nothing the police or scientists can do about what's happening—or what's *going* to happen." She groped for his hand and held it tightly against one pale breast. Her lips were dry. "I believe that it's all entirely of—some weird and supernatural origin. And that when it's finally done at last—when what's happened is finally over——" She paused, unable, or unwilling, to finish.

"Yes?" he prompted her, cupping her small

pointed chin and lifting her weary, worried face to his. He kissed her eyelids gently. "What then, sweetheart?"

"I feel that it's not going to be very pleasant for —for the rest of us," she finished in a whisper, eyes closed but moving fearfully beneath the fragile lids. "The ones who *haven't* been—taken. Oh, hold me. Jed, *please*—hold me and help me forget about it all for a while."

Jed did, gladly; he held her close and dear. Even with her frightened words in his mind, it seemed like magic to be holding against him a woman whom he hadn't even known until so recently, a woman whom he now knew he loved more than life. Everything about her was so warm, so feathery or yielding to the touch, innocent and well-meaning and wise, that Jed scarcely noticed when she fell asleep in his arms.

Odd, he thought, briefly puzzled. One instant she was still quite awake, breathing almost in pants against his bare chest; the next she was snoring, just faintly, in deep sleep.

Throughout the night, even when he awakened foggily and idly contemplated sex, Stacy remained so sound asleep that she scarcely moved a muscle. Once he hovered protectively above her, waiting until he saw her breasts rise in a breath. And the next morning, when he was ready to rise for the day, she was still dead to the world. He yawned and scratched his head. Stacy appeared virtually drugged.

Poor kid, he thought compassionately, getting up as quickly as possible and covering her sweet body with a light blanket. *She's just beat from all this.*

Meaning well, he let her sleep. . . .

8

Two days until April 22, 1984
8:51 A.M., EST

In Indianapolis, Monument Circle—*not* the Speedway, home of the legendary 500-Mile Race—is the traditional heart of town, with major streets fanning out from its rickety nucleus. Newcomers to the city are likely to find themselves going in frustrating circles rather than race-style ovals, since the 500 is actually on the outskirts of another town entirely, many difficult miles to the north and west. But such is the preeminent justice of power.

Monument Circle itself was recently red-bricked for beauty, in tribute to the economics-sustaining race and to replace a host of heretofore welcoming chuckholes. At its center towers an aging, modestly tall megalith erected to the honor of Hoosiers killed in war. At Christmastime the monument is laboriously bedecked in green and red—with chilled high school students singing wistful carols beneath its concrete branches—and proclaimed "the world's largest Christmas tree." No one, not even the city fathers who haven't been in treacherous downtown Indianapolis all year, finds the slightest incongruity in a parlay of the military, the Prince of Peace, and valiantly dead people.

Once upon a time, when Indianapolis was

young and innocent (and high-stepping horses trotted around the Circle), it was said that a visitor to the monument could see all the city from its apex. Now, if the wind does not shift, it is possible to make out the beginning of the better residential sections to which suburbanites have thoughtfully fled. Or, putting it another way, one can see the primary regions of crime without needing to squint.

Once, on the old Circle (say the social-security-bound), there was a liveliness and jaunty sense of being "in the know." Although New Yorkers did not believe it, the English Theatre—no longer permitted to stand—featured the nation's finest actors and playwrights in *off*-off-Broadway productions. The Circle Theatre offered, for half a dollar, one of the top dance bands of the thirties or forties, a first-run film, color cartoons, a newsreel, and coming attractions. Now that garish theater lets you have martial arts, black militant, or R-rated comedy flicks for possibly four dollars. Police cars meander slowly around the Circle, constantly making their unadmitted daily quotas.

Now, on the Circle, locals—who are not legally permitted to park their vehicles—can locate such indispensables as a failed department store, the Columbia Club (power base for wealthier Republicans), a nut house, a place that sells foreign cigarettes, a venerable shoe store, and the altogether democratic Power and Light Company. The latter is a vast, immensely expensive modern structure in front of which cars incessantly double-park with impunity and in the lurking bowels of which poor people, pouring through in droves, are often humiliated right alongside those who have simply neglected to pay their soaring monthly bills.

Today, midway between the once-splendiferous

theater and the monolithic light company, a small but effective coterie of young people called the Pathfinders were plying their persuasive trade. In a contemporary twist on the Robin Hood legend, these religious faithful—clean-cut, recently bathed, and dressed in drab suits or modest dresses— were doing their level best to take from the rich and give to themselves. Sherwood Forest, for the Pathfinders, was any evil modern woods where many helpless people were afoot and the authorities could be lulled into a charitable *laissez-faire* disposition. Rather than wearing the green, à la Robin, the Pathfinders collected it; rather than being merry men, the Pathfinders were earnest to a fault, good-looking, slightly glassy-eyed youths whose fundamental task was to please their founder, the Reverend Carlton Blant, who many —including the reverend himself, whose idea it was—said was the returning messiah.

Should anyone have looked closely at the dozen boys and girls working the Circle like so many highly trained encyclopedia salesmen, rather than averting their gazes from the dolefully convincing young eyes, they might have noticed that one of the young men was somewhat different.

Where the other eleven Pathfinders sidled up to their prey, Lonnie Malone approached them openly, unashamedly, and unfailingly said, "Pardon me." Where the others found their paths directly in front of people, Lonnie sidestepped and merely trailed after them. Where the others used high-pressure sales techniques drummed into them by a corps of hard-eyed, enormously skilled men called "Speakers of the Path," Lonnie spoke of Jesus Christ and his work, quoted the Bible, and *believed* it when he told people that the Pathfinders helped the poor.

Some such observant would-be customer might also have noticed that Lonnie Malone's eyes were red-rimmed from crying: his father had died last night.

At seventeen, Lonnie was over six feet tall, excessively lanky to the point of seeming in need of a good meal, a teen-ager with black hair combed straight back, a naturally serious manner, and a cheek-splotching array of blackheads. He might one day, when his acne war was won, be handsome; now it was necessary to speak with Lonnie, see the attentive way he listened, and hear the thoughtful things he said before one responded to his charm. He might one day, when he was older and confident enough, be a speaker of remarkable authority.

He'd heard of the Pathfinders on and off for nearly two years, learning that the organization flourished in the Midwest and was determined to become a national force. What he'd heard he'd taken with a grain of salt, since most of the others at school considered organized religion a laugh, and the Pathfinders didn't even seem to be organized. But what he'd read six months ago was a different story. In one of the same booklets that he was disseminating today, Lonnie had read that war was not necessarily wrong if it were righteous, but that only believers in God's word had the right to instigate war. He'd read that nobody but the Pathfinders seemed to care about reaching the religious heart of America's teen-agers and steering them away from evil to a life of purpose and meaning. He'd read that the Pathfinders planned to become the most charitable force on the face of the earth, but that they would screen applicants for help instead of giving welfare money away blindly—the way Dad said that government organizations did—and if you were an honest, industrious, God-fearing person in need, you might get *any* kind of help or *any* amount of money required to put you on your feet. You didn't have to be sixty-five or crippled.

He liked those things, the Pathfinder approach. He'd joined them a few months ago because he'd always believed more deeply in God than others around him seemed to and because he found society in general so hypocritical that the faintest exposure to it made him feel unclean. He liked the fact that the Pathfinders encouraged dating among its membership and hoped to find a young woman who shared his views fully. Although he wasn't sure that he wanted to remain a Pathfinder all his life, the way they wanted him to be, he'd been told that the leaders of the religion would personally counsel him in his vocational plans and, when he was ready, work out the best way for him to attend college. And because he passionately believed that worship of the dollar was wrong but that any real man earned his way in the world, he hadn't minded at all working ten or twelve hours a day for the Pathfinders and turning over every penny in return for a rude dormitory room shared with three other boys. Arithmetic and economics had never been among Lonnie's strong suits at school.

What Lonnie *hadn't* liked was the Reverend Carlton Blant, the leader of the Pathfinders, or some of the things he did—like allowing some of his followers to proclaim him the new messiah. But at seventeen Lonnie tried to be a man of the world in some things and figured this way: The Pathfinders was a growing organization *of* many, *for* the many, and the reverend would simply step aside when a better man came along. Lonnie figured, too, that any mortal man was essentially prone to errors of judgment and that the Reverend Mr. Blant merely enjoyed such praise and was certainly smart enough to know that people would give more to a man who was compared to Christ. This, Lonnie felt, was improper but not necessarily sinful—not unless the reverend believed it himself. But he often appeared before them, on the platform in the auditorium, softly inquiring, "Who is it they say I am?"—and then shaking his head, smiling, and leading them in prayer.

Today Lonnie Malone was grief-stricken not only by the death of his father but because he felt that his own enlistment in the ranks of the Pathfinders might have contributed to his dad's demise. He felt that it was his fault that he could not adequately explain his feelings, his commitment, to his parents, to make it clear that he was not turning against them so much as turning *for* his faith. He'd never gotten them to understand that it was right for him to be away from them entirely for a while, as Jesus himself had left his parents at an early age to "be about his Father's business." He couldn't get them to see that he missed them as much as they missed him but that the world was in a dreadful condition and it was the young men and women who would have to spend most of their time in it.

Lonnie was, of course, wrong about almost all the conclusions he had drawn. Among them were the cold facts that the Reverend Carlton Blant would let death alone remove him from leadership of the Pathfinders; that only the pittance recorded on tax returns had been given to the needy, and *that* only because it was a write-off; that the reverend's primary aspiration was to acquire a tax-exempt status, not to save people, not teen-agers or anybody; that war in general was condemned merely because the tactic appealed to youngsters who feared the military; that young men and women were sought as recruits solely because they were both gullible and a source of cheap labor; that they were removed from their parents because Dad and Mom were far greater adversaries of the Pathfinders than Satan or adversity; that nobody had ever been prepared for college or assisted in entering a university by any member of the Pathfinders; and that the Reverend Carlton Blant sincerely believed he was divine and could never die.

There was another fact, too, that escaped young Lonnie: because he insisted on approaching would-be contributors in his own passionately God-fearing way, because he preferred studying the Bible to the official Pathfinder tracts, and because living as morally and decently as he could seemed *natural* to him, several of the padres, or deacons, seriously questioned his value to the organization. At times the essential *goodness* of Lonnie Malone drove the padres to distraction. A few of them had implied cautiously that Lonnie would make a good "sacrifice," when one was required. That decision would be reached before they moved out to the west side for the hundreds of thousands of people who would be attending practices and time trials for this year's 500-Mile Race. There was considerable loose talk recently that the Reverend Mr. Blant, on the actual day of the big event, while in the midst of several thousand additional Pathfinders summoned from other midwestern chapters for the event, would allow one of his faithful to throw himself beneath the wheels of thirty-three cars traveling at two hundred miles per hour—as a symbol of his command and their unity of purpose, as an advertisement that would be unparalleled in answering questions concerning their devotion or dedication. "Let any piddly-ass Protestant or casino-bred Catholic match *that* one," the reverend had said warmly to one of his trusted padres.

He had also said privately that Lonnie Malone would be an outstanding choice.

While the teen-ager and his eleven companions were winding up the day's solicitation of funds on Monument Circle, Carlton Blant was himself locked in his study in stately Pathfinder Place. The mansion squatted like a huge frog on an uncultivatable plot of ground to the northwest side of Indianapolis, and this hour was, Blant's followers understood, the time of their leader's daily meditation. At this time, they whispered, the reverend was given divine instruction concerning future developments. A few simply remarked, "This is when he talks with his Father."

Blant stood before a great desk on which were conspicuously stacked a Pathfinder version of the Holy Bible, a dozen Pathfinder T-shirts, some Pathfinder posters, a ceramic Pathfinder Panther with a miniature red devil gripped in its teeth, and several editions of the Pathfinder Press's weekly newsletter. He wasn't communing with God or getting any divine instructions: he was appraising a business chart on the wall. Any interloper would have been impressed by the Pathfinder priest. He was one of those men in the six-foot range who succeeded, without trying, at seeming large and powerful. A lot of it came from his immense torso and broad back, but he was aided, too, by virtue of short-waistedness. The longer legs, frail by comparison to the muscular upper portions, gave an impression of greater height, and the fact that his skull and neck were much too big for the rest of his body completed the productive image.

And the image was bolstered by a basso voice

with unusual range and disciplined force. If shrilling tenors could crack crystal glasses with their high notes, Carlton Blant could dig furrows of earth with his. It had taken him years to learn how to use his wondrous voice box properly, years of practicing before mirrors and into tape recorders. He had even taken singing lessons, both to enhance his use of his diaphragm and as an extension of his boyhood longing to become a great popular vocalist. Emerging rock 'n' roll had ruined his plans; a message expressing his detestation of rock, his certainty that it was Satan's musical tool, was contained now in every Pathfinder pamphlet. On a day when the reverend was neither hung over nor exhausted from athletically pursuing the cultivation of obedience and generosity in the breasts of his nubile female members, his soaring, sonorous tones had often proved more useful to him than simple debating techniques. "Maybe I'm not another Como or Crosby, but knowing how to drown out the opposition without appearing to shout," he sometimes intoned to an intimate, "shit, that's worth at least fifty thou' a year to me."

Just about the time Lonnie and his companions were climbing back into the bus, dozens of envelopes in their pockets bursting with bills for him, the Reverend Mr. Blant was intensely studying his wall chart. It hung beneath a large, colorful banner boasting the name of the organization and a variety of quotations from both the (Pathfinder-authorized) Bible and the reverend himself. And the chart enabled the viewer, at a glance, to learn all about current profit margins in several endeavors as well as to plot future-growth curves. Some of the successful investments outside the Pathfinders were also recorded, kept up-to-date by a trusted ally. Now Blant was especially interested in estimating the likely gain from this year's 500 Pathfinder Panorama of Faith—both with and without the human sacrifice. While his own personal percentage of the overall take wasn't displayed on the chart, it didn't need to be. He knew it even better than he knew the real Bible—and he'd memorized every *word* of that!

Arriving back at Pathfinder Place, Lonnie Malone felt tired and gloomy. He knew why he was extra-unhappy but tried not to think about it. He sank down on his cot in the dorm and ran his hand over his face. His thoughts turned to his father's death and what would become of Mom, who had no other children. He lay back and tried to tune out the other boys, who were discussing their day's "take" like so many storm-door or ad-space salesmen. One of them, nearby, sat on the edge of his cot glancing through a porno magazine, hand languid against his crotch. Conversation among the other boys switched to the Memorial Day plans and how many suckers might be fleeced at the 500. Danny Bucher, who hadn't quite abandoned street talk since he'd come to the Pathfinders, wondered aloud if "the Rev" would really have "the guts" it took to "splatter some sucker right out on the track."

As evening came on and moonlight trickled through the small window high in the wall above the bed, Lonnie tried to read his Pathfinder Bible. Unable to recall exactly what portions had been changed, he turned to prayer. Now he faced what he had tried to ignore, the fact that the Reverend Carlton Blant and his padres wouldn't allow him to attend his father's funeral. Lonnie shut his eyes and prayed both for Dad's soul and for the well-being of his mother. He tried very hard not to question the leader's decision, because that was one of the diamond-hard rules at Pathfinder Place; instead, he tried to understand it, and he prayed that he would be strong and just for Christ and always do the Father's bidding. When he prayed that, Lonnie distinctly had God in mind and not Carlton Blant.

But something troubled Lonnie, and he could not concentrate on this prayer. The trail of moonlight from the tiny window distracted him; it seemed to be gathering instead of dispersing into strands of nothingness. He sat up, worried because he felt it was wrong to be here instead of with his mother at the funeral. Nervous, Lonnie ran a hand through his straight black hair and thought to himself, how far did a man go in obeying a leader here, when his own conscience told him that the leader was wrong? As a Pathfinder, he was a soldier for God—but what about the soldiers in World War II who did everything Hitler asked them to do? Wasn't it really a man's duty to obey his own conscience when it spoke to him as strongly as it was doing now? Didn't the Bible *used* to say, "Honor thy father and mother," instead of, "Honor thy leaders," the way it did now in the Pathfinder book?

Lonnie got up. It was almost lights-out, and nobody left the dorm then. Unless the reverend summoned them, *never*. Lonnie walked down the aisle between the beds and put his hand on the doorknob. "Where the hell you think you're goin', Malone?" called Danny Bucher, and Lonnie heard the other boy get to his feet.

"I'm going to make a phone call and then go into town," Lonnie said, his back still turned to them and his hand on the doorknob. "It's right that I do."

Danny and another boy, unseen, started moving

toward him from behind. "The hell you say," Danny growled.

"No," Lonnie said, "it's the hell *you* say." And he knew, somehow, that the two boys had stopped, unable to get around an invisible shield that had formed between them and him.

Untouched and thereafter unaddressed, Lonnie walked through the quiet corridors of Pathfinder Place, past rooms with open doors and startled, even amazed comrades. "Let 'im go," one boy growled. "That Malone's an oddball." "Pray that he will find the way," replied a more pious boy.

But all who had seen him leave went quickly, curiously, to their windows to look outside after Lonnie had made his phone call. His seeming daring fascinated them. None of them knew that he had said, simply, "God bless you, Mom. I will be looking out for you," and then hung up the phone.

Now they saw the boy step slowly to the center of the broad front yard of Pathfinder Place. Bathed in moonlight, he seemed pale, unreal; the grass looked like a peaceful pool of water. When the *other* light formed, above Lonnie, someone remem-study window to look wonderingly down upon young Lonnie Malone.

The shimmering, circular white light—deep and as absorbent as cotton—slowly lowered until it haloed, then engulfed the seventeen-year-old. And when the light lifted, cleared, and was gone, Lonnie Malone had vanished.

Inside Pathfinder Place that night, the other boys who'd seen it were astonished and, without exception, were greatly relieved it was not they who had been taken. They talked wildly among themselves, their exclamations coming in sharp outbursts. "They took the creep!" one said. "Good bered to call the reverend, and he, too, went to his

THE BANISHED 205

riddance to the outsider, the miserable oddball," another replied. And a third chimed in gladly, "He never fit in *nowheres!*" They were all so happy still to be there.

All except the Pathfinder priest, alone in his upstairs study. Because the Reverend Carlton Blant had been *told* something and because he also had *seen* more than they. And for the reason that the deep-voiced, powerfully built Blant was a genuine student of the Bible before he had revised it, he fell to his knees. He meant to offer the first honest prayer he'd made since his dreams of becoming a singer were ruined and left him a bitter opportunist.

"It should have been *me!* Why *not* me, Lord?" he asked, his excellent voice beseeching. There was no noticeable answer. "Please, God, don't just take the kid—take *me,* too!" It was hotter in the study now, but that was the only evident answer to his prayer. Annoyed by being ignored, Carlton Blant lifted his voice in anger. "Well, come *on,* damn it!" he shouted, staring about him. "Haven't I done your work, Lord? *Answer me!* Haven't I dedicated it all to you?"

Instantly the chart on which he had labored burst into crackling yellow-orange flames. They began to lick hungrily at the PATHFINDER banner above it. Most of both chart and banner was swiftly burned as Carlton Blant stared in speechless fright.

But a *single word* remained when the fire had gone out—*one word* was left of all the hectic, deceiving, self-serving words that had made Carlton Blant such a success. He read it, looked at how the wall and desk had not even been singed, and read the word again, knowing he had been answered.

Half an hour later a Pathfinder entered the priest's study to notify the leader that newspaper reporters were arriving in droves. They wanted to know what had happened to young Lonnie Malone.

But the Reverend Carlton Blant couldn't tell them. He was hanging from the ornate chandelier in the middle of the study, the cord of his expensive robe around his throat. A chair, kicked away, was sprawled a few feet from the body. And on Carlton Blant's forehead, in ashes taken from his burnt financial chart, was printed a single word: REPENT.

9

One day until April 22, 1984
1:15 P.M., EST

The news in Indianapolis, Indiana, of the disappearance of a single young member of a widely feared religious cult was interesting. Under normal circumstances, particularly considering the earlier Vanishments, it would have been picked up by the wire services. But today Lonnie Malone's absence was not nearly enough to take precedence over the international news, which was fired into this midwestern American city, as in most civilized cities, like a devastating rocket shell: war in the Middle East had begun in earnest.

Israel, prepared to defend its ancient heritage and its disputed capital of Jerusalem, whatever the cost, openly threatened the use of atomic devices. "We have waited too long and we have fought forever to possess this, our own homeland," said the new prime minister, "and we assert our intention to protect this sacred land, this sacred right." Did this mean to the point of using nuclear missiles? He did not hesitate. "It means that they *will* be used if this terrible thing becomes necessary." In the meanwhile, planes and tanks poured like angry lava from Israeli borders, and every man, woman, and child was mobilized for action.

Pakistan took a similar retaliatory stance and added ominously, without further explanation, "We think the time has come." In Egypt the president refused further discussion, stating that the arbitration period had ended, that he was considering expulsion of both the United States and Russian ambassadors.

Iran's new and younger ayatollah broke his self-enforced vow of silence to claim that his infamous predecessor was correct after all, that the "Satan's dogs" of America and Russia were determined to end the world. He called for the "Islamic brotherhood of every nation" to do what it could to sabotage the "war effort."

Hundreds of thousands of followers of the assassinated would-be Indian messiah appeared to be on the verge of seizing the country. In Libya, oil and other essential supplies were nationalized. Kosygin's recent replacement in the Soviet hierarchy called an urgent meeting of the Presidium; China said very little, indeed; and in Washington, D.C., White House staff meetings lasted into the small hours of the night. The president, said one source, was nearing exhaustion "but valiantly fighting on in the interests of international and world peace."

Meanwhile, everywhere on the globe, secret underground detonations were rumored, even "reliably reported." In London, among other places, it was whispered that "dissident factions" and "wholly unauthorized terrorist groups linked to the IRA" were carelessly traveling about with atomic devices concealed in attaché cases, even in lunch boxes. Defense, nuclear shelters, energy potential, worldwide famine, and inflation were on the lips of virtually everybody in the world in preference to the three words they universally feared to speak: World War III.

Yet the general feeling was that it would be extremely difficult to avoid.

Jed Westphal was appalled by the news in his morning paper; he listened to late-breaking news on his television set and then warmed up the coffee left from last night's meal. For some time he sat with the cup in his hand, sipping from it only twice, trying to decide if what was happening locally had any connection with international developments. He'd never been a man who attended church with any frequency. He had few organizational affiliations of any kind, including the religious. But he had heard for years now the rumors of Apocalypse and, with them, the centuries-old premonitions. He remembered the words of one prophet: *"There will be signs of the end to come, clear warnings that a man may just have the time to save his soul, if not his life."*

And every time he had thought of those terrifying words or read others like them, Jed had enunciated clearly the sentiment of every practical, hopeful man in the world: "Bullshit!" He had shelved his twinges of anxiety and done his level best to ignore the strangely changing patterns of weather throughout the world, the emerging nations and those suddenly making impossible demands, the ominous rattling of sabers everywhere, the bizarre outbreak of UFOs and all manner of otherworldly oddities that left scientists sputtering even while Bigfoot and his eccentric friends climbed right in front of their noses. *"We are the signs,"* they seemed to shout. *"Take heed."*

But he had behaved normally—rationally—knowing that doomsday screamers had been shrieking their neurotic fears in every culture since the dawn of time. There'd probably been a plethora of them when Christ was born: "Repent, repent, the hour has come." And when the bow and arrow were invented: "Man is not meant to possess such destructive knowledge." When science converted the atom to peaceful uses and created life itself in a test tube, Jed tried hard to applaud, to call it progress and stay in the company of true sophisticates.

And now, for the first time, he wondered if he'd been wrong.

In common with millions of other men this pregnant morning, he tried to put the world news out of his mind. There was nothing that one man could do—*now,* he thought guiltily—to change matters. If it was going to happen—if a hydrogen warhead was going to drop on his dinner plate tonight—well, it would simply have to occur. He just hoped he'd have a chance to taste the steak before it was gone.

But it *was* possible, he felt, somehow to solve the problem of the Vanishments. He and Stacy alone might find the solution. He got his notebook from his jacket pocket and sat at the table in his dining room, his coffee growing cold before him. Perhaps if he began collating and appraising the facts for his projected book, it would do some slight good. Financially, at least, it would help for the glorious day when he and Stacy lived together —assuming that anybody *lived* at all. There was more than the Vanishments to consider: there was the burning of Lionel Hartberg; there was yesterday's disappearance-motivated hanging of the Reverend Carlton Blant. He was even ready to wager that there were *other* peculiar things going on, things that had not been discovered yet or that the authorities had quieted to avoid panic.

It went smoothly in outline form for over an hour. Before Jed knew he even intended to do it, he was beginning a prologue for the book. Unlike his first novel, he instinctively resorted to a first-person format. Using actual thoughts he'd had, as well as quotations he could recall, Jed scribbled out the start of his investigation, noting how it had begun on the heels of a personal crisis, almost cathartically. The love that had developed between Stacy and him would add a romantic, even idyllic tone that the intelligent reader might never believe!

At that point Jed put down his pen and rubbed his jaw. Rosalyn and Darren were due back soon —very soon. If she should happen to arrive early, today, she would discover Stacy Bennett in her bed! My God, Jed groaned, horrified at the consequences of the terrible scene, the routine personal things could sure catch a guy off guard at times! Why, he still needed a place to live, and he hadn't made the first arrangement yet. For all he knew, Rosalyn would evict him without batting an eyelash.

For the first time Jed considered the possibility of asking Stacy if she would mind his moving in with her. That would allow him time to find a halfway respectable place for them both to occupy. Of course, given her professional reticence and his own puritanical background—his mind constantly cluttered with self-imposed standards that his chums found quaint, and haunted by restrictions from a distant childhood—it seemed hard to consider. A recent virgin and a recently separated man didn't become swingers overnight. But *was* it actually so unthinkable, he mused, when he already felt totally married to Stacy—

when she was already his woman, and he her man, in all but the legal sense of the word?

He would have to discuss it with her, Jed thought with a sigh, and got up to awaken Stacy. It was after one o'clock in the afternoon, after all—was she going to sleep all day? "Stacy, honey?" he called from the foot of the stairs. No answer. "Time to rise and shine, darling!" Again no answer.

He took a quick step forward, his heartbeat accelerating. If she, too, had vanished, he wouldn't know how to live without her. He rushed up the remainder of the stairs, threw the bedroom door open—and sighed in happy relief. She was still curled up where he'd left her, breathing heavily. He crossed the room to her and shook her shoulder gently. "Stacy, honey?" he called. She tossed a bit in her sleep but did not awaken. He was frightened again. "Stacy!" he exclaimed, shaking her shoulder hard. One rounded arm swept past him, in reflex, but her eyes stayed shut.

Jed sat down on the edge of the bed, staring at her. Did she *always* sleep this way? Did *anybody*? He leaned over her, kissed her full on the mouth. But nothing happened. He felt her forehead; it felt normal to the touch, perhaps even a trifle cool. There was certainly no fever. "Damn it, darling," he shouted, "wake *up!*"

When nothing happened this time, Jed drew her up from the mattress, like an obstinate pet dog who wouldn't do what she was told, and again shook her shoulders. No response. When he let go of her entirely, just for a moment, her body began to slump back to the bed. He eased her down, then rested his ear between her breasts to listen. The heartbeat was steady; it sounded just fine.

But Stacy was completely unconscious and as

absent from him as if she had been in her own apartment. Nervous, he gripped her wrist between his fingers and took her pulse. Normal. Everything was normal; there wasn't one damned clue.

Then he snapped his fingers and rushed to the bathroom, where he got a washcloth sopping wet and icy cold, ran back to the bedroom, and held the cloth against her forehead. She didn't budge; her eyelids didn't flicker. Frantic, he held her sweet, bare body to him and rocked her like a child, calling her name.

To no avail. Suddenly determined to phone a doctor, he placed her carefully on the bed, covered her, and hurried downstairs to the phone. There, he paced back and forth, uncertain about the decision he should reach. Stacy would be horrified for his family physician to find her there. He picked up the phone, put it down again. Then he rushed back up to the bedroom, thinking he had heard her moan his name.

But she hadn't. Looking perfectly well, and perfectly unconscious, Stacy slept imperviously on, and the terror in Jed Westphal's breast blossomed like a cancer.

This time when he went downstairs to call the doctor, he intended to do it. But when he picked up the telephone, through a Bell Company miracle of synchronism, he found someone had already called in. "Hello?" the voice said. *"Hello?"*

"It's an emergency, damn it, get off the phone!" Jed shouted into the receiver.

"Wait, please, Mr. Westphal," said the familiar young voice at the other end of the line. "This is Phillip Hanzlik calling, sir." He paused before speaking again and then did so with great care and tact. "You, ah, you cannot awaken Dr. Bennett, can you, Mr. Westphal?"

Jed's heart stopped. "How d-do you know that?" he demanded tremorously.

"I—I know."

Jed's fingers tightened on the phone in anger. *"You* did it, didn't you, you little freak? *Answer me!"*

The young voice was soft, compassionate. "Only in the sense that we're all involved in this together now," he replied. "But I can help you, sir."

"How?"

"Please listen carefully to me. First of all you must accept what I am going to say. You are *both* in terrible danger—the worst danger you've ever faced in your lives. You must stay with her and *protect* her, Mr. Westphal—and be on guard yourself, for the hour of your tribulation has come."

The boyish voice on the other end of the phone was tight with concern for them, but the emotions were under control, used as a knife edge to prepare Jed. He did not know why, but he believed Phillip —yet the boy frightened him badly. "What the hell are you *saying,* kid?" Jed cried, feeling that he had somehow strolled into a madhouse. "What kind of lunatic talk *is* this?"

"You know that I'm telling you the truth," Phillip said with certainty. "Watch Dr. Bennett carefully and be prepared to save her—and yourself." His high-pitched voice paused. "And don't forget prayer. I'll be there as fast as I can."

The phone went dead. Marvelous, Jed thought sarcastically, staring at it. He and his lady were in mortal peril, and a teen-age boy was coming to save them.

Slowly he replaced the phone in its cradle and stood up. He moved, dazed, toward the stairs, ready to sit beside Stacy. Then he remembered what Phillip had said earlier, about the terrible actions of what the boy termed "the Opposition"—someone or something that stood against Phillip and the others who had disappeared. What *was* the Opposition, and how could he, Jed Westphal, defend against it, when he had no idea what it was or why it opposed him and Stacy?

He was halfway up the stairs when the implications, full and deadly, struck him—fearfully.

He ran the rest of the distance to the bedroom.

4:24 P.M., EST

Minutes dragged by, trailing their tiny maimed feet on the broken glass of fear, and Jedediah N. Westphal saw every second of them seep away while his heart bled in sympathy and in worry. He had tried twice to awaken Stacy and failed, although the second time, just for a moment, he was rewarded by a sweet, contented angel's smile that gave the small, pretty woman the appearance of a sleeping madonna.

Jed nodded in grim satisfaction. Whatever Stacy was dreaming then, he thought with a measure of relief, it made her happy. He hoped she'd stay in that particular chamber of dreamland until she awoke.

For another minute he looked at her bare, unconscious form, realizing both how much he truly loved her and, with the kind of masculine bad timing he'd always been plagued by, how much he wanted her—awake, vibrantly alive, thrilling to his touch. Memory of the way her large breasts felt against his own naked chest, how the warm furriness of Stacy welcomed his awkward prodding, disturbed him, when the possibility of her remaining this way occurred to him.

He released her hand, kissed her forehead, and

went in search of his bathrobe. The boy was coming sooner or later, and she would hate to be seen this way. In the closet, next to his robe, he saw one of Rosalyn's and, realizing it would be a closer fit, started to take it down. But then he shook his head distastefully, not because Rosalyn might see Stacy in it, but because he didn't want any part of his ex-wife to touch the woman he loved. He took his own robe back to Stacy and laboriously worked her arms into the sleeves and ended by closing the robe across her breasts.

Sighing, he sat back in the chair he'd put between the bed and the window and looked out. For a while he had doubted that Phillip Hanzlik was correct, had felt that the boy didn't make an iota of sense. What secret knowledge of a mysterious attack could a teen-age boy have? But in most of us there is a layer of common sense underlying our acquiescence to that which is acceptably practical—the kind that told Jed, finally, that he had been right before in fearing the end of the world. Maybe it would happen and maybe it wouldn't, but any open-minded fool could detect the signs of possibility. Perhaps latent knowing comes, appropriately enough, with the kind of subterranean fear he felt for both of them, then. Because the truth was that Phillip was no ordinary child, whatever he'd been before the Vanishments. Possibly that even meant that the ubiquitous term *special*, in place of *retarded*, had more logic than he'd considered.

Very simply, he knew now with all his being that the little blond boy was right. Somehow— whether he'd been told about it while he was away or experienced some kind of cosmic telepathy unknown to others—Phillip understood the truth:

Jed and Stacy were in serious danger from something otherworldly, something potent and ugly.

So he pushed back the drapes and stared out the window, where he supposed the attack would originate, and found with mild surprise that it was a bright, sunny day with a delicious, careless breeze—a lovely spring day in an unhaunted and ordinary Hoosier city. The trees in the block were budding; there were signs of roses beginning anew on his own bushes, beneath the window; and in the distance he could hear a sure sign of spring: a lawn mower coughing twice, three times, before it began purring wasplike to itself.

Again, just for a moment, it all seemed absurd, even silly. It was difficult to imagine anything even as bad as a fender bender or an elderly neighbor getting the flu happening in such a middle-class neighborhood on such a day. Even threatening bills refused to come when it was so pleasant out!

But Jed shook off the mood and began trying to peer into the windows of every house in the block and every passing car. Apparently the Opposition, as Phillip had called it, was clever; it might come from anywhere. An off-duty police car crept past silently; Jed could make out the Band-Aid above the left eyebrow of the shirt-sleeved cop. Three girls under sixteen, two of them rushing the season in gaily patterned shorts, walked nonchalantly by, one balancing her bicycle in the gutter of the street and sneaking an illicit cigarette with her free hand.

A plane went by, miles above them, silver wings glinting in the sun and its sound arriving late. There was a particularly large robin sitting on a telephone wire across the street, and Jed's writer's imagination wondered if the Opposition could take animal form. He studied the mailman, several houses away, waiting until he drew close enough to identify. But it was only Mr. Book, the proselytizing Baptist who left notes in early December suggesting what he'd like for Christmas. The mailman was running hours late, the way he always did on this route. It had driven Jed mad for years.

Jed caught a motion in the Carl Plummer house, across the street and down two; he could see the curtains twitch, and he watched carefully until he saw the person. It was only good-looking Tony, the Japanese-American boyfriend of the Plummer girl, looking out at his aging Chevy. Probably worried about the tires going flat.

I feel paranoid, utterly paranoid, Jed thought suddenly, ducking back into the bedroom. *I feel like an old maid with nothing better to do than stare at her neighbors. I feel like an idiot—but please, dear God, though I don't always pray to you the way I should, make all this torment and insanity go away. Let me have the simple happiness of a loving wife.*

He sighed and, hand trembling, reached for the cigarettes in his shirt pocket.

Which is when it began.

The whole room shook in desperate palsy. Beneath Jed's feet the floor distinctly quivered, and he looked down, fearing he would see it crack. It didn't, but before he could look up again, the bed on which Stacy lay asleep sidled two inches closer to him.

He looked back out the window, to see if other houses were experiencing an earthquake, but the world looked perfectly normal.

Except for his own house. The shaking was growing much worse, and Jed jumped to his unsteady feet, casting his eyes about for some clue to the origin of the violence. In the ceiling above him a jagged crack suddenly opened and continued to spread, like the premonitional handwriting of some secret god—or demon.

Behind him the window he'd been using cracked fiercely into a thousand pieces, and for a flashing instant that Jed would not forget, there was a ghastly and demonic face, formed by the shattering, which leered in wild glee at his panic. Then the glass shot into the room. Frightened, Jed looked toward Stacy, but she was uninjured, still blissfully asleep.

Now, for the first time, he could *hear* the quake!

It sounded as if it began ten thousand miles below his feet and rumbled devastatingly upward. For a moment he thought the very bowels of the earth were churning, soon to empty their stony and lavalike contents in his home. And still the sound increased, gathering force. It was like thunder from hell, almost deafening now and still growing, a nightmare noise that conveyed immense, unstoppable power and, with that, some fiendishly shrewd sense of *purpose.*

His hands squeezed over his ears, Jed started toward Stacy Bennett, when all the forces of the quake appeared to concentrate upon the sleeping psychologist. Beneath her bed the floor hopped and skipped and jumped in terrible, orgasmic ripples; the bed itself began a frenetic, lunatic disco dance, leaping and jittering against the floor till it seemed the flooring must split and drop the bed, and Stacy, below. Now Stacy appeared, even in sleep, to notice; her face twisted in one of her old disapproving frowns, projecting a measure of fear even while her eyes remained closed.

Jed dashed across the room toward the bed, filled now with the desperate urgency of getting them both out of the house. He put out his frantic hand

—and felt a dreadful, arcing electrical shock course through his fingers and hand, up through his wincing forearm and into the bicep and shoulder. He yowled aloud with pain, instinctively yanking back his arm and staring, shocked, down at the bed. He had touched *it,* not Stacy; but she lay in the center of the bed, and it was quite impossible to get to her without touching the electrified sheets and mattress. But he reached out again, experimentally, as the floor beneath the bed continued to rise and warp—and again the excruciating, forbidding pain jerked like a million tiny knives through his groping hand and arm.

He spun around looking for help, aware that, rather than remaining numb, his hand and arm felt frozen with a dreadful iciness, like the coldness of death itself. When he faced the opposite wall, he saw, with wild and disbelieving eyes, a torrent of reddish liquid gushing from the seams of the wall and clotting on the floor around his cringing feet. It reeked of blood, fresh human blood; Jed gagged and threw his hand across his mouth.

The gloves! He dashed to his chest of drawers, yanked open the top drawer, and scrabbled through it for the heavy gloves he'd worn in the last horrendous Indianapolis winter. As he searched, he knew vaguely that he was making terrible little sounds and that spittle flecked his lips. Above him, plaster from the ceiling was beginning to fall, at first so many false flakes of snow and then a large, craggy chunk that narrowly missed the sleeping Stacy. He looked back toward the bed, desperately, as he found the gloves and slipped rapidly into them. They went over his wrists, protectively, and warmed his freezing hands as he turned back to Stacy.

For an agonizing moment he believed what his

eyes told him: Stacy was sitting up naked in bed, her lovely head at an impossible angle, her white spinal column showing. She seemed to have just died, and yet her arms were raised beseechingly to him, blood from the wound coursing over her full breasts.

"*No!*" Jed roared. He would never know if he made the sound or not—it was swallowed up immediately in the furor of the thunderous quake—but he knew that he *rejected* what his eyes told him, would *not believe* what he was urged to see, because he believed, truly, that God would answer his prayers.

And when he reached the bed, stumbling every inch of the way over the convulsive floor, he saw that he'd been right—that Stacy lay where he'd left her, in the middle of the bed, unconscious, still wearing his robe. She was all right! It had been a terrible illusion! He reached out quickly for her with his gloved hands and, though he was keenly aware of shocks of pain searing parts of his body that touched the bed, succeeded in tucking her into his arms.

Then he jumped over most of the gory chunks of scarlet strewn on the floor as the dresser crashed in on itself with a sound like a million bowls of crunching breakfast flakes, and he ran, Stacy hugged close to him, out the bedroom door to the stairs.

But after he'd leaped down two steps, Jed heard a sound and was awestruck. The rumbling quake was *in pursuit,* was *following* them like a snuffling hound along the path of his run, shaking the flooring of the hallway as it came toward the head of the stairs. His jaw set grimly, Jed looked ahead and vaulted two more steps down—then stared in terror and sick dismay as the remaining steps in the long flight of stairs crumbled away, as though trying themselves to flee the monstrous tremor, leaving only the concrete basement yawning far below.

Balanced precariously, buffeted by fierce winds that had begun howling wolflike behind him, seeking to shove him forward, Jed looked down and saw the unyielding floor and dangerous jutting pipes below and *knew,* with certainty, that they would break their necks in such a fall.

A sound! He glanced wildly over his shoulder in time to see the door to his bedroom *peeled* from its hinges, ripped away as if by a behemoth's paw, then tossed past him, where it clattered through the hole left by the stairway and crashed into the distant basement. Another giant sound whirled Jed's head to the right. Beside him, a gigantic crack had formed in the wall of the stairwell and, as he stared in dismay, became a moving, mighty fissure. From above, another huge patch of plaster fell away, striking his shoulder and almost causing him to relinquish his grip on his precious burden. The shoulder immediately reacted with internal shrieks of agony.

Suddenly Jed reached his decision. It was possible, *barely* possible, that he could jump far enough to clear the yawning cavity in the stairs and land on the first floor instead of in the basement. If he remained where he was, it was obvious, the entire upstairs and stairway would be ripped asunder until nothing was left but to plunge into the cellar. Something roared by his ear, a sound that was nearly human but not quite, the words unintelligible but the meaning clear: *I will kill you both,* the message came to Jed's mind. *I will stop you with death.*

You won't, Jed thought with determination, and,

gritting his teeth and pressing the sleeping Stacy to his chest, he leaped into space.

Together they landed in a heap on the floor at the foot of the stairs, freed of peril from the basement but with Jed's ankle turned agonizingly beneath him. Stacy had fallen from his arms, but only after they had landed safely, and he saw her eyes moving beneath her lids as if she might awaken. He tried to shove himself to his feet, to straighten his leg, and unbearable pain shot up from his instep into the calf like an ascending dagger. Moaning, Jed slumped back to the floor, holding his ankle.

But the sounds resumed. The quake had followed them downstairs! The Opposition had not given up, for above them, in the living-room ceiling, an awesome tear formed. The thunderous rumbling began overhead, and the fissure was suddenly a ghastly drawing, curving and curling until, with a hail of plaster, the fanatical, lunatic, and certainly demonic face he'd seen at the window peered down at them with intense hatred and a look of leering joy at their helplessness. Soon, Jed realized, the rest of the ceiling would collapse upon them and bury them alive in rubble and roofing.

What was *that*? A noise. His head turned in time to spy several field mice, which had made their home there the past winter, scurrying up from the basement. Squealing in terror and ignoring the fallen humans, they scrabbled across the floor to the front door. Jed saw it was open, the screen ajar. The mice were gone. But before he could think, he felt the tingling *vibration* begin beneath him. It quickly became intense, hurtful, numbing; it was almost electric. And then, in a single shocking burst, it literally lifted his heel and a hip an inch off the floor. He shouted in pain and saw Stacy wince. *If it doesn't get us with the caved-in ceiling,* Jed thought with near admiration for his ingenious opposition, *it'll settle for cooking us where we sit!*

Biting his upper lip, Jed muttered another quick prayer and lurched to his knees, pulling Stacy awkwardly back into his arms. He had time to be glad the front door was open, with only the screen between them and the posible safety of the front yard. Then, allowing full pressure on his injured ankle for the first time, half running and half hopping, he hurtled toward the door. Behind them, the ceiling gave way completely, crashing to the floor where they'd been in a thunderclap of destruction—and somewhere beneath, or perhaps above, the rending noise Jed heard, to his horror, the stomach-wrenching sound of jeering, demonic laughter.

The screen shot off its hinges as they catapulted through and collapsed in a tangle of limbs on the front lawn. Instantly Jed was on his knees, ignoring the pain in his leg to look warily back at the house he'd occupied for nearly a decade.

It was veering drunkenly to one side, teetering impossibly like a silly house of cards poked by a child's finger. And then, when the house was on the verge of tumbling entirely upon itself, the earthquake stopped and the sound began to ebb away.

Jed stared at his house a long while, his eyes absorbing it all and not believing what he witnessed through the gaping front door.

Inside, the living-room ceiling was still intact; the stairway was in place as well, each and every step where it had been put when it was built. Apparently nothing had happened—nothing at all.

Then a gush of putrescent odor—like that of

sulphur mingled with the stench of scorched and burning flesh—rushed past Jed and was gone.

A hand touching the author's arm made his head spin, his eyes open in abject terror.

"I'm here, finally, Mr. Westphal, and you did very well. I'm so glad you and Dr. Bennett survived." Phillip Hanzlik smiled down on them from his modest height, his golden hair catching and reflecting light from the dying yellow sun. "I think it's time—time you were told what is happening. And I assure you, Mr. Westphal, it will be all right now, for you and for her."

5:15 P.M., EST

Jed and Phillip began the lengthy and awkward process of carrying Stacy back into the house and to the sofa in the living room. The writer could barely walk on his ankle now—the pain was intense, and the ankle tended to buckle beneath him—but the boy was simply not strong enough to carry her alone. Entering the house, Jed glanced with concern at the ceiling, amazed that it was still there after all.

When at last Stacy was on the couch, still asleep, Jed sagged wearily to the floor beside her, and little Phillip companionably took a seat next to him. The boy wore walking shorts and a bright pullover sweater; at a glance, he might have been an early teen-ager anywhere.

But as Jed studied him, he sensed many different things about the Hanzlik offspring, qualities or attributes of character and perhaps ability that he knew he'd never recognized in another living being. Something about Phillip radiated . . . goodness. "What the hell *was* it?" Jed asked softly. "Phillip, what in hell was *happening*?"

Phillip looked steadily into Jed's eyes. "The enemy. It was all the work of the Opposition, the *ultimate* Opposition."

Jed wriggled, seeking lessened pain. His whole body ached. "And what is it opposed *to?*" he asked.

"Our Creator," the boy said easily, soberly, "and mankind, of course. It's been mankind's greatest enemy since the dawn of time. It's what's made whites fear blacks, and vice versa; it's what's made yellow hate yellow. It is what sets nation against nation, beliefs against other beliefs. It is what seeks 'elbowroom,' as Hitler called it, to expand —into land belonging to others. It is what has perverted religions and businesses, governments and individuals—what has perverted them morally, politically, legally, spiritually, in any way and all ways. It is the ultimate egoist, the ultimate opportunist; it is everyone who urges, 'Win at all costs,' and who whispers, 'It's OK because no one knows.' "

Jed nodded slowly. "Satan. The Opposition is Satan, then."

To the writer's mild surprise, Phillip shook his head. "We do not care to personify him, to honor him with a name, because in the deeper sense there is no 'he.' "

"But I saw his face in the window glass, in the ceiling," Jed protested, "the familiar, twisted countenance of Satan—the face that might be handsome except for the evil that shows through."

The boy smiled. "Reflectivity, they called that," he replied, scratching a bare knee with a scab formed over an old wound, a wound made when he was retarded, when he was clumsy. "The forces underlying this universe, alive in other dimensions and in other ways, are quick to show man what he *expects* to see—what he *believes in.*"

"Then, who *is* the Opposition?" Jed asked. "Or *what*, if that's the correct word?"

"I cannot tell you just what *God* is, either," Phillip answered after a pause. "In the ancient Hebrew language, you remember, they called him 'Jahweh' because they did not dare use his real name. To do so, they felt, would have shown disrespect." He frowned thoughtfully. "There also was one called a demon, to whom they would build no temple and whom they would not name. I was taught simply to refer to that creature as the Opposition. But, you see, it's not a *he* in reality, Mr. Westphal, so much as it is a *force*—a conscious force of enormous, unguessable power for all that is bad and wrong. While I was . . . *away*, they taught me about Dr. Jung, the great psychologist, and his theory of the *collective unconscious*—a sort of repository of all mankind's thoughts and wishes, into which man sometimes plugs, producing archetypal images of reality. But, in fact, sir, there are *two* collective unconsciouses—and one is evil alone. One is a stockpiling of all the evil words, ideas, actions, and desires that have occurred throughout the world, even the universe, *wherever* there is intelligent life. Because this amassed evil is from many different worlds, when man plugs into it—draws from it—we sometimes get things that seem monstrous, to us, alien and bizarre, because they had life only on *other* sentient planets.

Jed was trying hard to follow the amazing boy. "What does the Opposition want?"

"Destruction," Phillip said simply. "But more than that, it seeks to *claim*—man's mind, man's soul, and man's world. Because many men have believed absolutely in that which is evil, this dark collective unconscious has gathered vitality and purpose steadily through the centuries. Once, when the Creator expelled the Opposition from Paradise, it could merely think and plan, cunningly, occasionally interfering through the perversion of specific human minds. Now, however, it is prepared, potent, and anxious to . . . *take over*."

Jed shrugged, indicating his home. "But the house," he argued, "it's unharmed! Apparently I was merely hypnotized in some way, and what seemed to happen *didn't* really. So how could it produce any serious, farflung destruction?"

"Your ankle"—Phillip pointed to it with a smile —"is severely sprained. What happened was real enough to almost get killed over, especially if you'd panicked. Why, there must have been a *dozen* ways you might have taken your life, and Dr. Bennett's, inadvertently. Or you might well have gone mad, something the Opposition achieves much of the time. It would have served the Opposition just as well as your dying. Either way, you'd have been no threat to its power."

"But—what's real and what *isn't*?"

"You were in an *altered* state of reality, Mr. Westphal, but it was still a *kind* of reality. In a reversed way, it was like poltergeist activity. In such paranormal experiences, there really isn't any evil force present, but try telling *that* to someone who's seen everything in his house destroyed! Your case is a reversal of that: there really wasn't any destruction, but an evil force *was* present. As for not literally *seeing* the Opposition, nonmaterial entities have been around for thousands of years: angels, devils, leprechauns, and now the Loch Ness monster, Bigfoot, and the Men in Black of the UFO mythology—all apparently substantial and real but nonetheless creatures of altered reality, so that when a person *isn't* in that state, he concludes that they are nonexistent." Phillip paused. "The forces you can't see, behind the surface reality of life, *are* there and always *have* been—gently regulating our behavior and giving us little shoves toward new insights. Unless they are the creatures of the Opposition, in which case that force isn't at all gentle."

"*What* forces?" Jed pressed. "Let's stop talking in vague terms, son." Jed shifted his weight; he hurt everywhere, body and mind. "Maybe I'm thick, but I do *not* understand what's been happening, and I think you do."

"*She* understands," Phillip said, smiling, tilting his blond head to the sleeping psychologist, "and she'll tell you more about it when she returns. She is what much of this was all about, all that happened in your house. The Opposition was trying to stop both of you. Dr. Bennett was first."

Jed shook his head. "Then, why didn't it simply kill her, or us? Why go to all that trouble?"

"The Opposition rarely kills anyone or anything," Phillip answered, his tone serious. "Murdering someone does not make the soul automatically the property of the Opposition. But it *causes men* to kill for it, himself or other persons; *then* it can exercise its claim of property." Phillip looked over at Stacy again and tenderly smoothed back her tousled hair from her forehead. "This is a fine woman, Mr. Westphal. I recall now how hard she tried to aid me while I was—well, confined at Clemora. Like you, sir, she is pure. An innocent."

Jed's laugh was nearly bitter. "An innocent?" His mind went back to last night, what they'd done upstairs together. "I think you're mistaking me for somebody else, kid."

"Oh, no, I'm not." Phillip's gaze moved from

Stacy to Jed, his expression both solemn and kind. "Man makes too much of the importance of his anatomy. It's only a shell. God does not judge goodness or badness by man's laws or by anything man says; He judges by His own laws. It is the Opposition and its people who are quick to condemn or to curse persons in whom there remains a chance for salvation. Man tries too often to imagine what God would prefer—what He finds right or wrong—and sometimes, despite the presumptuousness of it, he's succeeded in doing so, in *little* ways. More times, however, he has fallen far short of God's choices. And many times when man guessed right, he has seen fit to 'interpret' the laws and then affix penalties for failure to adhere to them. He forgets that God claims vengeance is *His*—and so are all penalties for our mistakes."

"You speak with such ringing authority, son," Jed said softly, resting his hand on the boy's wrist. "With almost anyone else I'd be irritated, even angry, that he was taking such liberties with the Lord's wishes. But *you*—well, you seem not merely to believe but to *know*. You even seem to have been *told! How* do you know, Phillip? What's happened to change you from a—from a——"

"From a retarded child to a mature young adult?" Phillip smiled obliquely. "Stacy will know when she awakens. What I meant by your innocence is actually simple, Mr. Westphal. You and Stacy are among those whom man's worst corruptions cannot permanently mar. You know instinctively there is a distinction between good and bad. If, somehow, either of you has done wrong, you do your best to make amends."

"Oh, I don't know," Jed argued, reddening with embarrassment.

"It's *true,* sir," the boy insisted, grinning. "You

both are simply not motivated to do anything evil *for the sake of* evil. More than that, most of what either of you sincerely wants, or wants to accomplish, is *never* evil. If some deeds turn out that way, you neither meant for that nor seek to benefit from it. You don't tell yourself you've done nothing wrong. You accept responsibility for your own actions and consistently try to do the *right* thing."

"Thanks, but what's special in that?" Jed asked. "I suppose we both *try* always to do what's right, but doesn't everybody?"

"So innocent." Phillip shook his boyish head. "In a world where there are supposedly only underprivileged or underpaid people, undereducated people, and people who require psychiatric help, the words *evil* and *wrong* have no meaning to most individuals. But they exist. You have no idea, though you're a writer, how important words *are* in coloring our outlook and our morality. The Opposition's done its work well, creating a climate in which it's unpopular to speak of a deed that's either obviously *wrong* or *evil*—even if the deed gets your wife raped, your child killed, your home or your nation wrested away. No, Mr. Westphal, most people do *not* try always to do 'the right thing.' They act, and they justify it. They try not to be embarrassed, uncool, or caught."

"I find that a bit hard to accept. Or that *trying* to do right is enough."

Phillip's smile was both benign and reassuring. "Basically, that's all God asks of you—not to kid yourself, but always *try* for good. Of course, one must stop to *think* of his consequences before he *knows* if they're decent! Not that you and Stacy Bennett have no faults. You're both vain about talent and knowledge; in the little ways you always look after number one; you're overly interested in things of this world, this moment. You, sir, are a little impatient and sometimes crude. But none of *that,* you see, keeps you or the woman or the world's *other* innocents from first feeling a sense of responsibility to the important rules of life, the permanent ones. You were *tested* upstairs today, and you finally put someone *else* first. Your sins have been considered inconsequential, then, mere indulgences of a human spirit. They're seen as free of viciousness, absolute self-interest, or any unconscious urge to destroy: some of the major sins." The boy shrugged lightly. "Innocents, just as I said. More important than *my* saying it is that *others* say that of you and the woman."

Jed remembered how Stacy had put it about the boy, that he'd become "the very best Phillip" he could be. But it wasn't enough of an answer. "Who *are* you?" he asked in a voice just above a whisper. His eyes burned into the young, unlined face near his. "And—*what* are you?"

Phillip held the gaze without difficulty; indeed, he smiled into it.

Then he arose without answering, murmured, "Let's allow Stacy to inform you," and knelt beside the sleeping woman. He bowed his blond head, folded his hands, and prayed.

It occurred to Jed that he very much wanted to hear the words of this extraordinary youth. He inclined his head to listen; then he realized that was wrong and straightened, trying *not* to hear. But he'd already caught a few words of Phillip's prayer nonetheless: "I will behold thy face in righteousness; I shall be satisfied, when I awake, with thy likeness."

Then the boy was taking Stacy's hand lightly in his own, and he was saying, not loudly or dramatically, his face serene and confident, "Awaken, Stacy Bennett. Return to us."

She opened her eyes, blinked a few times, and once more was with them.

Jed thought he had never seen her more beautiful, more radiant. As she struggled to sit up on the sofa, the sweeping lines of her light-brown hair untangled and curved sweetly round her shoulders. Her eyes, rather than being fearful or startled, unaware of where she was or yet partly in her extended dreamworld, were instantly alert, intelligent, and kind. She was a revelation to Jed Westphal. It was, thought he, as if Stacy had rested away for good every selfish, angry, or passingly cruel word or deed of her whole life and then been fully restored to the fresh and guileless condition of early youth—even of newborn infancy. Her complexion and her gaze were that free of earthly corruption. There was no fear there, either, no apprehension, anxiety, or concern. There was, quite simply, the best and purest Stacy Bennett that one Stacy Bennett could ever be in this life.

And suddenly the author recognized in this crystal radiance and beauty some traces reminding him of the enigmatic, calmly dazzling light that had descended upon those who were banished by society but sought by *Others,* those who had been, if one judged by Phillip Hanzlik, cleansed, made whole and new, and made *best.* Jed stared wonderingly at her, and in the warmth of the loving look she returned to him, he knew she still adored him equally.

"Jed." She found her voice at last, in a glad little breath. She put out a hand to squeeze his, then turned to pat the boy's cheek. "And Phillip." Her slight arms lifted in a light stretch as she yawned. When again she looked at Jed, it was with a glint of wonder and an urge to tell all shining in her dazzling hazel eyes. "I know now why everyone was taken, Jed darling," she told him as she saw his anxiety. "I understand it all, and I can tell you, too."

"How?" he asked, baffled. "How can you know such things when you're—you've been *here* all this time?"

"But I haven't been. I was taken, too"—she smiled, again squeezing his hand—"in what some people call 'astral travel' or 'out-of-body experience,' only better. My mind and my soul were elsewhere, Jed, and it wasn't like sleep at all. You see, I've been where all the others were taken." She glanced from him to Phillip and back once more. While there was wonder in her eyes, there was no doubt, no confusion or fear. "And I've seen *what must happen*."

"Darling, for God's sake," Jed began intently, gripping her by the shoulders, *"tell* me, please. Where *were* you?"

She caught Phillip's eye, knowing he shared her knowledge, then kissed Jed's lips and whispered against his cheek with all the soft, unquesting passion in her soul, "I've been in a far place, my dearest: to the seashore and to the pasture. I've been to a city of towering gold and silver structures that soar sublimely into cloudless skies—and I've moved among the stars. I've been to a land of plenty, of sweet liberty, and of genuine freedom. Jed, honey—*we call it Paradise.*"

10

Six hours until April 22, 1984
6:00 P.M., EST

Stacy felt uncomfortable and wanted to change out of Jed's massively oversized bathrobe to her own clothes. While she went upstairs, taking her secrets with her, the author and little Phillip moved out to the dining room. Jed glanced down at the boy, wanting to ask another question, but he didn't. Instead, sighing, he went to the kitchen and prepared a snack for the three of them

Yesterday Jed, with his unmechanical mind, had watched as Stacy made coffee, and now he laboriously and faithfully duplicated the simple steps, determined to make a respectable pot for once in his life. It seemed vaguely important to perform one of mankind's little routines; deep inside Jed sensed that most of them were about to be eliminated or severely damaged.

After he'd plugged the pot in, he stood for a moment, aching and exhausted, with his forehead resting against the kitchen wall that his own eyes had said no longer existed. Maybe it had only been symbolic of the way the entire world was caving in on people, he thought. Elsewhere, civilized people who claimed they did not want war were saying and doing all the things that might very well guarantee it—a war that, as most leaders claimed, could not be won by anyone. The shock of absolute change was difficult for him to rebuff, even if he was dealing only with the essence of evil and not obliged to find a way to deter total mobilization. If this was only a warning of what was coming, Jed thought tiredly, he would require every ounce of willpower, insight, imagination, and personal faith to handle it. Not to mention courage— and he felt stripped just then of every brave emotion he'd ever known.

Finally, he dropped some of yesterday's breakfast rolls onto a plate, limpingly brought them to the dining-room table, and waited impatiently for Stacy to rejoin them. When his gaze happened to meet Phillip's, the boy looked quietly, almost respectfully away, as if sympathetic to Jed's burden of sorting out the incredible. Beyond the window, the writer saw, night was coming on in a rush of blackness, apparently unable to wait for the fearful culminations lying immediately ahead. A tiny sparrow had perched on the sill till he lifted his gaze to it; Jed hoped it had flown to safety, if safety still existed anywhere.

Stacy looked brand-new, morning-fresh, as she hurried into the room and took a chair at the table opposite Jed. "Ohh, coffee!" she murmured happily, taking a sip. "Thank you."

"Are you going to tell me everything now?" Jed asked with tense anticipation.

"I certainly am, honey," she promised. "After all, you're part of this. You *have* to know."

"Nice to hear that I still carry a little weight," he replied, forcing a grin. "You realize, of course, that I don't have a single idea what you're talking about. Start with . . . when you were away."

"As I told you, it was entirely legitimate." She

put her cup down, her eyes absolutely solemn. "While I was there in spirit, it was entirely real. I even had a—a *form,* so that others could see me. Darling, I was in Paradise as literally as I'm sitting now with you and Phillip. I don't want to start sounding 'preachy,' but if everyone could see what it'll be like for them someday, they'd behave themselves—so they'd be sure of going!" Her eyes shone. "It was exquisitely beautiful—beyond anything I ever saw before—and quite real. Really, I could never describe it."

"Then, don't," Jed said tightly. "Stacy, *please* —explain!"

She took a breath. "OK. Many, many people have known for hundreds of years that a final confrontation between good and evil was bound to happen. It's not recorded in the Bible alone— although Revelations speaks of it at length—but also in many ancient records. And the reason they knew it would happen is simply because it's already happened in the *past,* many more times than is written down. The Ice Age, for example, was only *one* time the world was ended—but, even then, just in a single sense of the word."

"You're saying there can be more than *one* 'final' confrontation of good and evil?" he inquired, dubious. "How can that be?"

"As each civilization has reached its peak—the end of its current course of evolution—it's come to an end, right on schedule."

"Like the fall of the Roman Empire?" he pressed her. *"That* kind of ending?"

"Well, yes and no," Stacy replied, tapping her long nails thoughtfully. "The mighty civilizations must eventually reach a point of confrontation, but sometimes they aren't, um, totaled. Instead, they may be permitted to endure with a relative handful of people, absorbed by a different challenging culture that increases their knowledge in the new realms. But in the literal sense of Armageddon—of the world *as man knows it* drawing to a close—it's happened hundreds of times." Her gaze held his. "Because, Jed darling, there've been hundreds of ages just as modern as this one in every way, or even more so!"

"Where have they gone?" he asked, sipping coffee and feeling perplexed.

"They've been literally buried by the rubble of their own endings. Much was destroyed, of course, by the earlier nuclear wars. But as archeologists continue to dig, deeper and deeper, they will continue finding concrete evidence of more and more ancient civilizations. Do you recall the battery they found from *thousands* of years ago? They'll go on finding evidence forever. The *good* part, Jed, is that there *must be a remnant* with which to start anew." She sighed. "The current peak of progress throughout the world—*this* impending end—was prophesied, as I told you, in many places. Particularly in the past century and in this one, hundreds of wise and decent people—ministers, philosophers, astrologers, psychics and occultists—have warned others that the end is coming and that one must be prepared for it."

"But in every ending," Phillip interposed gently, entering the conversation, "there is a *beginning,* a time of transition, or what they call a 'cusp' in astrology. The world never *literally* ends, despite atomic power and the other similarly devastating ways in which former advanced civilizations eliminated themselves. You see, Mr. Westphal, the world has never ended and never will"—the boy touched Jed's arm to emphasize the importance of what he was saying—"because *it never began.*"

THE BANISHED 239

"Never began!" Jed echoed, astonished. "What do you mean by that?"

"People with good intentions have been trying for thousands of years to explain how the earth and the universe were formed. Do you have any idea how many different ways both scientists and religionists have proposed?" Phillip's eyes gleamed. "There must be dozens of proposed moments and ways of Creation. The big-bang theory is just one of the newer ones, and even cosmologists are stumped when they're asked to explain the origin of that *first* puff of gas."

"Do you recall," Stacy asked Jed, "how foolish science once was made to feel about its notion that the earth was the center of the universe? It isn't, of course, but it *is* the very *first* planet in the universe to support any form of life. Remember the 'ancient astronaut' theories of the seventies? I've learned the truth—that mankind wasn't 'seeded' by people from other planets, but by people who were *returning home* to Earth—people who had left this mother planet thousands of years before the dinosaurs and, of course, before Neanderthal man!"

"There was only a remnant left here at that time, and our homecoming ancestors continued the race. Earth has always been the jumping-off place," Phillip observed, "for the handful of civilizations that have been good enough to avoid Armageddon, who became *truly* evolved and left to spread man's seed to other galaxies, other worlds. Most of them, of course, found they had not escaped the Creator's judgment when they were supposedly 'safe' on other planets. God is literally universal."

"Earth is a beehive of birthing activity, as everyone should realize when they see how the planet swarms with life and then compare it to the lifelessness of the moon," Stacy put in. "It's also a buried storehouse of the memories of advanced peoples who go back not tens of thousands of years, but tens of *millions*. And we are their descendants—descendants of the remnants."

"Obliged once more to face an ending," Phillip finished, "and required once more to provide a remnant. Already, in the thousands of unexplained reports of unidentified flying objects, we see our living ancestors waiting to reseed and replenish, to guide us in new directions as they have done for ages since departing the planet."

"It's utterly staggering," Jed remarked. His fingers trembled when he lit a cigarette. "But what *proof* . . . ?"

Stacy shut her eyes for a moment and smiled. "Truth has never required proof—only believers, accepters. But think for a second of the way science goes on finding artifacts from the past, year after year. They continue pushing back the origins of man another half-million years or so every five to ten years! Why, just before you and I were born, Jed, there were still folks around who believed that the earth was created only a few hundred years before Christ—even though it was clear to anyone who could *reason* that mankind couldn't possibly have formed societies and religion, discovered fire and the wheel, started agricultural communities and government, in such a limited amount of time!"

Phillip cleared his throat. "It was timeless where Stacy and I and the others were taken, Mr. Westphal. And I learned how science asked us to believe there was once a thick-skulled, scarcely erect, hulking man-ape called Neanderthal who, just a few thousand years later, became Cro-Magnon

THE BANISHED 241

man—Cro-Magnon, who made cave paintings as complex and beautiful as any modern man can do!" He laughed, a burst of boyishness. "Wow! From no concept of roots in a real home—earlier life was nomadic, including dumb old Neanderthal —man built villages, houses, conceived of gods, initiated burial and began creating language!" He shook his head and giggled. "Man, people are weird!"

"The truth, Jed, was that Neanderthal was never in the Homo sapiens line and that Cro-Magnon was the remnant of another modern civilization which had destroyed itself. It was guided anew by visitors, not really from outer space, but our *own* ancestors returning to Earth." Stacy got up to pour more coffee for the astonished writer. "I learned, darling, that in the sense of something newly formed, devised from nothingness, Earth and man were never begun. That's part of the nature of eternity. It never began; it never will *end*—not wholly. And that is why the planet is cosmically important, despite being located in what scientists call a 'middle-class galaxy' —that is why our ancient forebears continue returning to it, some in spaceships, some interdimensionally when they've reached the point of living as sheer energy." She looked earnestly but sweetly into Jed's eyes. "It is, quite simply, the *only* planet that has always existed and always will."

"World without end, but also without beginning, amen," Phillip paraphrased. "No more coffee, thanks—physically I'm still a kid. Now, life developing on other worlds is often insubstantial, lacking the nervous systems with which to experience human sensations. Some of our visitors to Earth are such people; but, as Dr. Bennett said, sir, the majority are our own people who departed possibly *millions* of years ago."

"The trouble is," Stacy told Jed, touching his hand, "most advances man makes during his millions of years on earth are primarily in *technology* —the Opposition making sure man is concerned first with comfort, convenience, matters of pleasure. The progress is seldom in terms of the individual's mind or his spirit or of definite moves toward genuine goodness. Progress toward true decency, compassion, Godliness, a willingness to live in peace, is made with each new advanced civilization, *yes*. We've learned better ways to live together with those who are different, or *appear* different. But always——"

"—*always the Opposition interferes*," Phillip interjected flatly, with a surge of anger. "It makes us recognize differences that would otherwise be too tiny, too microscopic, for our minds to *see!* That damned countering force of pure evil which literally makes *possible* the continuing existence of the force of pure *good* we call God!"

"What do you mean?" Jed asked, breathless.

"Balance between good and evil is the principle of the universe and the payment mankind must make in return for life," Stacy said slowly. "The final confrontation, thousands of times, has come down to the effort made by the Opposition to *cast that balance aside*. Each time, much has been altered; much is destroyed in our final wars. But myths endure by word of mouth; racial memories are retained, often in archetypal form, distorted but important in fostering a—a *continuity* of moral growth." She sighed. "And always, for hundreds of years during each rising phase of man, there've been the words of warning, recollections of what transpired before—such as the Deluge, for example."

Jed nodded, starting to understand. "And always there is a remnant left, to project the myths, to advance from where we left off."

Phillip looked out the window a moment at a nightfall grown thick with blackness, heavy with the foreshadowing of doom. "Pockets of innocents remain, Mr. Westphal, who remember what once had been and go on seeking the victory of good over evil. I was fortunate enough to be in one of those pockets, charged with remembering and restarting—even pointing, if I must, toward the *next* almost inevitable period of confrontation, perhaps three or four thousand years from now."

"This time, Jed," Stacy murmured, "I was told, the Opposition has done its work unusually well. It has almost achieved victory, a victory that would overbalance and truly finish the world."

"What precisely would happen if evil won?" he asked softly.

"No one knows. No one must ever find out." Her eyes were frightened.

"And what would happen if *good* won the confrontation?" he pressed.

Phillip answered wearily. "No one knows that, either, not for sure. But good's winning has never been further in the future than today. Part of my task, and that of the others who will be returning, is to locate enough innocents to endure. They must demonstrate and enact the good faith of Jesus, the great prophet of this millennium."

Stacy nodded firmly. "Those who survive must see that He kept his promises."

"What promises are those?" Jed asked softly and knew suddenly that he believed now, that he accepted.

Phillip gave him a sweet and gentle smile. "Those from Matthew 5:1-5: 'And seeing the multitudes, he went up into a mountain: and when he was set, his disciples came unto him: And he opened his mouth, and taught them, saying, Blessed *are* the poor in spirit: for theirs is the kingdom of heaven. Blessed *are* they that mourn: for they shall be comforted. Blessed *are* the meek: for they shall inherit the earth.' You see, Mr. Westphal, we mentally retarded at Clemora were taken because, in our absolute ignorance, *we could not sin*. Yet we had been sinned against: unwanted by our own families, exploited by Mr. Hartberg. We were never responsible for our acts or our words, and we were certainly poor in spirit, confused, lonely. In the broad sense of the word, *everyone* who was taken—not just those at Clemora—was meek."

"The unwed mothers who were seized by the white light, that strange shining globe, were already banished by their own parents and friends," Stacy continued. "They'd been abandoned by the young men who were responsible for the babies they carried."

"But surely some of those young women brought it on themselves," Jed remarked slowly.

She nodded. "The ones who were taken had acted only from ignorance or an absence of real love in their lives—or from a deep craving to know and to share love *somehow*. But the girls who were pregnant for selfish reasons alone, who had allowed it to happen without a thought to what it might do to their families, or even to the innocent babies they would deliver, were left behind. Remember, not all were taken—just the poor in spirit, as it was with the old people from the Logan Memorial Home, who mourned personal losses including that of the self-respect that was denied them. Those old folks had earned the regard of others, rest and comfort, and a chance to prepare for afterlife; but each of them was banished by society and wanted, thankfully, elsewhere."

"Yes, I think I do understand," Jed replied thoughtfully. "And the young man who was taken from the religious cult called the Pathfinders—he'd lost his father the day before and sensed that he was unwelcome there; yet he still meekly accepted God."

"Even in a place of hypocrisy, self-interest, and false gods," Phillip put in. "And the Creator chose him from all the phonies at Pathfinder Place, one genuinely decent human being from all those who lived there. On a planet of billions, he found Lonnie Malone."

"The one thing that concerns me," Jed began, "is the biblical saying about it being easier for a camel to pass through the eye of a needle than for a rich man to go to heaven. Are those who are genuinely successful to be automatically turned down—*all* of them? Is it serving the Opposition to do the best you can with your life?"

Phillip shook his head. "What has happened in Indianapolis is occurring elsewhere. Many of the most successful people are said, unfairly, to have achieved their accomplishments by stabbing others in the back or by simply knowing the 'right' people." He grinned. "Yes, even corporation presidents, politicians, and military generals will be taken—if they deserve it. But, as the Bible said, it's harder for them to have lived decent lives."

For a moment it was silent in the dining room. It was getting darker out, and Jed arose to switch on the lights. Phillip reached for a breakfast roll and chewed it contentedly. Jed smiled as he noticed the boy was so short his feet didn't quite reach the floor.

Then Phillip's eyes moved to Jed's face impishly. "You two are also chosen," he said lightly.

"Us?" Jed repeated, incredulous. "Me? They would take *me?*"

Phillip bobbed his blond head. "Yep!" Stacy smiled as he looked to her and murmured, "Why else do you think I was summoned? I was told to notify you."

Jed swallowed hard and peered down at his hands. "I'm not worthy," he mumbled.

"That's an example of why you *are*," the boy said brightly. "Yes, Mr. Westphal. We're all inheritors of the earth."

11

Five hours until April 22, 1984
7:00 P.M., EST

Jed was stunned, unable to comprehend his rarefied status in a world that was about to undergo sweeping change. He felt a surge of genuine humility flood his mind and body for the first time since he was a small child and daily marveled at what incredible things adults could do. Marvels and miracles, he thought, like beauty and perhaps truth, were in the eye of the beholder. "What are we supposed to do, Stacy and I?" he asked the boy at last, his voice barely audible. "I'm not especially ... a courageous man."

"Let's go outside," Stacy said, quietly standing and smoothing her skirt. Phillip arose, too, without a word. The psychologist looked very serious. "I think we should take a final look at the world the way it has been for so many, many years. We'll talk about it there."

Jed found that his legs did not wish to move properly; they had grown stiff with tension. He felt drunk on the wines of revelation and astonishment, inhibited by the only true magic.

But when they opened his front door and moved out to the front yard, he was invigorated by a sturdy spring breeze that rumpled his gray-sprinkled hair and made the skin on his arms tingle. He reached for Stacy's hand. A teen-age boy scarcely older than Phillip drifted by, ghostlike, on his bicycle, making no sound. Several birds were perched silently on power lines in a neighbor's backyard, immobile and waiting. Through a window Jed could detect the noiseless motion of Diana Fuller, a neighbor, clearing her dining table. But no automobile sped angrily past, and except for a television eye beaming from within Diana's house, it might have been the time of an ancient Passover.

Jed glanced at Stacy, saw that she felt it, too. There was something distinctly *unusual* about this night. While there was no fog, the streetlight across the way was barely discernible, muted as if in respect. The houses of his neighbors appeared strangely distant, shrouded in the wan, uncaring curtains of shifting time. Even the breeze was different. Some wayward, disarming, and slightly frightening suggestion of unseen currents, twisting and commingling, indicated imminent upheaval. Jed remembered when he was a boy who spent more time out of doors and sometimes sensed a storm coming from the way his hair twitched and the very cells in his skin seemed to adapt.

He lifted his head, listening intently, and thought he could just make out the far-off rattle of urgent sticks on a tight drumhead, the swift, bloodless clicking of drawn sabers, the hopeless murmur of a brave and resigned chaplain. Napoleon might have experienced this on the eve of Waterloo, Eisenhower on the brink of D day, Moses before he led his people out of Egypt. But he was mixing his memories wildly at a time when war began with missile silos springing open mechanically and when slick, sweatless cylinders rose slowly from their beds like incongruous vampires from their eternal caskets. Yet at that instant, for Jed, the mists of swirling time converged; godlike, he could glimpse the secret heart of eternity and see that its steady beat foretold life's only alternative.

Manlike, he turned wildly to his woman and the mysterious boy, his face a thunderclap of comprehension and misery. "I'm not up to this," he said. "I have no right to survive; I have nothing to offer the remnant."

"Let's think only of the wonderful, good things that are going to come from this," Stacy said anxiously, holding Jed's arm and peering up with a loving concern that parted the gathering shadows. "Do you *hear* me, darling? It's *too late* now to think about what will begin to happen in the world tomorrow. We had that chance for a very long time, right up to this *year;* but now it is simply too late."

"Why can't God stop it?" Jed demanded angrily, staring off down the block and thinking of people he knew, people he liked and loved.

"Because he gave us free will," Phillip replied lightly, standing beside the author. "Because the Opposition again chose to play the contest out, all the way to confrontation. *We* let it happen, you realize; people did, not God. We've had the choice to make for centuries, and it remained in balance right up to now, some going one way, some going the other. And now the spoils of the confrontation are evenly divided: souls and lives to the Creator, souls and lives to the Opposition. An earth ruined by the Opposition, on which it can urge the remnant to despoil, loot, and kill and on which the Creator begins the *next* confrontation—gently urging mankind's tattered remnant to choose *his* way."

"We must plan for that new world, Jed, and be grateful we're a part of it," Stacy whispered in the night. "Perhaps we can contribute toward making it a better place in the future—even a place where, one day, no one worthwhile will ever again be banished by his fellow man."

"We're *nothing*," Jed argued harshly, whirling to them, "ordinary little human things—just a *pocket*, as you put it—an insignificant pocket in Daddy's big, impressive suit: the *whole world!*"

"Haven't you guessed yet, honey?" Stacy asked him, searching his shadowed and forlorn face. "Haven't you seen the truth, that we are only *one* pocket—that the same things have been going on *everywhere* in the world? Why, people like Phillip and the others exist in Europe, Mexico, China, Russia—even Iran! But the international press isn't as *open* as ours." She watched his face brighten, but only slightly. "Wherever portions of the planet survive, wherever it is habitable, the banished will return to start it all over again."

"My *boy*," Jed said at last. Although it was a whisper, the words were uttered with absolute clarity. His face underscored his anguish. "My *son*—and my ex-wife, even; my friends, members of the family..."

"You asked what you two are meant to do," Phillip said, taking a seat on a step in Jed's front lawn. "Dr. Bennett, as I heard it, will become one of those providing psychological counsel and reassurance to people who can't quite grasp what's happened: ordinary folks, like my mom and dad, who are deeply troubled by the chaos; people like your son, many of your friends, perhaps even your ex-wife." Jed turned to stare at the speaker, this wondrous boy, a dawning realization of what was said moving into his mind and heart. Abruptly, he sat heavily beside Phillip. "That's right, sir, the remnant *isn't* just those who were taken around the world. We're the inspirations, the guides." His almost turquoise eyes flickered, bearing encouragement. "There will be others, a good many others, actually. One will definitely be your son."

"Thank God," Jed said with tears in his eyes, his facial muscles convulsive.

"Others, too, you may know. And they will need all kinds of help and guidance, sir. Obviously, the world will need numerous skilled people, and certainly labor to rebuild from the terrible mess left behind. It will need——"

"Thank G-God," Jed said with tears streaming down his cheeks, "we won't be *alone* h-here."

"And *you,* Mr. Westphal," Phillip said with obvious pleasure, "are one of our scribes, our recorders. You will have the task of writing down and explaining what has happened and conveying the ideas of new leadership, to point out what we must try now to achieve *genuine* progress at last. By the way, that is an example of the advancement mankind *has* made this time—that we won't have to start off at a level of abject ignorance. You will be one of those keeping the written word alive, *this* time to teach and to enlighten, to uplift and inspire, as well as to entertain. When all those who were removed throughout the planet begin now to return, in the midst of chaos and awful loss, it will be clear that a miracle has occurred. And the remnant will join us in witnessing the Creator's new beginning toward victory over the Opposition— and celebrating the fact that, even now, the Opposition has not enjoyed its final triumph!"

"Just what *will* the banished do when they return?" Jed wondered.

Stacy grinned. "That's a happy part. People like

Phillip, as you can see from listening to him—the *very best Phillip he can be*—will retain their identities but be endowed with similar extraordinary insight and knowledge. As the younger ones grow to maturity, they will be our true teachers and seers."

"The unwed mothers, when they return," Phillip explained, plucking a blade of grass and sucking on it, "well, *their* kids are the children of the Apocalypse—the surviving, new generation on which existing mankind will pin all its hopes for the future. They are, in a way, like the descendants of Adam and Eve. It will be their task to repopulate the world."

"What of the aged?" Jed asked, beginning to catch the feeling of their optimism. "What's their job?"

"They know better than any of us what has happened in the past, especially during this century," Stacy replied. "They know the mistakes man has made. Rather than carrying the forgetfulness of senility—which is motivated by an absence of love and purpose, by the way—they will return with an *absolute knowledge* of how those mistakes occurred; they will be given extra years to live, and they will not permit us to repeat our errors. They will be our *living memories,* computers with compassion and the ability to reason—the wise men and wise women every society needs as examples of what we may one day become if we are both obedient and fortunate."

"When?" Jed asked in a breath. *"When?"*

"That depends on something else you don't know about," Stacy said softly, "another . . . person." She looked down at her man and rested her hand gently on his head. The three of them went on looking at the ordinary and familiar sights of

THE BANISHED 253

an American neighborhood, almost as though memorizing them. "It concerns the one person you haven't asked us about."

"Of course. The Pathfinder boy," Jed said, nodding. "Lonnie Malone."

The moon was struggling to come through ebon clouds as Phillip replied in a small, low voice. "We cannot tell you much about him, because you need to learn about him on your own, to draw your own conclusions."

A chill trickled along Jed's spine. "I don't understand," he said.

Stacy reached down to urge Jed to his feet and hugged him. He noticed that her hazel eyes were hot, intense with a meaning she could not quite express. "Lonnie Malone has a very . . . *special* role to play," she said slowly, trying to choose her words with care. "It is . . . unique in this new world."

Phillip also arose, brushing his knees. He took a final, long look around him, but Jed could tell with puzzlement that the boy was looking farther away than the black horizon. "You asked when it begins. Well, it begins for real when Lonnie Malone *returns*." His gaze touched Jed. "And he returns tomorrow."

"Let's go back inside," Stacy said suddenly. Her shiver was involuntary, unpleasant; she made a face as she looked back over her shoulder and urged Jed in. "It's getting cold out now, don't you think? *Very* cold," she added.

Jed held the door for them. "I'm not entirely sure I understand everything you're telling me at this point," he remarked, clearing his throat. There seemed to be dust forming in the air; the breeze was clearly picking up. "What do you mean when you say I must learn about this boy Lonnie myself?"

Phillip paused in the doorway and said it calmly to Jed Westphal, said it matter-of-factly, with utter seriousness, and not as obliquely as it sounded at first. "The rest of your job, sir, is quite important. *You've* been chosen to write one of the new gospels."

"The others will return with him tomorrow, Jed," Stacy said, preceding him through the front door. He gaped openly at her. "In answer to your question, sweetheart," she finished, "that's *when*."

He stepped through the door in amazement and with a feeling of boundless awe and wonder spreading through the cells of his mind and body. Instinctively he put out his arms to Stacy, and she came close, kissing him. "Inheritors," she said simply, her arms enfolding him. "The meek shall inherit the old world after all."

Jed wasn't quite at peace. "Why does everyone return *tomorrow?*" he asked, reaching behind him to close the door. "I don't really get the significance. If everything is according to plans that were set in motion as long as *thousands* of years ago, *what in the world is special about tomorrow?*"

Phillip looked up at Jed with a sober, sweet smile, and his knowing gaze met Stacy's. "Why, it's Sunday, Mr. Westphal—Sunday, April the twenty-second, the day of Resurrection. Tomorrow, sir, is Easter Sunday—*the most important Easter Sunday in two thousand years.*"

Jed closed the drapes. Then he sat on the couch beside his beloved Stacy and the once-retarded boy named Phillip. Together, they waited.

Epilogue

"And every one that heareth these sayings of mine, and doeth them not, shall be likened unto a foolish man, which built his house upon the sands:

"And the rain descended, and the floods came, and the winds blew, and beat upon the house; and it fell: and great was the fall of it."

Matthew 7:26-27

"Sometimes of late years I find myself thinking the most beautiful sight in the world might be the birds taking over New York after the last man has run away to the hills. I will never live to see it, of course, but I know just how it will sound because I've lived up high and I know the sort of watch birds keep on us. I've listened to sparrows tapping tentatively on the outside of air conditioners when they thought no one was listening, and I know how other birds test the vibrations that come to them through the television aerials.

" 'Is he gone?' they ask, and the vibrations come up from below, 'Not yet, not yet.' "

Loren Eisley,
Immense Journey,
Random House: N.Y., 1946

WE HOPE YOU ENJOYED THIS BOOK
IF YOU'D LIKE A FREE LIST
OF OTHER BOOKS AVAILABLE FROM
PLAYBOY PAPERBACKS,
JUST SEND YOUR REQUEST TO:
**PLAYBOY PAPERBACKS
BOOK MAILING SERVICE
P.O. BOX 690
ROCKVILLE CENTRE, NEW YORK 11571**